Spitting feathers

KELLY HARTE

RED DRESS INK™

SAN BRUNO PUBLIC LIBRARY

If you purchased this book without a cover you should be aware
that this book is stolen property. It was reported as "unsold and
destroyed" to the publisher, and neither the author nor the
publisher has received any payment for this "stripped book."

First edition March 2004

SPITTING FEATHERS

A Red Dress Ink novel

ISBN 0-373-25051-7

© 2004 by Kelly Harte.

All rights reserved. The reproduction, transmission or utilization
of this work in whole or in part in any form by any electronic, mechanical
or other means, now known or hereafter invented, including xerography,
photocopying and recording, or in any information storage or retrieval
system, is forbidden without written permission. For permission please
contact Red Dress Ink, Editorial Office, 225 Duncan Mill Road,
Don Mills, Ontario, Canada M3B 3K9.

This book is a work of fiction. The names, characters, incidents and places
are the products of the author's imaginaton, and are not to be construed
as real. While the author was inspired in part by actual events, none of the
characters in the book is based on an actual person. Any resemblance to
persons living or dead is entirely coincidental and unintentional.

® and TM are trademarks. Trademarks indicated with ® are registered in
the United States Patent and Trademark Office, the Canadian Trade Marks
Office and/or other countries.

Visit Red Dress Ink at www.reddressink.com

Printed in U.S.A.

ACKNOWLEDGEMENTS

A big THANK-YOU to all those people
who matter to me; you know who you are....

To Joanna, Christian and Martin Harris

1

It could be said that I owe everything that's happened to me in recent months to a mouldering, putrefied watermelon. I was coming to the end of my photographic course when my mother bought two for the price of one at her local market, and because she couldn't fit both into her fridge she hauled the spare one all the way across town and gave it to me. I'd never had one before, and didn't much fancy it either. I prefer my food with a few more calories, so I placed it on my ugly bed-sit windowsill and there it stayed until it finally began to collapse in on itself.

It was obviously decomposing from the inside, and it was as I was lying on my bed, noting the still glossy greenness of its skin set against the grey, disused gasometer that had been the view from my window for the past year, that I got my brilliant idea.

I'd been racking my brains for inspiration that would sneak me the end-of-year exhibition prize. I hadn't been a particularly good student, I am sorry to say. In fact, I'd only just managed to scrape a pass on the course, and my future did not look especially rosy. The best I could hope for was a job in a second-rate studio, taking photos of uncooperative kids and perhaps the odd wedding, if I was lucky. And the only thing that could rescue me now was to win that prize.

It was a very long shot, but one thing I had over the others on my course was a tip-off from a sympathetic tutor about the judge. I'd been told she was one of those arty types, with a penchant for bleak social realism and pretentious titles. And, with this in mind, I set to at once, carefully cutting an artistic slice out of the gourd to expose the festering red flesh inside. Then, with the aid of some carefully positioned lights, I contrasted it sharply against the dreary monochrome background. My masterstroke, though, was the title of the composition. I called it *Urban Decay,* and the judge loved it.

It got me the prize—a place on the books of a well-known photographic agency—and a whole new future in the Capital. And so there I was, two weeks later, crashing on the sofa at Sophie's Shoreditch flat while I waited for the expected deluge of offers.

Partly because my prize-wining photo had been of something vaguely edible—before it went off, that was— I'd decided to register myself as a specialist in food photography. It seemed a sensible move to me, what with the many images of food that surround us daily, not to mention that fact that I like the particular subject so much. Another thing that hadn't escaped me was the possibility of an opening for a Celebrity in that particular area. There are Celebrity everything else, after all—Celebrity chefs, interior designers, hairdressers, gardeners… There are even Celebrity photographers, of course, but none, so far, that I knew about, that specialised in food. None, anyway, famous enough to have their 'sumptuous homes' featured in *Hello!* magazine, and that's what I mean by Celebrity.

Except that my plans weren't going too well at that particular moment. To date, in fact, there hadn't even been a trickle of offers, let alone a flood. Which was why I dived at my mobile phone when it let out its little frog croak that sunny late-September afternoon.

'Tao Tandy,' I said eagerly into the mouthpiece, ever hopeful it was the agency calling.

'It's me,' Sophie said, and I tried not to show my disappointment. She'd been ringing me daily from her place of gainful employment to check on my progress—or, more accurately, lack of it. 'I might have some good news for you,' she added chirpily.

'A job?'

'Better than that.'

'What could be better than a job?'

'I sent an internal e-mail memo to all departments of the bank today,' she pressed on regardless.

'What kind of memo?' I asked her with caution.

'Asking if anyone knew of any affordable accommodation going, of course.'

Of course. Getting rid of me seemed to be her main priority at the moment, and to be honest I couldn't blame her. She was getting a lot of grief from her snooty flatmates about me staying there in the flat. 'And?'

'I think we might have hit the jackpot.'

'What's the catch?' I said.

'Don't be a cynic all your life, Tao. I reckon we could be really on to something here. A once-in-a-lifetime offer.'

Which sounded very fishy to me indeed. 'Where?' I asked, picturing some bed-sitter-land dive in a run-down part of the city, much like the one I'd left behind in Manchester.

'Hampstead…'

Now even I, with my limited knowledge, had a good idea that Hampstead wasn't a run-down part of the city. 'I thought you said that it was affordable.'

'But that's the best bit,' Sophie said with glee. 'It's free. Gratis. Buckshee.'

'Free as in in exchange for my body?'

'Free as in in exchange for looking after a pet while the owner's away.'

'So there is a catch.'

'God, Tao. Listen to yourself! You get the chance to live in the most sought-after part of London, for *nothing,* and you're still complaining.'

'I'm not complaining if this is for real, but it just seems too good to be true. You can't blame me for being a teeny bit sceptical.'

'Well, it's certainly not a foregone conclusion. You'll have to go for an interview—see if the pet owner likes you, trusts you, whatever.'

'How long is this person planning on being away?'

'Two months, which would be brilliant. It would give you loads of time to get established before looking for some-where more permanent to live.'

It would indeed be brilliant, but then something else oc-curred to me. 'Who told you about this amazing opportu-nity anyway?'

'Someone in Foreign Investments e-mailed me back and we had a chat during our lunch break.'

Foreign Investments... I couldn't help feeling a tiny bit jealous of Sophie at that moment. We'd both started out at the bank together in Manchester, but it had always been clear that she was the smart one, and so when she was duly promoted to the bank's head office in London I'd decided to go back to college and study photography. It was the push I had needed to get me out of a rut and into something that appeared from the outside a lot more glamorous and exciting.

'Male or female?' I wanted to know.

'Male,' she said, suspiciously coy. 'A very nice male, as a matter of fact, and it's his great-aunt who owns the house in Hampstead.'

'Why doesn't *he* look after her pet while she's away?'

There was a slight hesitation. 'He's not very good with animals, apparently, and he has his own place to think of. He can't just drop everything to help Auntie out.'

'He doesn't sound all that nice to me. Hates animals, and unhelpful to old ladies. What's his name, anyway?'

'Jerome Audesley, and if he moved in you wouldn't be able to, so you should be grateful.'

'But what makes you think this aunt of his will like me?'

'I'm not saying she will. But she's a bit eccentric, apparently, so you've got a better chance than most, I suppose.'

It wasn't a particularly encouraging response, but I didn't have anything to lose so I asked for the woman's name and number. 'And what sort of pet are we talking about?' I said when I'd finished jotting it down.

Another slight pause. 'It's a parrot,' she said. 'And the old lady is extremely fond of him.'

I got the impression she was holding something back, but since I was beginning to like the idea of spending some time in a smart part of town I let it pass. 'I'll give her a ring straight away,' I said.

Mrs Adrienne Audesley had at least three plums in her mouth, and possibly a citrus fruit as well. She sounded posher than the Queen on the phone, and as formidable as Margaret Thatcher. I thought it would be helpful to mention the name of her great-nephew, but it nearly blew my chances there and then.

'Are you a friend of his?' Mrs Audesley demanded to know.

'No,' I said quickly, guessing the lie of the land by her tone. 'He just works with a friend of mine.'

There was a slightly suspicious pause, then: 'Can you come over immediately?'

I could, but, having no idea how long it would take, I said I'd be there within the hour.

'That will have to do, I suppose,' she growled at me. 'Only don't be any longer or I might have gone out.'

She gave me the address and, worried I might not get there in time via public transport, I decided to take a taxi. I couldn't believe it when the driver announced that we had arrived, on two different counts: one, because he proceeded to charge me the equivalent of a small ransom demand, and two, because the house that we were parked outside was frankly amazing.

I'd already taken a fancy to Hampstead, which looked more like a large village to me than a part of London—and a very nice one at that. The house itself was just off the main drag, a mellow-bricked Georgian end of terrace with three elegant storeys, plus basement, and a run of steps leading up to a shiny black-painted door. And as I grudgingly parted with my money to the driver, who could not be persuaded that I deserved a discount on account of the fact that I was out of work, I set to wondering which part of the house Mrs Audesley lived in. She hadn't mentioned a flat number during our phone conversation, but I assumed that her name would be listed along with the other occupants at the main door.

On my way up the tiled steps, I glanced over the wrought-iron railing to the basement, which had its own separate entrance, and guessed that this was where the old lady lived with her parrot. By now I could already see that there was only one buzzer at the front door, which seemed to suggest that the upper part of the house had not been turned into flats after all. And, because I was sort of curious to see who my rich neighbours might be, I pressed it anyway.

The voice went so well with her appearance that I knew it was Mrs Audesley the moment she opened the door. She was tall and well built, and there was nothing about her that suggested frailty despite the obvious advancement of her years. I took a quick guess that she was in her mid-seventies, which would roughly be the same age as my gran, but unlike my gran, with her perm and blue rinse, Mrs Audesley's silvery hair had been fashioned into an elegant, upper crust, cottage loaf bun.

'Miss Tandy?' the woman said, peering at me with alarming scrutiny. I was glad I'd slipped into something smart—well, smart for me, anyway—but I did feel a bit lower-end-of-the-High-Street next to someone who was dressed like a dowager duchess. I'd been living as a student again for the past year, and as money had been very tight, the budget cream trousers and jacket I wore looked a bit shoddy beside her pale blue cashmere twin-set and matching linen skirt.

'Tao,' I said, thrusting my hand firmly towards her in pretence of a confident manner. 'That's T-A-O,' I spelled out, 'pronounced like *towel* without the E and L on the end.' I was talking fast, like I always do when I'm nervous. 'My parents were sort of hippies,' I offered by way of explanation. 'Well, my mother mostly. Still is, as a matter of fact. She's into all that Eastern stuff. And Tao—well, it's—'

'It's from Taoism,' Mrs Audesley interrupted me, letting go of my sticky hand. 'A system of religion and philosophy based on the teachings of the sixth-century Chinese philosopher Lao Zi. Come inside, Miss Tandy.'

'I'm impressed,' I said, following her into the wide hallway. 'I don't think I've ever met anyone who wasn't one of my mother's friends whose heard of all that stuff.'

'I studied eastern religions in my youth,' Mrs Audesley replied. 'But I remain a committed atheist,' she added almost cheerfully.

I just had time to glance at myself in the gilt hall mirror before we moved on, and I squirmed at the state that my hair was in. I'd pulled it into an elastic band before leaving Sophie's flat, but being fine, and having a mind of its own, a considerable amount had already managed to disengage itself from the fastening. I was desperately trying to tuck it back as I was shown into a spectacular sitting room, complete with stunning chandelier, that overlooked the quiet street at the front of the house. It was decorated in pale blues and creams, with which we, in our current outfits, blended nicely. I sat down when she waved her hand at a brocade-upholstered chair and watched as she moved elegantly towards the black marble fire-

place. Above it was what I imagined to be a family portrait—
a painting of a good-looking man in military uniform.

'My husband Larry,' she said, following my eyes. 'He died
twenty years ago, and although he was handsome he was also
very annoying at times, and quite honestly I don't miss him
one jot.'

It wasn't what I'd expected to hear, but I was beginning
to quite like Mrs Audesley's blunt honesty. 'I understand that
you're going away for a couple of months,' I said, deciding
to cut to the chase, 'and that you need someone to look after
your parrot.'

'He's not a mere *parrot*,' Mrs Audesley responded severely.
'He's an African Grey. A *Congo* African Grey, to be precise,
and he is very choosy about the company he keeps.'

She gave me a quick up and down again, and I got the
distinct impression she didn't hold out very much hope for
me.

'He's already turned down several applicants, and if we
don't find somebody soon I may have to cancel my trip.' She
told me that she'd been invited to spend some time with her
son and his family in Portugal, and would have taken Sir
Galahad—the name of the Congo African Grey—but he'd
never been a very good traveller. I got the feeling that she
didn't much care if the trip did have to be cancelled, and that
there was an element of simply going through the motions
so that she could truthfully tell her son that no suitable par-
rot-sitter could be found.

We discussed my current situation, which seemed to sat-
isfy her. She didn't want anyone with regular working hours.
It was important, she said, that Sir Galahad wasn't left alone
for more than an hour at a time.

'My gardener lives in the basement, and he has agreed to

step in where possible during absences beyond an hour, but he is often away himself, so close consultation with him will be a necessary part of the sitter's responsibilities.'

I had no complaints about that, so I showed her copies of my references—from the bank in Manchester and two previous landlords—and she seemed happy enough with them—subject to confirmation by telephone.

'And when do I get to meet Sir…er…um…Galahad?' I eventually asked. May as well get it over and done with, I thought, because, despite her tentative approval of my situation, Mrs Audesley had made it perfectly clear that the real test was still to come.

'He's waiting for you in the adjoining room,' the woman said, and it seemed to me that there was a sinister edge to her tone, as if she was getting some morbid pleasure from what was about to take place.

I stood up and, frowning now, made my way towards the door that she indicated by a queenly nod of her head.

'I'll leave you alone together for five minutes,' she said, 'and we'll see how the two of you get along.'

One of the joys of ignorance is that you don't have any preconceived ideas, and I had none whatsoever about African Greys, Congo or otherwise. I was a bit apprehensive, certainly. If it was true that the parrot had already rejected several would-be sitters, then there was a very good chance that he wouldn't like me either. But I hadn't lost hope entirely yet, and, most importantly, I didn't at that stage have any idea what these particular birds are capable of if they take a serious dislike to someone. Had I done so I would probably never have set foot in the same room as him.

I closed the door behind me, because if I was going to make a fool of myself I preferred not to be overheard doing it. I entered what appeared to be some sort of anteroom—not large, like the one I'd just left, but huge by the standards of Sophie's Shoreditch flat. It was tastefully furnished, with a couple of squashy armchairs and its own blocked-off white marble fireplace, but apart from a couple of landscapes on the walls it was void of any kind of ornamentation. The cage was enormous and hung from a solid-looking brass stand in the far corner of the room. And Sir Galahad was perched on the top of it with his back to me.

I walked up to him slowly and quietly, instinctively aware that this was not the time for my usual slightly-too-loud and sometimes over-the-top friendly approach. I stood watching his back for some time. He wasn't the most beautiful bird I'd ever seen, but he was certainly handsome, with his dark grey feathers and red-tipped tail.

'How do, Sirg?' I eventually said. I couldn't quite bring myself to use his name in full, because it sounded so daft, and when he manoeuvred his stringy feet around on the bars of the cage to face me I thought I detected a look of puzzlement in his dark eyes. They were surrounded by a circle of white naked skin that I found slightly revolting, but I did my level best not to show it.

He stared back at me hard for some time, and then shuffled a little closer. I lifted my hand to him tentatively and he took one of my fingers gently in his black beak. Or at least it seemed gentle enough until I tried removing it, at which point it turned into a vice-like grip. And as he hung on his eyes never left mine. This lasted for at least a minute, when I decided on two possible options.

One: panic and call for Mrs Audesley.

Or two: show the little varmint just who was the boss.

And, since Option One would guarantee failure, I stared

back at him hard, giving him my best evil eye, and then in a low and harsh voice said, 'Let go of my fricking finger…'

Like Ali Baba and his cave, the bird's beak sprang open immediately and his head jerked back in surprise. He twisted it away from me sulkily and then slowly turned it back again, and although I must have been imagining it, I could have sworn that he actually winked at me.

Then he waddled to the edge of the cage, hopped onto my shoulder and proceeded to nibble my ear for a moment or two. When I was happy it wasn't some sneaky trick before taking a piece out of my lobe, I reached up and scratched the feathers on his throat, and he responded by doing a very good impersonation of a vacuum cleaner.

By this time, my five minutes must have been up, because Mrs Audesley entered the room. She seemed rather shocked by the scene of her precious African Grey whispering his version of sweet nothings into my ear, and for a moment, her mouth very slightly agape, she couldn't say anything.

'Do I pass the test?' I wanted to know, and she and the African Grey nodded their heads in unison.

2

The two Cs—Miss Cordial and Miss Congenial—were in the flat by the time I got back to Shoreditch. They were a couple of Home Counties fee-paying-girls-only-school types, who thought it was 'a lark' to live in a part of the city famed for its artists, Asian restaurants, and Jack the Ripper— although strictly speaking the fame of the latter is mostly associated with neighbouring Whitechapel. At least that was what they said, but my guess is that they'd far sooner have been within strolling distance of a branch of Waitrose and an exclusive little frock shop if their Daddies' allowances had only run to it. They were budding would-be *It* Girls who worked in advertising and marketing respectively, read *Tatler* avidly, and who both had ambitions of marrying some wealthy, possibly polo-playing chinless wonder who would take them away from the stresses and strains of earning their own living.

Apart from their usual conspicuous consumption, their favourite occupation was making fun of my northern accent.

Sophie, my fellow Mancunian, had been in London long enough to soften the edges of hers slightly. Besides which she is very good-looking, wears a thirty-four Double-D cup bra, and has a habit of dating the sort of men the two Cs could only dream about. Which had earned her a certain amount of grudging respect.

How she came to be sharing a flat with two such unlikely females was down to an overheard conversation between what had then been a couple of strangers. In a pub not far from where she worked, Sophie had listened to Jemima and Fiona—as they are known to each other—cattily discussing the recent departure of their former flat-sharer. She'd been swept off her kitten-heel-shod feet by a Brazilian back-packer, apparently, who'd whisked her off to Buenos Aires, and Sophie, desperate for accommodation and never one to miss an opportunity, stepped into the breach.

She told me she could put up with them because the flat was not only handy for work it was also surprisingly comfortable. It was a council flat, as a matter of fact, sublet by the official tenant—which was strictly against the council rules but, since the rent was cheap by London standards, the Cs hadn't asked any awkward questions when they took over the place. It was a scam, basically, but as I'd seen their land-lord—a big burly bloke with a tattoo of a spider's web on his cheek and a serious attitude—I didn't blame Sophie for not asking questions either.

They stopped talking when I entered the sitting room and I knew they'd been having one of their bitches about me. Another favourite occupation was pretending to trip over the tools of what I hoped would soon be my trade in order to make a point about clutter.

'Good news,' I announced as I slumped on the couch opposite them. They were still in their work clothes, almost matching black suits, and sipping Chardonnay from glasses that were almost as frosted as the atmosphere. They looked at each other and then back at me with narrow-eyed suspicion.

'I'm moving out at the weekend.'

'Well, that *is* good news,' Jemima said with a smirk.

'Never mind, dear,' Fiona piped in pityingly, 'you tried your best.'

'I'm not moving back to Manchester, if that's what you mean,' I said, in no rush to get to the good bit.

'Oh dear, you're not moving into a hostel, are you?' Jemima sneered. 'You'll have to be careful with that equipment of yours. Those places are full of undesirables.'

'Try again,' I suggested, and I pulled the elastic band out of my hair and shook it loose. It was well over my shoulders now, and in need of a trim, but that was another thing that would have to wait until I'd earned some money. The two Cs both had expensive hairdos: one short and spiky, one bobbed—both bottled blonde.

'A cardboard box?' Jemima quipped.

'Hampstead,' I said with a lazy sigh as I heeled my shoes off my aching feet.

They glanced at each other, then glared at me.

'Hampstead!' they repeated as one.

' 'Fraid so,' said I with a sigh. 'But someone's got to live there, I suppose.'

They naturally assumed that this was an example of northern humour.

'Where are you *really* going?' Fiona wanted to know, trying to smile now.

'Hampstead,' I repeated patiently, crossing my budget-trouser-covered legs. 'That place with the Heath—surely you know it?'

They did another quick exchange of glances, and then seemed to lose the use of their tongues for a while. Except as an aid to swallow large gulps of wine. I watched as they fumbled for something to say, and was glad I was me and neither of them. They might have nice clothes and well-paid jobs, but they were essentially soulless. And my hair might need a trim, but at least I didn't have to touch up the roots every three weeks. At least my almost-though-not-quite blonde hair was natural.

'I expect there are bad parts even in Hampstead,' Jemima eventually said, but she didn't sound quite so cocksure now.

'I expect there are,' I agreed as I stretched my arms over my head. 'But where I'm going isn't one of them.'

It was getting on for six o'clock now. I was later back than I should have been, due to the fact that I'd spent a couple of hours mooching around what was to be my new stomping ground. Before that Mrs Audesley had shown me over the house and assured me that I was welcome to use as much or as little of it as I liked. I think she was a bit hurt at first, to discover that her one-woman African Grey had taken a shine to another. She kept glancing at me curiously, as if trying to work out what it was about me that had captured Sir Galahad's heart. She told me he'd only taken to one other person in his thirty-nine years. This was her gardener, whom she'd said she would contact later in order to fix up a time for us to discuss our shared parrot-sitting duties.

And then she said something about her great-nephew, the one who worked at the bank with Sophie. And I'm not sure why but it was still bothering me even now.

'So when exactly are you going?' Jemima asked, inter-rupting my thoughts.

'Saturday morning. You could give me a lift over in your car, if you like.'

Normally there would have been a stock reply to such a wild suggestion that included words like 'dreams' and 'in your', but I could see she was battling between her natural inclination to be rude and unhelpful and desperate curios-ity about my apparent turn of fortune. She skilfully managed to overcome the dilemma with her eventual reply.

'Well, if it will get you and your junk out from under our feet any quicker I don't see why not.'

Fiona, who didn't have a car and was a little less sharp than her partner in malice, looked and sounded appalled. 'You're not really going to help move her awful stuff in your car?' she demanded of Jemima.

'That way she gets to see my new gaff,' I answered for her. 'But it's okay, Fiona, *you* don't have to come.'

She got it at last, and twittered a bit before insisting on helping with the move, at which point Sophie got back and, shocked at this display of co-operation, asked what was going on.

I hadn't got round to ringing her yet, to telling her the outcome of my interview with Mrs Audesley, and she was clearly delighted when I told her my news. But I didn't want to go into details with the two Cs around, so I suggested we went and had something to eat at Felix's Place. 'My treat,' I insisted, 'as a thank-you for tipping me off.'

The café is handily placed on the corner of the street. It's a genuine old-fashioned greasy spoon, which Sophie and I loved a lot because there wasn't a bagel or French stick in sight. Just proper bread baps, the size of a side plate, that we had filled with chips and washed down with huge mugs of tea. It's a sort of endangered species really, Felix's Place. Somewhere you can fill yourself up for around a quid and where no single item contains less than one thousand calories. It is heaven on earth.

Felix, who runs the place with his wife and whichever one of his seven children happens to be available at any given time, has been there for twenty-two years, ever since he arrived from County Donegal with his lovely wife Angie. They live in the flat over the café and it is not unusual to hear Angie bawling at the kids, which just kind of adds to the homely atmosphere of the place. It was John on duty with his father tonight, a fourteenish-year-old Arsenal fan who flaunted his allegiance with his red and white shirt.

'You look as if you've lost a euro and found a fiver,' Felix said to me as I rolled up to the counter. Sophie had grabbed the last available table, which happened to be our favourite, and waved to Felix as she slumped triumphantly into a seat. He is one of those men who will insist on living a lie as far as his hair is concerned. The central area of his head is completely bald, but he grows the remainder just long enough to draw it up over the bare patch and then he secures it with a dab of something that could well be chip fat, but I very much hope isn't—for Angie's sake. With their pale skin and curly rust-coloured locks, most of the children are clones of their father, and with John at his side it was easy to imagine how Felix must have looked before most of his own hair sadly forsook him.

'I've found somewhere to live,' I told him, then ordered two of our usual specials.

'Around here?' he wanted to know, and I said that it unfortunately wasn't. He seemed a bit sorry for me when I filled him in, especially when I mentioned the parrot.

'An ould aunt of mine had one of them fellers, and her life was never her own after he cem through the door. Ruled her with a rod of iron, he did, and he had the foullest mouth that side of the Shannon.' He'd belonged to a sailor, according to Felix, and as he piled chips into heavily buttered baps, and poured steaming tea into horizontally striped blue mugs, he gave me some milder examples of the parrot's revolting way with words. 'T'would make a maiden blush, some of things that he said,' Felix concluded, 'so it was lucky, I suppose, that my aunt was as deaf as the hinge on a gatepost.'

Felix had a fine turn of phrase that was all part of the colour and charm of the place, and even though I'd only known him a couple of weeks I felt a bit sad that I would no longer be seeing him on a daily basis. I popped in every morning for a cup of tea, and although I could rarely face cooked food at the start of the day Felix had let me take the odd snap of his mega fry-ups by way of keeping my hand in.

'But you'll come back now and then,' he said as he took my money, and it sounded more of a prediction than a question.

'For someone with your particular ambitions, you're not exactly a gastronome,' Sophie said when I'd squeezed past tables and put the tray down on ours. It was positioned right next to the window, which was, as usual, misted over with condensation.

Her statement was a perfectly true one but I didn't see why it mattered. 'Food's food,' I told her blithely, 'and I'm as happy to take pictures of the humble fish finger as I am of squid *à la* Up Yer Posh Bum.'

'So,' she said as she lifted the lid of her bap and squeezed brown sauce over the pile of golden glistening chips, 'how did you manage it? I've heard that the parrot is a hard bird to please.'

'Which I note that you failed to mention,' I said sternly when I'd slipped into the seat opposite her.

She smiled at me slyly. 'I thought if you knew in advance you'd have chickened out.'

'I would have done if I'd known how vicious he can be if he takes a dislike to someone. Mrs Audesley said that three of the previous applicants are threatening to sue.'

'So what *is* your secret?' Sophie asked me curiously. 'I didn't know you had a way with parrots.'

'African Greys,' I corrected her as I, being a tomato sauce person myself, coated my chips accordingly. 'Which his proud owner assures me are a cut above your average parrot.' To be honest I was just as bewildered as Mrs Audesley had been as to why Sir Galahad had liked me so much. But there was no denying that he did from the way he'd clung to my shoulder and nuzzled into my neck as he made shockingly perfect imitations of all manner of sounds, from an old-fashioned telephone ringing to a toilet cistern being flushed. He also had a lot to say for himself, in Mrs Audesley's own imperious tones. 'Do take a seat,' was one of his favourites, as was, 'One lump or two?'

'Maybe I was an African Grey in a previous life,' I suggested wildly, at a loss for any more reasonable explanation. Then I remembered something—the something that had been bothering me. 'Mrs Audesley said that he was being very polite today, but that he had a much wider vocabulary which, and I quote, "includes some very extreme vulgarities", that she blames entirely on her great-nephew.'

'Who? Jerome?'

I nodded as I pressed down on the butty to make it easier to put in my mouth.

'She doesn't seem to like him much,' I said as I looked over at Sophie now. 'In fact she was at pains to make sure I understood that he wasn't to be admitted into the house while she was away.'

'I can't think why,' Sophie replied indignantly. 'He seems very pleasant to me.' Which I happened to know was Sophie-speak for, *I fancy the pants off him.*

'And she's not alone in her opinion. As soon as his name came up Sir Galahad announced that he was a "ghastly young man",' I said, impersonating the bird's impersonation of Mrs Audesley's disapproving tones.

Sophie was munching now, and managing to look defiant at the same time. 'You don't expect me to accept that a parrot actually knows what he's talking about?' she eventually said. 'He's obviously been brainwashed.'

I shrugged as I swallowed. 'You're probably right,' I said, even though she was plainly missing the point. But it didn't seem wise to labour the point that Mrs Audesley might have had good reason for brainwashing her bird. 'And if he's so "ghastly," why is he trying to be so helpful? Good point,' I said, deciding to let the matter drop. 'And you must really pass on my thanks to him.'

Sophie began to thaw a little now and promised she would. We ate in lip-smacking silence for a while then, until we got to the empty-plate, finger-licking stage.

'I'm so glad you decided to change your life,' Sophie said thoughtfully then. 'For a while there I thought you would fade into suburban oblivion.'

'Me too,' I said, and for a while there this had indeed been a very distinct possibility.

For years I'd been trying so hard to rebel against the mantra-chanting, Zen-aspiring upbringing provided by my well-meaning but flaky mother that I'd gone too far the other way. This had not only involved seven years' hard labour in the bank, but also a series of decent, hard-working boyfriends and, finally, the joint purchase of a semi-detached starter home in a respectable neighbourhood with an insurance salesman named Malcolm—Mal, to his friends and former fiancée. It lasted almost a year, until I suddenly came to my senses and told Mal it was over. He was bewildered and angry, of course, but I was determined, and with my share of the money we made from the sale of the semi—there had been a small property boom during our time together—I paid for the photography course and kept a bit back for emergencies.

I know that Sophie still worked in a bank, but it was different for her. Quite apart from her ample chest, she had Snow White looks, with milky skin and raven-black hair, and a game plan in which starter homes had never figured.

'Oh, God,' she said. 'Don't look now, but I think someone's heading our way.'

He arrived before I had a chance to ignore her warning, shoving past me to get near to Sophie.

'Room for a little one?' her landlord said, briefly showing a set of teeth that would make an orthodontist twitchy. He had on trainers and a grubby grey jogging suit that I'd bet had seen little of the action intended.

'We're just finishing up,' Sophie said, which was thankfully true. She was wearing her smart charcoal work suit, and I was still in my African Grey-beguiling garb, and I suddenly felt that we were a bit overdressed.

He squeezed himself into the space at our table with his

rear end spread well over the sides of the chair. He didn't have any food with him, and when I glanced up at Felix he gave me a wink of encouragement. 'John will be bringing Mr Parker's order when it's ready,' he called out.

'Mr *Parker?*' I queried with a frown, before I had time to engage caution and prudence. I knew that his first name was Peter, so was this the explanation for the spider's web tattoo on his face? Did he think he was Spider-Man? I was about to laugh, but I felt a sharp kick on my leg from under the table, and when I glanced at Sophie I realised that pursuing this particular line of enquiry might be a mistake.

He dragged his attention away from Sophie's Double-D chest and looked at me questioningly.

'Oh,' I fumbled, 'it's just that my mum's name is Parker, but I don't expect there's a connection.' It was completely untrue, and a very poor effort as cover-up stories go, but he seemed to swallow it whole. He had very thick, very black hair that I'd never been this close to before. Now that I was it seemed strangely unnatural, and I was finding it difficult to take my eyes off it as he turned his attention back on Sophie. If I distorted my focus by narrowing my eyes it looked exactly as if a fluffy black cat had curled up and gone to sleep on his head.

'There's Karaoke at the Peeler Saturday,' he said to her now. 'Coming?'

The Peeler was a local dive that you'd only dream of going into if you were especially drunk and happened you have in your company several prize-fighting escorts, and I was curious to see how Sophie would handle turning down such an attractive and beautifully extended invitation.

'I'd love to,' she answered sweetly, 'but I'll be helping Tao move into her new place, I'm afraid.'

He glanced at me dangerously, as if I was personally responsible for all the troubles of the world. I was tempted to say that I could manage without her help, but I could feel the daggers being aimed at me across the table.

'Sorry,' I said, 'but I'm depending on her.'

There was an almost audible sigh of relief from Sophie, who stood up now and gave me the nod. 'Another time, maybe,' I heard her say, and after wishing Felix a fond farewell we left the place, trying not to giggle till we were well out of sight of the café.

'Is that a wig he was wearing?' I eventually asked, and it set her off all over again.

'Of course it's a bloody wig,' she finally managed, 'but the secret is to pretend not to notice. The way you were looking at it I was afraid you were about to give it a tug.'

We took a little diversion on the way back and bought a bottle of Château Cheapo from the local offy. And, because neither of us was in the mood for the Cs, we drank it in Sophie's bedroom—her sprawled on the bed, me in the lotus position. (Some things die hard, I'm afraid.)

We talked for a while about my prospects, and I got the feeling that Sophie didn't think all that much of them—at least not on the strength of my work.

'But then you've always been a good bluffer,' she said, trying to make amends now. 'And in this town that's far more important than actual talent.'

I thanked her a bunch, but didn't take this vote of no-confidence to heart. I was hopeful and optimistic after today and I had a good feeling about the future.

And then, just as we were finishing off the wine, just as we were at that rosy, happy stage where nothing in life seems impossible, she went and spoilt everything by telling me that she might just have met the man she was going to spend the rest of her life with. The only crumb of comfort I was able to take from this alarming statement was the fact that she almost certainly wasn't referring to someone who wore a dubious wig and had delusions of being an arachnified superhero.

3

There is always a price to pay for a chip butty, and I paid it next day by missing out on lunch as well as breakfast. Having been brought up on an apparently healthy but deadly boring macrobiotic diet, I am nowadays an enthusiastic eater of junk food, but I know that I have to be careful. Despite the faddiness of my mother's former regime, she now weighs fifteen stone and, much as it suits her, I don't want to end up the same way—not for a good few years yet anyway. But, rather than eat a sensible, balanced diet, I eat what I want with big gaps in between.

I took a call from Mrs Audesley first thing that morning, with instructions for me to go to the house at three o'clock 'sharp' in order to meet her gardener. Since that meant I had about six hours to kill, I decided to take the tube to Covent Garden, so that I could have several rolls of film developed at the photographic lab recommended by the agency. I knew how to process the stuff myself, of course—just about—but it was such a faff, and I didn't think the Cs would appreciate me turning their bathroom into a makeshift chemical-filled darkroom.

The Linford Laboratory was in a fairly run-down-looking building in a side road off King Street, and for a moment I thought I must have the wrong address. I was used to labs on industrial estates, and although there aren't too many of those in central London, I was still very surprised. I wasn't really sure what I'd expected to find, but since many top professionals apparently used the place, I suppose I thought it would appear a little more on the up-market side. There was just a small, unimposing shop front, and inside a dizzy-looking chilli-pepper redhead behind an old-fashioned oak-topped counter. She greeted me with a hugely welcoming smile, however, and before I'd even opened my mouth asked me what kind of work I did.

'Food,' I said, and the smile immediately turned to an expression of disappointment. She was wearing a deep V-necked red sweater that revealed rather desperate-looking breasts that were squashed together by a ferocious up-lift bra. She was heavily made up, and it occurred to me that she was working there in the hope of being 'discovered'.

'Are you a model?' I asked, in an effort to cheer her up.

'If only,' she said unhappily.

'Have you tried the agents?' I asked as I dug five rolls of film out of my bag.

'A couple,' she replied gloomily, 'but they seem to think that my look is too strong.'

And they could have a point, I thought as I passed the film over the counter. But it was very possible that if she removed some of the slap, and maybe stopped using the chilli-pepper dye, she could look pretty good. She was the right height and weight, and her features looked fairly photogenic.

'You should try toning things down and then go somewhere else.'

She gave me a *What-the-hell-would-a-food-photographer-know?* sort of look, and without any response to what was meant to be a helpful suggestion she asked me my name and address so she could write it down on a slip.

I supplied the information and asked how quickly I could have the prints back.

'It's usually a day, but you can pay extra, if you like, and we can have them ready in three hours.'

It was a curt response, and I wondered if it was time for some toning down myself. My plain speaking clearly wasn't going down too well in this town. 'I'll pay the extra,' I said, 'and I'm sorry for being so blunt. It's just that you really are very pretty, but it's kind of hidden behind all the make-up.'

She softened visibly now, and I made a mental note to engage sensitivity before offering any further advice to strangers.

'Standard E6 okay?' she said, and I nodded that it was.

'Do you do the processing here?' I said curiously as she deposited my films in a large envelope.

She shook her head. 'This is just the drop-off and collection point. A despatch rider picks up every hour and takes them on to the lab.' She glanced at her watch. 'He's due any minute, so with a bit of luck these might be back in two hours, not three.'

I thanked her, and looked forward to picking up the prints. As well as Felix's wonderful fry-ups, I'd taken quite a few shots of the Brick Lane Sunday market with my brand-new Hasselblad, and I was hoping they'd turned out well.

They certainly should have if the price of the camera had anything to do with the quality of the finished product.

All through the photographic course I'd managed well enough with an old Pentax my father had given to me, but since it was pretty old I'd recently sacrificed an arm and a leg for a brand-new Hasselblad 201F. And that, plus a digital camera, a computer, and all the rest of the paraphernalia required by a present-day pro photographer, had just about cleared me out of what was left of the sale of the semi. But I kept telling myself that it was an investment, that it was necessary to speculate to accumulate, and, having now done a great deal of the former, it seemed high time I started to get some rewards. Which was why I headed straight for the Front Page Agency after dropping off my film.

Naff name, I know, but they seemed a pretty pukka sort of set-up—smart offices, cool-looking people working in them. A bit *too* cool, though, if you ask me. The receptionist, for example, wasn't the most approachable person in the world. I'd tried being friendly with her when I first landed in London, in the hope that she'd keep me in mind if anything good came in, but it had been like trying to befriend a refrigerator. Poker-thin—and faced—I think she was afraid to smile for fear of disturbing her magnificently applied make-up. Either that or she'd had radical Botox treatment that had left her incapable of using her facial muscles.

'Hi, Amber,' I said. 'Remember me?'

She cast me a vaguely hostile look and pursed her full, beautifully lipsticked lips disapprovingly. She was sitting behind a glass-topped desk which had on it just a phone, a slimline computer screen and a cerise leather appointment book. She herself was dressed in matching cerise that, because she'd been wearing it before, I assumed was a uniform.

'We haven't got anything for you, if that's why you're here,' Amber replied in an accent that was supposed to be posh but didn't quite cut the mustard. There was a hint of twang there in her vowels that I think I recognised as Midland in origin.

'Well, I think I'd like to see someone who's a little more senior in the organisation, if you don't mind.' It wasn't a comment designed to win favour, exactly, but I was getting fed up with nasty, bitchy women, and I was wondering what had happened to all that sisterhood stuff my mother still gamely talked about. I certainly hadn't seen much evidence of it in the past fortnight.

She seemed taken aback by my remark, but soon recovered her icy equilibrium. 'You'll have to make an appointment,' she said, opening the diary in front of her, 'but I don't have anything available for at least a month.'

'A month!'

She seemed pleased by my dismay, and delighted with her own power. She might just be a receptionist, but she was God as far as appointments were concerned. I was debating whether to take the appointment or tell her what she could do with it, when a door to the left of the desk opened and two men appeared in the foyer.

They were clearly at the end of a meeting, and as they shook hands I recognised one of the men as Taylor Wiseman, the famous American chef. He had his own hit TV show and a legion of adoring female fans, and while I wouldn't have counted myself amongst their number, I had to admit that he did look pretty good in the flesh. He was tall and dark and lean, and although I was used to seeing him in the sexy kitchen whites he wore so well to present his shows, the smart suit he'd donned for the meeting gave him a nice touch of the urbane that certainly did not go amiss.

'We'll contact a few of our best,' the other man assured him, with a smile that was midway between charm and smarm.

'It's real important that we get along,' Taylor Wiseman replied in the husky tones that added greatly to his small screen appeal. 'We'll be working together closely on this project, so I'm going to have to like the guy, as well as his ideas.'

The other man nodded sympathetically. 'If I shortlist a few then you can meet them and make your decision.'

'I'll wait to hear from you,' Taylor said, and turned to leave. At which point I moved sideways and blocked his path past the desk.

'Mr Wiseman,' I said, thrusting my hand out. I was wearing faded jeans and a good-quality tweed hacking jacket that I'd bought in a charity shop a few years ago. Not exactly how I'd choose to be dressed when meeting a celebrity, especially with my wayward hair and lack of any cosmetic enhancements, but I didn't have a chance to think about all that. 'Delighted to meet you.'

I'd taken this unusually bold step with Sophie's words writ large in my mind. She was forever advising me to 'get out there and *network*', and although I had no real idea what was going on my hunger for work told me there might just be an opportunity here.

'Likewise,' he said in his friendly all-American way. I could see his teeth now, which looked even more perfect in real life than they did on the small screen. Their whiteness was exaggerated by his lightly tanned skin and his brown eyes were smiling at me. 'And you are?'

'Tao Tandy,' I replied. 'Food photographer extraordinare...' I added with a cheeky wink and a grin, remembering what Sophie had said about my good bluffing skills.

By now the man with whom the meeting had just taken place was at Taylor's side, an expression of surprised concern on his face. He was quite a pleasant-looking man, with thinning hair and pudgy plasticine features; in his mid-forties, I'd say. He plainly didn't know me from the Boston Strangler, but I snatched the advantage.

'I joined the agency a couple of weeks ago,' I explained to them both, 'and I thought it was time I introduced myself.'

I glanced at Amber behind her desk and saw that her face was frozen in impotent fury. 'Amber here was helpfully arranging an appointment for me to meet someone,' I added with a slight smile in her direction.

'Jerry Marlin,' the man said as he extended his hand warmly to me. I recognised the name as that of the agency's top dog, and gave him flash of my own excellent teeth. They might not be as white as Taylor's but I pride myself on their neatness.

'You're the prizewinner from Manchester, aren't you?' he added, and I nodded my head modestly.

'Well, that's great,' Jerry said. 'I've been wanting to meet you as well. Only we don't seem to have a contact number.'

'That's strange,' I said, glancing towards the reception desk. 'I left it with Amber a fortnight ago.'

'It was unfortunately mislaid,' Amber said quickly, when Jerry looked at her questioningly.

He glanced at his watch. 'Damn,' he said. 'I've got a lunch appointment in ten minutes, but I could meet up with you later.'

I was about to agree when I remembered my instructions

from Mrs Audesley and offered him a little grimace of regret. 'I'm afraid I have to be somewhere at three,' I said, thinking now that it wouldn't do any harm to appear a little less desperate than I actually felt. 'But I could come back tomorrow.'

Jerry looked at Amber again, and she sniffed as she looked in the diary. 'You have a window between ten and ten-thirty in the morning,' she said glacially.

'Ten it is, then,' Jerry said, and with a final appraising glance at me and a sly wink in Taylor's direction he took his leave of us.

'And what are you doing for lunch?' Taylor said when the two of us were left alone—apart from Amber, that is, whose eyes were boring a hole into the side of my face.

'Missing it, I'm afraid. Making up for a bit of over-indulgence last night.'

He raised one of his thick dark eyebrows curiously, so that it seemed to form an unspoken question mark. 'How about a coffee, then? There's a place not far from here that does a great cappuccino.'

'With cinnamon topping?'

'You bet.' He smiled captivatingly.

I slid a look at Amber as I hoisted my bag higher on my shoulder and fell into step with one of TV's hottest properties. 'See you tomorrow,' I said, but failed to get so much as a grunt by way of response.

Things had happened quickly for Taylor since he'd arrived in London, I learnt. He'd been spotted by a TV producer almost straight away, and offered a show there and then. It had been an immediate hit, but clearly took everyone by surprise because no one had thought of a spin-off book to go with the series. So a big glossy had been planned this time, and was due to be launched with series two of the show.

'Trouble is,' he said, 'most of the illustrations are stills from the show, and I just think it needs something else to make it different. Some additional shots to set it apart from the usual stuff. Which is why I went to the agency.'

I could feel my heart beginning to pound as the words BIG BREAK burst into my mind. 'I might have some ideas,' I said, without thinking first. He looked at me with interest and I tried not to panic. 'Maybe we could meet again to discuss them,' I said, because I didn't actually have any ideas at that particular moment.

I felt a bit stupid when he didn't respond directly—when he completely changed the subject, in fact. 'So,' he said, when we were half way through cappuccino number one, 'what kind of food do you like yourself?'

Slightly deflated, but not yet defeated, I lowered my eyes a little as we sat opposite one another in a two-seater booth near the café's counter. The place looked new—not one of the chains of coffee shops that seemed to be on almost every street corner now, but an independent, run by what I took to be South Americans. I was trying to decide whether to lie and say Mediterranean, which covered a multitude and which, along with Pan Australasian, seemed to be what everyone seemed to be into these days. Or just be honest. I went for the honest option in the end, because by now, having already provided a quick rundown of my credentials, I was beginning to suffer from bluffing fatigue.

'Being from the north,' I began, 'I have a particular partiality to anything which contains a lot of cholesterol—suet, pastry and chips being at the top of my list.'

He grinned uncertainly, not sure if I was serious or not. 'But how come you manage to keep such a neat little figure?' he said when he finally accepted I was telling the truth.

His lovely dark eyes were constantly smiling, and from him it felt like a genuine compliment.

'Long periods of abstinence between binges,' I said, warming to him all the more. I explained why I wouldn't be having lunch that day, and he seemed quite taken with my description of Felix's place.

'I've got some photos of it,' I told him. 'It's got a great atmosphere—like something from a different time.'

'I'd like to see them,' he said, and I asked him when…

Which was how we came to make the arrangement for me to go to his restaurant the following day. And if he liked what he saw, he casually told me, he might well consider using me on his book. I was naturally cock-a-hoop about this, but since I hadn't yet seen the results of my efforts I wasn't exactly counting my chickens. It didn't stop me indulging in a mental shopping binge, however, not to mention a few choice imaginings about being up close and personal with a popular TV chef. I'd be the envy of housewives everywhere.

I was a third of the way through the second delicious cinnamon-topped cappuccino when the conversation became a little more intimate. I was telling him about the problems I'd been having with certain females lately—no actual names mentioned—and he said it might have something to do with what he called my 'refreshing openness'.

'That's not a euphemism for crass insensitivity, is it?' I queried wryly, and then related the tale of Miss Chilli-Pepper.

'Sounds like good advice to me,' Taylor said with a shrug. 'Anyway,' he added after a moment's thought, 'why do you mind so much if people don't like you?'

'I don't know, but I do,' I said, surprised at my answer. I

did know, really—but, nice as he was, I didn't think it was time to tell Taylor the sad story of my early life.

'Well, I like you,' he declared, and the creases around his eyes deepened.

I felt my face colour slightly, and steered the focus back to him. It was obvious that things had worked out well for him professionally since he'd arrived in the city, so I threw in a few subtle questions about his social life.

'I haven't really had time for much relaxation,' he said. 'Sure, I *know* people, but there isn't anyone—well, you know…special.'

I found myself frowning as it struck me as odd that a man who was lusted after by thousands of women didn't have a girlfriend. Of course he could be gay, I supposed briefly, but it wasn't the signal he was giving out. I couldn't state with any certainty that he'd been flirting with me, that he was at-tracted in the *fancying* sense, but I did get the impression he was quite looking forward to meeting up with me again, and I couldn't help but be flattered.

It was getting on for two o'clock when I took my leave, having reluctantly declined a third cup of coffee. Which was just as well, really, because three large cups of full-fat milk would have been getting on for the equivalent of another chip butty, and that would have meant forgoing yet another meal if I was to stand any chance of hanging on to my 'neat little figure'. The reflection of which kept catching my eye in the windows of shops as I practically skipped down the road back to the tube station.

I was still on a high when I stepped off the train at Hamp-stead—still feeling hopeful about the future despite the un-comfortable proviso that I still had a few hurdles yet to overcome. I'd picked up the developed photographs on my way to the station, but I hadn't dared look at them yet for fear of spoiling my excellent state of mind. A lot was now riding on the shots having turned out well, and I was anxious to delay any disappointments. However, having arrived at my destination early, and with half an hour's heel-kicking time on my hands, temptation got the better of me.

Miss Chilli-Pepper had been nice enough, now that we'd got over our small misunderstanding, but for some reason dark thoughts had crept into my head. I began to imagine that I'd detected a hint of smirk on her face as I picked up the package, which I now felt certain had been directed at the quality of my work. I tried to adopt a *What-does-a-would-be-model-know?* sort of stance, but I didn't have the confidence to sustain it, and eventually, at the end of the street where Mrs Audesley lived, I decided to put an end to all the suspense.

There was quite a strong breeze going on, but it was warmish and fine, so taking out the pictures seemed safe enough as I perched on a low brick garden wall and delved into my bag. I was starting to have serious doubts now, because without any special lighting I'd resorted to flash, and that can look a little bit amateurish. Still, I tried assuring myself as I lifted the flap of the first envelope, if all else failed I still had my famous watermelon pic to fall back on.

I took a deep breath and slid out the prints, and the photo on top cheered me a bit. It was of a plate of bacon and egg, set on one of the Formica tables and with one of Felix's customers, knife and fork eagerly poised, grinning toothlessly at the camera. It wasn't a *great* photograph, but it was good. Encouraged, I thumbed through the rest and my heartbeat gradually slowed to its regular pace. The market shots weren't bad either, especially the ones of the French cheeses, which a genuine Frenchman brought over from France every week.

'Brick Lane market,' somebody said in my ear, and I jumped so much the photos nearly shot out of my hand. I looked up to see a youngish man leaning on the gatepost next to me. He wasn't bad-looking, with rich brown, longish hair and a cute smile, but he had a damn nerve looking over my shoulder, so I gave him my best haughty expression.

'Not bad,' he said now. 'Are you a professional?'

This warmed me slightly to him, I suppose—but, flattered or not, I still wasn't about to engage in cheery banter with a rather scruffy, ill-mannered stranger. He was wearing old jeans with mud on the knees, and a red and white striped rugby-type shirt that was clean enough but raggy and frayed at the edges. I slipped the photos back in their envelopes and glanced at my watch. It was five to three. Time to be off. I stood up and to my surprise, but not yet alarm, the stranger fell into step beside me.

'We seem to be going in the same direction,' he said nonchalantly.

'Not for long, I trust.'

'You're from the North, aren't you?' he said, not put off by my disdainful tone for a moment. 'Me too. From Black-pool, originally, but I've been living down here for a few years now.'

I recognised the familiar accent now, and I almost dropped my guard for a moment—until he spoilt it with his next words.

'I take it you're new in town.'

I didn't like him pointing out that it was so obvious, and since he was now following me down the path to Mrs Audesley's house I was getting a bit nervous at his persistence.

'I don't think that's any of your business,' I said, and then I stopped and looked at him sharply. 'Look, if this is how people do their pick-ups round here, forget it. I've come here for an important appointment and I'd like you leave now.'

'Can't do that, I'm afraid,' he said with a shrug of his admittedly broad shoulders. 'And, no, this isn't the way that we "do our pick-ups", as you so charmingly put it. It's got the same name here as it has in the North. It's called being *friendly*.'

But I was still stuck on the first bit of what he'd said. 'What do you mean, you *can't* leave?'

'I can't leave because I too have an *important* appointment with Mrs Audesley,' he answered lightly.

I was so busy feeling defensive and foolish at the way he put so much emphasis on the word 'important', as if he was making fun of me, that my confusion didn't kick in for a moment. Then, when he spoke again, it hit me big time.

'And I also happen to live here.'

I felt a bit queasy then, as I glanced over the railing to the gardener's flat in the basement.

'Oh,' I said, trying to make amends with a silly smile as the penny dropped, 'you must be the gardener, then.' He wasn't what I'd imagined at all. I'd being expecting an elderly retainer type, with a cap and dentures.

He looked amused at my discomfort. 'And I guessed who you were when I saw you sitting on the wall.' He glanced at his wristwatch. 'It's precisely three o'clock,' he added coolly now, 'and our Mrs Audesley sets great store by punctuality.'

4

'Ah,' Mrs Audesley declared when she opened the door, 'so the two of you have already met. Excellent.'

In fact we hadn't actually got as far as exchanging names, but she'd referred to him as Chris the day before, and I assumed she'd mentioned my name to him. I was feeling uncomfortable because of our small misunderstanding, and it wasn't helped by the ease Chris and his employer obviously felt in one another's company. I also noted that Mrs A didn't seem to mind in the least about his untidy appearance.

'How are the travel plans going?' he asked casually as we followed the lady of the house into the opulent sitting room.

'Not bad,' she replied. 'Marcus has arranged most things. It's just a matter of packing, really, though one needs so much for so many weeks away from home,' she added with a wistful sigh. She indicated that we should take a seat and then turned her attention on me. 'I've checked your references and everything seems to be in order.'

I nodded demurely and waited for her to continue. Chris had taken the seat next to me on the sofa and Mrs A remained on her feet, just as she had the day before. She was wearing an expensive-looking ensemble in beige today, with a single row of no doubt real pearls around her well-preserved neck. I'd taken to looking at women's necks of late. The last time I saw my mother I'd noticed that hers was looking rather scraggy, a bit turkeyfied, and if I took after her—as I already feared I might in the genes department—that was presumably another undesirable physical feature I had to look forward to in about twenty-five years.

'I'm making a list of dos and don'ts regarding Sir Galahad,' Mrs A went on, 'which I'll have ready for you on Saturday afternoon.'

'Is that when you're leaving?' Chris wanted to know.

'Yes. A taxi will be arriving for me at four p.m., by which time I trust that Tao will be settled in.'

'I thought I'd get here around midday,' I said. 'If that's okay with you.'

I didn't hear Mrs A's reply because at that moment an almighty squawk let rip from the adjoining room. Knowing looks were exchanged between the two other people in the room with me, and while I looked on blankly Chris got up.

'Come on, old feller,' I heard him say as he opened the door and went inside. When he reappeared Sir Galahad was perched importantly on his shoulder. Until he saw me, that is, at which point he squawked again, flapped his wings, and took off in my direction. He landed safely on the top of my head and immediately enquired whether I'd like 'one lump or two.'

'We haven't even poured out the tea yet,' said Chris, who was now standing next to a side table on which was arranged a formal looking tray of tea things. 'Shall I pour, Adrienne?' he asked his employer, and I was struck again by his easy familiarity with the dowager duchess, and the fact that he used her first name.

Mrs A nodded and finally sat in a chair at right angles to me.

'He's been very excited at the prospect of seeing you again,' she told me, which seemed a little bit far-fetched, but I didn't think it would be wise to say so.

'That screech was his welcome cry when he heard you speak,' Chris chimed in. 'I used to get it, but he takes me for granted these days.'

He brought tea over for Mrs Audesley and me, served in fine bone china cups—with saucers, of course—and placed them between us on a wine table. Meanwhile, Sir Galahad was gently plucking my hair, and purring like a contented cat. I reached up and ruffled his throat feathers a little, and he announced in the fondest of terms that my mother was sired by a German shepherd.

'Sir Galahad!' Mrs Audesley bellowed severely, and the bird instantly flopped down onto my shoulder. He extended his head round to my face and tut-tutted at me, as if I was the one with the foul mouth.

'I'm sorry about that, Tao,' his owner said, 'but I think I warned you that his language can be a little spicy at times. I think he does it for attention now. You're a naughty little show-off,' she said, wagging her finger at the bird indulgently.

'Adrienne blames her wayward nephew,' Chris said as he took his place next to me again. 'But I've heard him say things that couldn't possibly have come from Jerome.' He looked accusingly in Mrs Audesley's direction, and she gave in with the tiniest hint of a grin.

'My husband was a little deaf, and I'm afraid I used to say things under my breath which Sir Galahad later repeated.'

'Silly old fart!' Sir Galahad piped in, as if he understood what she was saying all too well and was obliging us with a small demonstration.

Mrs Audesley chuckled fondly at this, and then glanced at the portrait of her husband. 'He was a lot older than I was, and I'm afraid he could be very difficult at times. I was tempted to poison his pink gin on several occasions,' she said lightly, 'but I released my emotions with the occasional whispered insult.'

Just then the bird started making a noise that sounded as if he was imitating someone being strangled, and I glanced at Mrs Audesley questioningly. She was looking at the bird with surprise, as if this was a new one on her as well. I turned to Chris, and as he mirrored her expression the noise suddenly changed to a cough and I felt something land on my lap. A small ball of I wasn't sure what. I picked it up and examined it more closely. It looked like a tightly compressed orb of seeds and vegetable matter, and a quick sniff confirmed my suspicions. The strange object had come from within the bird. Luckily I am not particularly squeamish, so I held it up to the bird and thanked him for the presentation.

At which point Mrs Audesley let out a sigh. 'If there was any doubt about his affection for you,' she began mysteriously, 'then there is no longer.'

Still none the wiser, I frowned at Chris.

'I should be offended,' he said wryly. 'It's a regurgitation. They only do it for those that they love, and I'm afraid he's never done it for me.'

'That's because you're a man,' Mrs Audesley said soothingly. 'It's clearly something he saves for the women in his life—although until now it's only been me.' She glanced at me sadly, but without resentment. 'And I have to admit he hasn't performed for me in quite a long time.'

The bird appeared to be listening intently, and whether or not he understood—and I was sure, of course, that he couldn't—he lifted his wings and took off towards his mistress where, on the top of her perfectly coiffured head, he announced, 'Here is the shipping forecast,' in a perfectly enunciated BBC accent.

'It's no good trying to sweet-talk me now,' his mistress said in feigned hurt tones, but she ruffled his feathers just the same. She might have looked faintly ridiculous, with a bird on her head like some bizarrely plumed hat, but somehow she got away with it. She looked over at me then.

'Well, at least I won't have to worry that my old friend will be pining while I'm away, I suppose.'

'And I promise to take very good care of him,' I said, because I thought that was what she wanted to hear and also because that was exactly what I intended to do. Apart from anything else, I was flattered that the bird liked me so much, and it's hard not to like someone back when they make their feelings so clear. Not that he was exactly a 'someone', being a parrot and everything, but the way he spoke so well, and at times in just the right context, it was easy to fool yourself that he was really a miniature human in parrot costume. Quite spooky, really.

'Amen!' Sir Galahad said, and his mistress managed a chuckle.

When we'd finished tea, Mrs A suggested that Chris show me around the garden—which, I presume, was her way of providing an opportunity for us to get better acquainted. For obvious reasons it was important to her that we got along, and I didn't at this stage see why we shouldn't, despite our bad start. And it was obvious that Mrs A thought a lot of him, especially since she allowed him to live in part of her house.

'How long have you been working for Mrs Audesley?' I asked as we strolled slowly along the path which led from the terrace at the back of the house. The layout of the garden was fairly traditional. It was long and narrow, but broken up with areas of shrubs and beds crammed with old-fashioned flowers. I didn't know much about gardens, but I could see that this one was very well kept.

'Four years,' he said. 'Although I've only been in the flat for just over a year.'

It occurred to me that, although he was lucky to live somewhere as nice as this, he couldn't earn very much. And neither would a garden this size take up the whole of his time, I wouldn't have thought. 'So, do you look after other gardens as well as this one?' I asked him chattily.

He nodded absently as he took a penknife out of the back pocket of his jeans and deftly dead-headed a pale pink rose that was past its best. I don't think he was really listening to me.

'And what do you do for entertainment round here?' I pressed on regardless.

He shrugged. 'This and that, though I'm not really one for going out much. I work most evenings during summer.' He moved ahead of me and began slicing the stems of some blowsy red flowers that I didn't know the name of.

'They don't look dead,' I said.

He turned and looked at me as if I was stupid. 'They're not. I'm cutting them for the house.' He went back to what he was doing. 'Adrienne likes fresh flowers in the house. It's part of my job.'

It was beginning to feel like hard work, this getting acquainted with the gardener, and I wondered if this was his way of paying me back for being offhand with him earlier. Which would be a bit childish, but, since I obviously hadn't made a very good first impression, I made a final effort to be friendly.

'I could stick around for a while if you like. Till you finish up here. And then perhaps we could have a drink somewhere close by. Get to know each other better before I move in.'

He was kneeling on the grass now, and I realised how he came to have muddy jeans. When I finished speaking he looked up at me again briefly, and seemed to consider my suggestion.

'Can't, I'm afraid. I've got someone coming to see me at the flat shortly.' He glanced at his wristwatch and, after muttering something under his breath, got quickly to his feet. He gathered the flowers he'd cut and, without speaking again, headed away from me back to the house.

With nothing else for it I followed him, feeling a bit of a fool. I found him in the kitchen, pouring water into a plastic bucket. I was about to say something else, some snidey remark about his attempts to be friendly being pretty shortlived, but I didn't get the chance because Mrs A came in then, and made a big fuss of the flowers. They started talking about them, using the Latin name for the plant as they made favourable comparisons to last year's crop, and I, who knew the English names of only about three garden flowers, felt distinctly out of it.

I saw Chris look at his watch again, and after turning off

the tap and placing the flowers in the bucket he excused himself. 'Gotta go, Adrienne, though I'll see you before you leave, of course.' Then he seemed to remember me. 'Nice to meet you, Tao,' he said, without much conviction. 'Just give me a knock if you need any guidance on our mutual friend, and try and let me know in plenty if time if you're going to be away from the house.'

He left then, and after a quick farewell to Sir Galahad, which involved him making the sound of a mournful trumpet that Mrs Audesley informed me was a burst of *The Last Post*, I left as well. Just in time to see a very striking, wealthy-looking woman in her early, possibly middle forties, hobbling down the steps in silly high heels towards the door of Chris's basement flat.

I wandered down to the nearby shops and discovered a pricey little gift shop that I found hard to resist for two reasons. One, I wanted to get something nice as a thank-you to Sophie for everything, and two, I was feeling agitated after my brief encounter with Mrs Audesley's gardener, and spending always calmed my nerves.

I mean, who did he think he was? Ordering me about like that, and worse—much worse—snubbing my invitation to go for a friendly drink. I tried comforting myself with the old 'it's his loss' chestnut, but it didn't ring all that true when I thought of the woman he'd turned me down for. Though what she saw in him was a mystery—unless she considered him her bit of rough, of course, I thought nastily. It is well known that some women get their kicks from dirtying their hands on the hunky hired help, and since he'd said he did gardening for other people, she might well have been one of his clients.

An unpleasant thought suddenly crossed my mind as I was

examining a nice little crystal candlestick that seemed to absorb the colour of everything around it—an image of Mrs Audesley and Chris cosying up on her pale blue sofa. I ejected it with a shudder and told myself to behave. Just because the woman was on first-name terms with her gardener, just because she seemed very at ease with him about the place, that did not mean there was anything else going on between them. The woman was in her seventies, for goodness' sake, and okay, so she might have a good neck, but a fifty-year age gap was just too revolting to contemplate.

The candlestick was one of a pair and as I tipped it over and saw the price ticket stuck to the base, it emptied my head of all other thoughts. I'd almost decided that they would be perfect for Sophie, but could I really afford sixty-five pounds? And besides, unless I left the price tag on she wouldn't even appreciate the expense I'd gone to.

I was the only browser in the shop at that moment. Apart from me there was a smartly dressed brunette who was heavily involved in a book behind the counter. So I took the pair of candlesticks over to her and, after sucking in some air, asked if she could manage any discount.

From the look on her face it was clearly a question she hadn't been asked before, but when her mouth finally closed she smiled at me warmly. She had strange pale grey eyes, and one of the smallest noses I'd ever seen. She reminded me of a fairytale wood creature, a nymph or a fairy, or something. Definitely on the supernatural side.

'I'm afraid I don't have the authority to do that,' she said. 'But I can show you some like them that don't cost nearly so much.' She got up and glided gracefully across the shop to a shelf in the corner that I'd overlooked. She was quite small, and very slender—the sort of person who makes me feel big and clumsy. She picked up a similar pair of candle-sticks and held them up to the light. 'You can hardly tell the difference,' she said.

I looked at them closely and saw that she was right.

'Apart from the price,' she said with a grin. 'These are just under twenty pounds.'

'Do you giftwrap?' I asked.

'Beautifully,' she said.

I rang Sophie when I got out of the shop half an hour later. During that time I'd become quite friendly with Alina, whom I discovered was just standing in for a couple of days while the shop's owner was away at a gift trade event in North Wales. Alina herself was currently 'between' acting jobs—which was stretching the facts just a little, I'd thought, when I heard the details. Indeed, the last acting job she'd had was six months ago, when she'd played the part of a mugging victim in a *Crimewatch* reconstruction. But I liked her upbeat confidence, and her certainty that the right role was just around the corner. When she learned I was mov-ing into the area, and where, she told me that was 'com-pletely amazing', and promised to come round and see me. I'd left the shop feeling quite uplifted, encouraged to meet a female who wasn't a bitch, and hopeful that I'd found a new friend.

By now it was getting on for six, and I wasn't even sure if I'd catch Sophie before she left work, but I did. She was just on her way out of the building, as a matter of fact, and I asked if she'd meet me at a pub not far from her flat in about half an hour. I wanted to talk, tell her all about Taylor and my awkward new neighbour, and I wanted to give her the present. And I wanted to do it all beyond the prying eyes and ears of the two Cs.

But she sounded dubious, impatient almost. 'I just wanted to get straight back to the flat and have a soak in the bath.'

'Oh, go on,' I wheedled, 'just a quick one. It might be the last chance we get for ages.'

'Okay,' she said with a sigh. 'But it really will have to be a quick one. I'm going out at eight.'

I didn't get a chance to ask where she was going because she disconnected.

She was frowning and looking at her watch when I got to the pub forty minutes later. I was very apologetic, of course, but she refused another drink when I offered her one.

'I'm sorry, Tao, but I can only stay another ten minutes. As it is I'm going to miss out on my bath.'

I passed over the gift, which had indeed been beautifully giftwrapped in lime-green paper and purple ribbon by Alina, and hoped it would soften her up while I went to the bar. It was fairly quiet, thankfully, and the barman, a middle-aged man with a sad expression and sandy-coloured ponytail, nodded in silent, morose recognition when I ordered a glass of red wine.

Sophie seemed pleased enough when I got back, but there was still a look of elsewhereness in her eyes. She held up one of the candlesticks and smiled. 'They're fabulous, Tao, but you shouldn't have. I know how tight money is at the moment, and these must have cost a bomb.'

I didn't deny it, but I pooh-poohed her objections. 'I just wanted you to know how grateful I am for everything.'

'I know you are,' she said.

'I met Taylor Wiseman today,' I told her quickly. 'You know—the TV chef. And guess what?'

But I'd lost her again. She was putting the candlesticks back in their gift box and transferring them to her bag. She looked up at me blankly.

'He's asked me to go to his place tomorrow to talk about a possible job.'

'That's nice,' she said.

'It's more than nice! It's brilliant. It could be the start of something really big.'

She nodded. 'I'll keep my fingers crossed, then, shall I?'

I was beginning to get annoyed with her. She should have been gushing with excitement by now, not offering to keep her damn fingers crossed.

'What about the house?' she asked, sounding a bit more enthusiastic now. 'Everything still okay there?'

'Fine. I'll be moving in on Saturday, at twelve-ish, I told Mrs Audesley. Is that still okay for you?'

'Great,' she said. 'I'm looking forward to seeing the place.' She was slipping her bag onto her shoulder and there was a look of apology forming on her face. 'I'm sorry, Tao, but I really will have to leave now.'

'But where are you going?' I said. What could be more important than my exciting news? I was actually thinking, but managed not to say.

'I've got a hot date,' she said, getting up.

'Not with Mrs Audesley's prodigal nephew, by any chance?'

'As a matter of fact, yes,' she answered defensively. 'And I wish you wouldn't make it sound as if there's something dubious about his character. The only thing you know for certain about him is that he's done you an enormous favour.'

She was right, and I couldn't deny it. For all I knew, Mrs Audesley's reasons for disliking her nephew were quite un-reasonable. And, come to think of it, Chris had as good as defended him when he'd said that Jerome wasn't responsi-ble for *all* of Sir Galahad's bad language. 'Sorry,' I said, giving in to the inevitable of being left on my own to drink my wine. 'Have a great time.'

She gave me a grateful nod and then looked a bit coy. 'You can have my bed tonight, if you like. I might be late so I'll sleep on the sofa.'

Which was Sophie-speak for, *In all probability I won't be coming home tonight*.

Because I didn't want to get in the way while Sophie was preparing for her big date, I hung around the pub for a while. I had another glass of red wine, and a packet of pork scratchings, and when they were gone I dawdled home through the narrow, busy streets. I picked up a couple of cream cheese and smoked salmon bagels from the twenty-four-hour bagel shop, and found the flat empty when I got in. For once I was a bit disappointed. It would have been fun to tell the two Cs about Taylor, to rub their noses once more in my move to Hampstead. They went out a lot during the week, though I had no idea where they went or how they managed to fund their outings. As far as I knew neither one of them had a current boyfriend, so they must have been spending their own money.

I could have phoned my parents and told them my news, but I knew they wouldn't be all that impressed. Never having owned a TV, they wouldn't have heard of Taylor Wiseman, and besides, I wanted to be a little more sure of my ground first. I hadn't even told them about my move yet, so if anything definite came from my meeting with Taylor tomorrow I could tell them the whole lot together.

I spent part of the evening watching TV—a ghoulish hospital drama that involved close-ups of open wounds made wonderfully real by the make-up department. Then, although I still had another day to go, I made a feeble attempt at some packing before planning to use the hot water that I had deprived Sophie of. I was also planning to 'borrow' some of Fiona's expensive bubble bath, then rub out the marker line the suspicious cow had made on the bottle and create a new one. In fact I was just checking her make-up drawer for the right colour eyeliner when the front door-bell rang.

Luckily I hadn't got as far as stripping off yet, because when I answered the intercom I got a nasty shock. It was Peter Parker, the landlord, asking if he could come in.

'What for?' I asked cautiously.

'I had a message from one of those posh birds. She said there was a problem with the light fitting in her room.'

No one had told me that. And what was he doing, coming around here at this time of night? 'I'm sorry,' I said, 'but there's only me here at the moment. Can't you come back tomorrow?'

'No, I can't. Now, open the door like a good girl, or I'll just use my own key anyway.'

I sighed and pressed the buzzer to open the street door, alarmed for Sophie's sake to learn that he had such easy access to the flat, and alarmed for my own sake that I was about to be alone with him. I could hear him dragging his feet over the uncarpeted stairs, and I opened the door before he reached it. I left it open, just in case I needed to make a fast getaway.

He was dressed in two shades of denim tonight—black jeans, blue jacket—and he was carrying a metal box that I assumed contained his tools. I managed a smile as it didn't seem sensible to appear unfriendly.

'I'll leave you to it, then, shall I?' I said.

'I wouldn't mind a drink,' he said as he gave me the once-over.

I hesitated. I didn't want him hanging around, and yet I didn't want to antagonise him either. 'Tea okay?' I asked as I uttered a silent groan.

'Tea's good,' he said.

He followed me into the kitchen and I switched on the already fullish kettle. 'Better wait till it's boiled 'cause I may have to switch the electricity off.'

I shrugged, and then busied myself with teabags and things as he plonked himself down at the kitchen table.

'Had a helluva day,' he said with a heavy sigh.

Unfortunately I felt some response was necessary. 'Oh, yes?' I said, glancing around at him. 'What have you been up to?'

The kitchen was poky, with hardly room for a table, and his presence was overpowering. He smelt of very stale BO and I wondered if I could get away with spraying some air freshener without offending him. I decided I probably couldn't.

'Having a row with the Social. They're threatening to stop my benefits. Seem to think I might have some undisclosed income.'

I turned and looked at him properly. Like rent from a sub-let council flat, I thought, but wisely didn't say. His eyes were narrowed to a slit.

'I'd be really upset if I thought someone had grassed me up,' he said meaningfully.

'Why would anyone do that?' I asked as casually as I could manage. Luckily the kettle clicked off at that moment and I could get on with making the tea.

'All sorts of reasons,' I heard him say, 'but none worth the trouble they'd come up against if I found out who it was.'

I put some milk in the tea, removed the teabag, and turned to ask if he'd like some sugar. When I'd added the requested three spoonfuls, I decided it was high time to change the subject. 'So where do you live yourself?' I asked chattily.

'Not far,' he said, in a way that sounded to me like an additional threat.

'With anyone?' I pressed blithely on.

He looked a little bit embarrassed now. 'With my mum,' he murmured quietly.

Suddenly he didn't seem nearly so scary, this thirty-odd-year-old man with his big talk and his silly tattoo...who still lived with his mother.

'Does she give you a hard time?' I said, on a hunch.

'Does the Pope say his prayers?' Peter said dismally. 'She'll kill me if the Social carry out their threats. She's forever nagging me to get a job.'

'Why don't you, then?'

'Easy for you to say,' he said huffily. 'It's hard when you ain't got no qualifications.'

And I didn't suppose that his appearance helped much either. He could be smartened up if someone tried very hard, and made to smell a lot better, but it would be difficult to hide that thing on his face.

'Well, I haven't worked for over a year,' I said, to make him feel better, conveniently forgetting to mention that I'd been learning a trade for most of that time. 'But I'm hoping my luck's about to change.' He wasn't exactly first choice to share my news with, but I did it anyway. And to my surprise he seemed quite excited for me.

'My mum's a big fan,' he said, shaking his head with the sort of indulgence that made me realise how fond of his mother he was, despite everything. 'I'm not allowed to open my mouth when that American's on.' He looked at me slyly.

'If you get the job, I'll tell her you'll bring him round for a chat. That should keep her off my back for a while.'

I didn't dispel his hopes there and then, not when he seemed in such a good mood, but as he downed the last of his tea I reminded him why he'd come here. 'Whose room did you think has the lighting problem?' I said pointedly.

He got up reluctantly and went to Jemima's room. Two minutes later he reappeared. 'Got any lightbulbs?' he wanted to know.

I didn't have a clue, but guessed if we had that they'd be in the cupboard next to the sink. I was right, and I handed him one.

He was back again in less than a minute. 'Thought so,' he said with a slow shake of his bison-like head. 'Silly bitch probably doesn't know that you have to change them occasionally.'

And, don't ask me why, but there and then I decided that I quite liked Peter Parker.

Sophie must have gone straight to work from Jerome's place the following morning, and I couldn't help feeling a little prude-like disapproval. That's another thing I've reacted against. My mother remains so stuck in a Woodstock mind-set—all that *free love* and everything—that she insisted in putting me on the Pill on my fifteenth birthday, as if it was an accepted coming-of-age tradition. I was appalled, and deeply embarrassed, but for a quiet life I'd pretended to take the contraceptive while actually flushing it down the toilet. I would have been the envy of all my friends at school if I'd told them, for having such an enlightened parent, but I kept it to myself and secretly longed for the sort of mother who would lecture me on the folly of teenage sex.

I didn't get around to actually doing the deed until I was eighteen—much later than most of my friends—but I still wouldn't call myself particularly experienced by the time I moved in with Mal. As it turned out that was part of the problem for me. I kept wondering what it would be like with someone else, and it wouldn't have been fair to cheat on him. It's hard to know whether he'd have felt any better if I'd just told him the truth, but my guess is that it wouldn't have made much difference. It added up to rejection, whatever the reason, even the one I gave him about feeling too young for settling down.

I made up for my shortfall a little during my year at photography school, but I'd guess I was still way down on the scoring average of most twenty-five-year-olds.

I arrived at the Front Page with ten minutes to spare, and had to endure being glared at by Amber as I waited in the reception area. I'd have liked to ask her exactly what her problem was, in the manner I'd expect Peter Parker to use, but I didn't want to get into a slanging match in earshot of the boss's office. Besides, I knew the answer to the question anyway. At least I knew what her current problem was where I was concerned. Not only had I wangled an appointment with Jerry Marlin, but I had also been last seen leaving the building with one of the hottest TV properties around at the moment.

I could tell she was bursting to say something, but I tried to ignore her by closing my eyes and concentrating on the spiel I'd prepared to dazzle Jerry Marlin with. However, I got only as far as the firm, confident handshake in my imagination, when I heard her speak. It sounded more like a hiss, actually, and a decidedly venomous one.

'I'd be careful if I were you,' she began, and I opened my eyes cautiously. She had moved round the desk and was perched on the front edge of it now, her skinny arms folded tightly round her concave chest.

I smiled enquiringly. 'How so?' I said.

'With that TV chef.'

'Taylor?' I said, just to remind her I was on first-name terms with him.

'Rumour has it he's shacking up with Mary Deacon—you know, the producer who made him famous.'

I shrugged. I was sure she was lying, following my conversation with Taylor yesterday, but I didn't want her to think I gave a damn either way. 'What's that to me?' I said. 'My only interest in Mr Wiseman is the possibility that he might put some work my way.'

She didn't look as if she believed me. 'If you say so,' she said snidely. 'But he knows where his bread is buttered, and if it came to a contest my guess is that you'd lose hands down.'

Until then I hadn't seriously considered Taylor in the way she was hinting at. At least I don't think I had. I thought he was attractive, of course, and I'd been flattered by the attention he'd shown me. I also thought it might be fun to work with someone who was adored by so many women, but I hadn't seen it going any further than that. He wasn't really my type, for a start. There was something a bit obvious about his good looks for my particular tastes, but to tell Amber that would only invite her scorn. Of that I *was* certain. I was also annoyed with the suggestion that I was out of his league. While I could secretly acknowledge that it was true, I wasn't about to admit it to her.

'Thanks for the warning,' I said with what was meant to be a mysterious smile that I hoped would annoy her more than any further denials. 'I'll bear it in mind.'

She was saved from responding by the sound of the intercom buzzing on her desk. She kept hostile eyes firmly on me as she circled back round and took the call, then she told me, as if nothing had happened, that I could go in and see Jerry now.

His office was a shrine to minimalism—a touch of light-coloured wood here, a bit of chrome there, and a great deal of glass in the form of a huge plate window looking down over the busy street below. I felt dangerously exposed, as if I was on show to the public, and Jerry must have seen the expression on my face.

'It's one way,' he said as he took my limp hand. 'We can see them, but they can't see us.'

I nodded, remembering the building as it was from the outside. A modern glass and concrete infill between two elegant Georgian properties. The exterior was completely without architectural merit but it was definitely impressive on the inside, and he seemed pleased when I told him so.

I had my portfolio with me, carefully arranged the night before after Peter Parker left, and I put it down now on his virtually empty desk. I'd read somewhere that this was a good idea. I wasn't feeling nearly so brave as I did yesterday, when I had nothing to lose, and claiming space in alien territory was supposed to empower the newcomer. And as this man could make or break my future, I needed all the empowerment I could get.

He looked amused, as if he knew what I was up to, but before I could blush he shook his head. 'There's no need to show me your work,' he said as he waved me into the seat across from his own. 'This is meant to be an informal meeting, and besides, you've already won our Mr Wiseman over and that's good enough for me.'

It would not have been a shrewd move to bring up the fact that Taylor hadn't seen any of my work as yet. 'I'm meet-

ing him later at his restaurant,' I said, and he nodded as if he
already knew.

'I spoke to him yesterday afternoon,' Jerry said. 'He likes
the idea of you being new and fresh. He thinks you'll work
well together.'

It couldn't be that easy, surely! 'Are you saying that I've
got the job?'

Jerry smiled and produced several sheets of paper, as if
by magic. I certainly didn't see where they came from. He
put them down on my leather folder and asked me to read
it in my own time and, when it was signed, drop it off at
Reception.

'It's a contract,' he explained when I didn't respond. 'You've
been booked for two weeks by Featherweight Productions,
the company behind the book. Though you won't be working flat out during that time, of course. It will be a matter of
fitting in the shoots when Taylor Wiseman is available.'

I nodded stupidly, unable to open my mouth.

'Basic agency rates will apply,' he went on brightly. 'But if
you do a good job we might be able to upgrade you next
time. There's a buzz out already on this book. Big pre-or-
ders in place. And if the show is taken up in the States you
could well make a real name for yourself.'

The daze I was in deepened when I glanced at the fee.
Basic rates or not, it was more than I'd ever imagined I
would earn on my very first job. It just seemed too good to
be true, only I couldn't say what I was thinking, now, could
I? It would only make him suspect I didn't think I was worth
what I was being offered. I was tempted to sign there and
then, before he had time to change his mind, but I did what
was expected of me, and with a great deal of effort I unzipped
my folder and slipped the contract into it.

He looked at his wristwatch then, and let out a sigh. 'I know we scheduled in half an hour,' he said regretfully, 'but something's come up and I'm going to have to cut our meeting short, unfortunately.'

But I was relieved. I was beginning to feel distinctly unreal, and the quicker I got out of there the quicker I could pinch myself to make sure this was actually happening. So up I got up quickly, full of smiles now as I retrieved my portfolio. He got up too, and walked me to the door of his office. He held out his hand and this time I shook it firmly.

'I've got the feeling this is just the start of a long and successful association, Tao,' he said, and I must have been coming round a little now, because I found myself wishing he'd said it on the other side of the door, so that Amber could hear.

The Tulip, the restaurant where Taylor worked, was only a five-minute walk from the office, so I strolled around the old flower hall for a while, in order to kill some time. I didn't take much notice of the shops and the stalls, but I paused for a while on the balcony, to listen to a young man playing a classical piece on a violin. Quite a crowd had gathered and for one crazy moment I was tempted to make a public announcement about my new job.

Fortunately I managed to resist the temptation and I arrived at the restaurant at precisely the appointed time. It turned out to be one of those swanky places with a bay tree on either side of the entrance, and I would normally have found it intimidating. But not today, not in my state, which by then was bordering on euphoric. It wasn't due to open till twelve-thirty, and I had to ring on the outside bell and wait to be admitted.

A short and pleasant-looking young man eventually

opened the door, and looked as if he was expecting me. Which was a relief, because despite all the excitement my concerns about it all being too easy had begun to haunt me. What if it was just some horrible practical joke? What if, at this very moment, Taylor Wiseman was splitting his sides as he laughed down the phone at my expense with Jerry Marlin?

My paranoia receded when the young man informed me that 'Chef weel be weeth you soon,' in a thick French accent. He was wearing black trousers and an open-neck white shirt at the moment, but I presumed he'd be adding a tie soon enough, and possibly one of those tablecloth aprons that waiters in smart and pretentious restaurants are often given to wear. I followed him into the dining room, which was simple and chic. A lot of white linen and pictures of, well…tulips—one the few garden flowers that I did recognise. They were the sort that you find in early bound books on botany, set off nicely in old gold frames. There were also fresh yellow tulips in an enormous glass vase on a Georgian-style mahogany sideboard, and all in all it was a lot more cosy and comfortable than I'd somehow expected it to be.

I was shown to a table at the back of the dining room and refused the waiter's offer of coffee. I was already buzzing so much on adrenaline that caffeine would have had me climbing walls.

A few moments later Taylor appeared, dressed in the pristine kitchen whites that he wore on TV. I smiled as he sat down opposite me.

'Shouldn't they be all splattered in food by now?' I said.

He looked down at his double-breasted jacket and grinned. 'They will be later, I promise you. I'm the hands-on kind of chef, but we do everything to order.' He looked at me for a moment without speaking. 'Has Jerry told you?'

I hesitated briefly. 'You do know this will be my first professional job ever, don't you?'

'Of course I do.' He shrugged. 'Like you know that this is my first cookery book ever. We've all got to start somewhere. Now,' he said in a brisker tone, 'down to business, I suppose. You said you might have some ideas…'

Ah, yes. So I had. And I'd been racking my brains ever since the words had slipped out. To not much avail. Or at least not until I was wandering around the old flower hall, imagining how it used to be before it became a tourist attraction. My imaginings were mixed with a scene from *My Fair Lady,* with Audrey Hepburn as Eliza Doolittle in all her new finery. The one where she goes back to the market to see the people who had once been her friends before Mr Higgins changed her so much she didn't fit in any more. One thing had led to another in my head, and finally met up with something that Jerry had said about Taylor's show.

'Jerry said you were hoping the show would be taken up in the US,' I said.

He nodded, but didn't speak.

'Well, I was thinking that it might be nice to take some shots of you in parts of London that tourists—American *or* British—wouldn't normally see. With the sort of people they probably don't know exist. Real places, real people.'

He still didn't speak, and his eyes drifted off to a blank bit of wall on his left. It was impossible to guess what he was thinking, but he was clearly mulling something over. I opened my mouth to speak again, but he must have sensed it and he raised his hand as if to politely shut me up. Then, finally, when I was beginning to think my idea must be rubbish, he turned his eyes back on me.

'I love it!' he said. 'It's brilliant.'

'I'll show you the sort of thing I mean,' I said, trying not to seem too excited as I unzipped my portfolio and took out the recently developed prints of Brick Lane market, and of Felix's Place. I passed them to him and he nodded his head with enthusiasm as he flicked quickly through them.

'They're great,' he said. 'Just great.' He looked over at me. 'Can I borrow these? I'd like to show them to my producer, help sell the idea to her.'

'So you need to get her approval?' I said cautiously, remembering what Amber had said about Mary Deacon.

He shrugged again. 'I guess so. She is my boss…' He paused for a moment and I had the feeling that he wasn't telling me something. I wondered if it had anything to do with the fact that he'd taken me on. Maybe his boss hadn't liked the idea very much and had insisted he consult her about anything else to do with me. 'But I just know that she'll love it,' he added more confidently. He took hold of my hand suddenly across the table, as if he was going to shake it, but just held it instead. 'If we do get the go-ahead, when do you want to make a start?'

'That's up to you and your boss,' I answered, more coolly now. He'd told me there was no one special in his life at the moment, and if he really did have something going with his producer then that made him a liar. Someone not to be trusted. But, then again, so long as it was only in personal matters it should not affect me, I assured myself. Which made me feel better.

He nodded and let go of my hand. 'Let me have a contact number and I'll get back to you as soon as I can.'

I took a pen out of my bag and looked vaguely around me for something to write on.

'Here,' he said, offering me his arm, 'put it on there.'

'On your sleeve?'

He smiled. 'Sure, and don't worry—I won't lose it.'

So I wrote my mobile number on his jacket sleeve, and in doing so had to rest my other hand on his to gain some purchase. And I got a strange tingle in my fingers as a direct result. I think he might have been aware of the effect this bodily contact was having on me because he grinned when I went red and snatched my hand away from his. Then he got up and spoke as if nothing had happened.

'It's a pity we're fully booked for lunch, or I'd ask you to stay and sample the menu. We don't have any pies on today, but I think you'd enjoy it just the same.'

'Another time, maybe,' I said with a forced smile, still a bit shaky as I got up from the table. I wasn't remotely disappointed. I probably wouldn't have stayed if there had been a free table, because I just wanted to get out of there now and get some air.

I made a few calls when I got back to the flat, and left my parents till last. I'd already called five or six friends, three of whom had been on the photography course with me. In their case I tried not to sound too smug, especially when I learnt they were still out of work, but on the whole I think they were encouraged. If Tao Tandy could do it then surely they could as well...

It was still afternoon, and my father wouldn't be back from work for another couple of hours. He is senior social worker, and leads a team who specialise in the welfare of children. It's a job with lots of downsides and frustrations, but he firmly believes that it makes enough difference in some children's lives for it to be worthwhile. I'm not sure how worthwhile what my mother does is. She makes dreamcatchers, from willow and feathers and all sorts of things that she finds on the beach and in the countryside, and sells them on stalls at Green Fairs and festivals, where she hangs out with other ageing hippies to smoke pot, hug the odd tree, and talk mostly about *the environment*. I suppose the last bit is fairly worthy, or at least it would be if she and her friends did anything more than recycle a few bottles and keep up their annual Greenpeace membership subscriptions.

I don't think she goes in for 'free love' these days, I'm happy to say—not since she married my father, in fact—but I'm just so glad I've grown up now and can no longer be dragged along with her. It was bad enough being dressed like a miniature version of my mother in strange clothes that she bought mostly from charity shops, and beaded braids she put in my hair. It set me apart from the other kids when I was small, and made me a target for bullies as I got older. Until I was twelve, that is, when I moved to the senior school and got myself a job at the local newsagents, delivering newspapers from six-thirty till eight in the morning, then again after school. It was hard work, but worth it. It gave me enough money to buy my own clothes, so I could pretend I was like everyone else. That was the theory anyway, but I still felt like an Eliza Doolittle, neither quite fitting in at home anymore, or with the people at school that I wanted so badly to be like.

'It's Tao,' I said when the ringing tone ended. My mother had the unnerving habit of not speaking when she answered the phone—at least it unnerved people who didn't know her odd ways.

'How goes it, sweetie?' she replied in a far-off way that told me her mind was on other things.

'It goes well,' I said. 'Not only have I found somewhere to live, but I've also landed a job. And a good one at that.' As I was speaking I was reaching for the contract I'd left on the table, and I read out some of the details, including my fee for the fortnight.

'Two and a half thousand pounds!' she screeched, and I knew that I had her attention now. 'For two weeks' work! You've got to be kidding… Do you know how many dream-catchers I'd have to produce to make that much money?'

'No,' I said, annoyed with her for missing the point. 'Tell me.'

She didn't recognise irony when she heard it, and there was a silence as she was obviously totting things up in her head. After what seemed an interminable time, and about two pounds fifty in mobile phone charges, she came up with an answer. 'About five hundred—and it could take a couple of years to sell that many.'

'Then why don't you do something else,' I said, beginning to lose my patience now. 'It's not exactly a money-spinner, is it?'

'It isn't all about money, Tao,' she said huffily. 'I thought I'd taught you that much, at least.'

I must be a great disappointment to my mother. Not to my dad, thankfully, because he is a keen photographer too, and I think he was really pleased when I left the bank to give it a go. My mother was glad as well, but for different reasons. To her, working in a bank was practically evil, as if I was involved with the forces of darkness, or guilty of robbing the poor to pay the rich. She was certainly relieved when I renounced my formally wicked ways, but she'd have liked it much better if I'd kicked over the traces entirely and spent a year being completely irresponsible on the Indian sub-continent, as she wished *she'd* done in the glorious Sixties.

'It might sound good,' I said, trying hard to be reasonable, 'but it's a precarious career that I've chosen and I might not get another job for months.'

'Like you say, though, Tao,' she said disapprovingly, '*you* chose it.'

For someone who considered herself to be a gentle free spirit, she could still deliver a killer put-down. 'Yes, Mum,' I said, because I knew there was no sense in arguing, 'and I'm not complaining either. I'm very happy, and I just wanted you and Dad to know that. Now, I've got to pack everything up for my move tomorrow, so I'd better go.'

'Without giving us your address first?'

I sighed and gave it to her, and promised to be in touch very soon. Though I made my mind up that next time I called it would be when I was certain my father was in. He, at least, would be happy for me.

I did everything I had to do and then had a long soak in the bath. By the time I got out it was getting quite late, and there was still no sign of Sophie or the Cs. I was feeling a bit sorry for myself, as a matter of fact. I imagined that they'd all gone out straight from work for the evening—which was fine as far as the Cs were concerned, but I was disappointed in Sophie. It wasn't like her to put a man before friendship, and as well as my disappointment I couldn't help feeling uneasy. I know I hadn't met Jerome Audesley yet, but there was something about the whole situation that just didn't feel right.

And I didn't change my opinion even when I learnt I'd been wrong about Sophie letting me down.

I'd just made myself a sandwich, from some leftover

tuna and stale brown bread, and was looking ahead to a night in front of the television, when I heard the front door open. I was still wearing Sophie's bathrobe and had a towel wrapped round my head, so I wasn't best pleased when the two Cs stumbled in with several strange men in tow.

'Surprise!' they called out as I tried making a quick retreat to Sophie's room, and I saw that they were holding up a bottle of wine in each hand. Furthermore, they were smiling at me...

Then Sophie came in as well, and laughed when she saw the state I was in. 'I knew I should have warned you,' she said, 'but the girls thought it would be fun to surprise you.'

I'll bet they did, I thought as I looked a bit closer at the men who seemed to fill the small sitting room. There were four of them. One each, I thought ruefully, and guessed straight away which one was Sophie's. He was tall and very good-looking, in a confident, floppy-haired, public school-boyish sort of way, and he was eyeing me with amusement.

'This is Jerome,' Sophie said, taking his arm, and the two Cs looked on adoringly.

I held the neck of the robe together and extended my hand. 'I think I owe you a thank-you,' I said.

He took my hand nonchalantly and slipped the other round Sophie's shoulder. 'We're even,' he said. 'I'd never have met this beautiful woman if she hadn't circulated that e-mail on your behalf.'

And, yes, okay, so it was pleasant enough, what he'd just said, and I could see that Sophie was lapping it up, but I disliked him intensely. He just sounded so completely smarmy. But I didn't have time to respond, because then Sophie was introducing the rest of them—friends of Jerome's—who all looked a bit like him, strangely enough, but weren't quite so good-looking.

There was a Simon and a Lawrence and a Henry, and I think Henry was earmarked for me because the two Cs were moving rapidly in on Simon and Lawrence. I nodded and smiled and excused myself, and when I went to Sophie's room to dress I found myself longing now for that night on my own in front of the telly.

Sophie came in while I was slipping into a pair of jeans and asked me if I was okay. 'I thought you'd appreciate a decent send-off,' she said, 'and the Cs jumped at the idea when I rang them at work.'

'Especially when you mentioned bringing some friends of Jerome's along,' I said.

Sophie smiled wryly and sat on the edge of the bed. 'What do you think?' she asked in a whisper, her eyes larger than usual in her excitement.

'He's very good-looking,' I said truthfully. I pulled on a pink T-shirt with an embossed red heart on the front of it, which covered my face for a moment and hid my misgivings—I hoped.

'He is, isn't he?' she said happily. 'But it isn't just his looks. He's just so... I don't know, sooo *different*...'

He was that, all right. But I didn't want to spoil this last evening with Sophie by telling her what I really thought.

And so I spent a lot of it drinking wine, avoiding eye-contact with Jerome, and being as pleasant as possible—mostly to Henry, who worked in the City, liked sailing and fast cars, and spent most weekends at his parents' home in Surrey. I think he found me as boring as I found him, and I wasn't surprised, or sorry, when he made his excuses and left before the others. It gave me the opportunity to slip away, virtually unnoticed, after getting the wink from Sophie that she would be spending the night at Jerome's place.

And it was only when I crawled into bed, with cotton wool in my ears to drown out the sound of booming music, that I realised I'd got through the whole evening without a single sarcastic comment from the two Cs. They'd even opened a treasured bottle of champagne to toast me when they heard about my job. But they were pretty drunk by then, and I think their generosity had a lot to do with impressing Jerome and his friends—not to mention the hope I'd introduce them to Taylor. Even though I made it perfectly plain that wasn't ever likely to happen.

I had trouble getting the Cs out of bed the following morning. They both had raging hangovers, and for a while I feared they were going to renege on their promise of helping me with the move. However, after a lot of groans and a fair bit of extremely unladylike cursing, Jemima eventually gave me her keys and told me to load up the car myself. It ended up so crammed full that there wouldn't have been room for Sophie as well, so I phoned her mobile—which she had switched off—and left a message. I told her the situation and said that I'd ring again once I was installed and see if she'd like to come over later.

The Cs eventually emerged just before noon, and were surprisingly chatty—to one another—on the journey to Hampstead, while I sat squashed in the back with my things. The weather was good, and they were both full of their plans for an afternoon picnic with Lawrence and Simon, which suited me fine because it meant they probably wouldn't be hanging around too long.

They were as impressed as I expected them to be with the house, and by the cordial greeting we received from its distinguished owner. I caught them glancing at me now and then in a quizzical way, as if trying to work out how someone like me had pulled off such an amazingly lucky stroke. They were all over Mrs A, though. Smarming up to her in a way that made me embarrassed but which she seemed to take in her stride. Until Jemima unwittingly made a simpering reference to the family likeness between her and Jerome, that is.

'You think so, do you?' she said, pleasantly enough, but I sensed a spiky edge to her demeanour.

Having drooled over the first-floor bedroom that I would be using, and done as little as possible to help move my things in there, the Cs had been making small talk with Mrs Audesley in the drawing room before taking their leave. I'd forgotten to warn them that Jerome was a taboo subject, unfortunately, which is probably the reason I blame myself for what happened next.

'You haven't met Sir Galahad, have you?' Mrs A said out of the blue, and the Cs looked at one another blankly. They were both in their casual uniform today—jeans with preppy V-neck sweaters, one lemon, one pink—and despite being the worse for wear they'd still managed to apply full, if understated, make-up.

'It's the…' I began, but stopped just in time. I'd been about to say 'parrot', which would have been a big mistake. 'The African Grey that I'll be looking after,' I said.

The two Cs suppressed a smirk. 'No,' said Fiona, 'but we'd love to, wouldn't we, Jemima?'

'Oh, yes,' agreed Jemima. 'I simply adore parrots. They're just so clever and amusing.'

I was surprised when Mrs A failed to correct them. 'Please,' she said, indicating Sir Galahad's room with a wave of her hand. 'Only do shut the door after you.'

I watched with a certain amount of trepidation as they happily entered the room. There was just something about the look on Mrs A's face that bothered me. When the door closed behind them she looked at me, and there was a definite gleam in her eye. I frowned at her questioningly and she raised a hand to silence me.

Ten seconds later I heard a squawk. It sounded a little like the squawk of welcome I'd received the other day, but when it was followed almost immediately by a human scream, then another, I guessed that I must have been wrong about that. It all happened so quickly that I didn't have time to react, as such, and a moment later the door was flung open and with a look of sheer terror in their eyes the Cs staggered out in undignified disarray.

'He attacked me!' shrieked Fiona, holding her head as she slammed the door, then leant on it, hard, as if she was being pursued by an angry mob.

'He bit me!' Jemima howled bewilderedly, and she held up her index finger to prove it. It was bleeding profusely, dripping down her hand—and, call me unfeeling, but my first concern was for the cream carpet.

I ran over to her, pulling a tissue out of my pocket on the way.

'Why didn't you warn us that he was vicious?' Jemima said accusingly as I mopped up the blood.

'I didn't know he could be,' I told her lamely, and it was true as well. I'd genuinely believed that Mrs A was joking, or at least exaggerating, when she told me that some of the previous pet-sitting applicants were threatening to sue, but I wasn't so sure now.

I could see the old dislike back on Jemima's face as she shook her hand free. Mrs Audesley had been cursorily examining Fiona's head in the meantime, and at that moment let go of her dismissively.

'It's just a small scratch, but I'd recommend some TCP for that finger of yours,' she said to Jemima. 'If you go to the main bathroom with Tao, I'm sure she'll be able to find some for you.'

Jemima looked at her furiously. She was about deliver a tongue-lashing, I was sure, and I shrank uncomfortably into the background. It was perfectly obvious that Mrs A had guessed what was going to happen, that she'd sent them into the room intentionally—and all because of a throwaway comment about her resembling Jerome. I didn't know what to be shocked by most, her deliberate wickedness or the depth of dislike she clearly felt for her great-nephew. One thing I was certain of, though, and that was the strong desire I felt at the moment not to make her *my* enemy.

I held my breath and waited as Mrs A visibly took up the challenge, expanding her already ample chest in readiness. Maybe that was what did it, but suddenly, to my surprise and relief, Jemima's expression suddenly changed.

'It's okay,' she said, backing off. 'Fiona can drive and I'll stop off at a chemist on the way back. No real harm done,' she added as she looked askance at the gaping, bloody wound.

I actually felt bad about it, and from the nasty look I received at that moment I was clearly the one who was now taking the blame. They left quickly after that, without any further comment. Until I walked with them to the door, when Jemima turned on me.

'I suppose you think you're clever, don't you? Making us look stupid in front of Jerome's aunt. And after all we've done for you, too.'

I shook my head defensively. 'I'm sorry,' I said. 'I didn't mean for that to happen, and I'm grateful to you for helping me out. I really am.'

'Grateful and sorry enough to introduce us to Taylor Wiseman?' she said slyly.

'Yes,' I agreed after a pause, quite admiring her opportunistic cheek, 'as much as that.'

Jemima sucked her finger and nodded mournfully. 'Then we'll expect to hear from you soon.' She was silent for a moment, and then eyed me narrowly. 'And don't feel too bad about Henry abandoning you,' she said with transparently dressed-up spite. 'It was patently obvious that you weren't his type.'

I was ever so tempted to tell her what I really thought about Henry, and all the others for that matter, but I was bigger than that and I let it go. 'I'll try not to,' I said.

I saw Mrs Audesley off in her taxi at four o'clock, after a long and private farewell to Sir Galahad from which she emerged wearing elegant sunglasses, in order to hide, I imagine, her red-rimmed eyes. On her departure she'd issued me with two pages of carefully handwritten instructions, and I studied them while I drank Earl Grey tea with a slice of lemon in the luxurious kitchen.

It was a lot to take in. Everything from his complicated diet to the amount of social interaction he required—which was quite a lot, apparently. There was also a long and rather worrying list of things to look out for in regards to his health and well-being. *If in any doubt,* it read, underlined in bold red ink, *contact the vet immediately.* The number for which was writ large at the head of the page.

I was a little concerned about coping with all the attention he seemed to require, and I thought about calling on Chris for some old-fashioned reassurance. I was mulling things over in my mind, thinking how offhand he'd been with me, and weighing this against his obvious interest and concern for the bird, when somebody rang the front doorbell. And it turned out to be the man himself.

'Just checking to see how you're settling in,' he said, without smiling.

'Come in,' I said, standing back to allow him to pass. I didn't smile either.

He followed me into the living room and made himself comfortable on one of the sofas. I'd been thinking of letting Sirg out of his room anyway, so I opened the door and allowed him to join us. I'd had a little chat with him earlier. Told him what a naughty boy he was: but he was obviously unrepentant.

He flew straight onto Chris's head and began plucking out strands of his hair.

I told him what had happened earlier, and he made a perch with his finger and lifted Sir Galahad round where he could see him. 'How many times have I warned you about being unpleasant to guests?' he said.

'What shocked me was that Mrs Audesley seemed to do it deliberately,' I said with a frown. 'She must have known what was going to happen.'

'Then your friends must have upset her,' Chris replied as he stroked the bird's chest. 'She's a brilliant woman, but it doesn't do to cross her.'

I couldn't help noticing that he was looking a lot smarter than when I'd seen him last. Clean jeans, newish-looking plain navy sweatshirt. I wondered if he was expecting another 'client' later. By now I'd completely dismissed the idea of any improper conduct with Mrs A, but that didn't mean he wasn't providing additional services for his other employers.

'I wouldn't call them my friends, exactly,' I said. 'In fact they don't even like me much. They only agreed to help me out because they're so nosy.'

Chris shrugged. 'Well, there we are, then. Maybe the old feller will have taught them a lesson.'

'I doubt it,' I said gloomily. 'They've just used the incident as a means of manipulating me.' Which made me think about my job and the fact that I was going to need Chris's help. So I'd told him I'd been offered some work.

'I know the timing's not great, but it's not full-time or anything,' I added quickly.

'Well, let's just hope we can sort something out between us,' he said doubtfully. 'I've got a busy schedule myself next week.'

I shouldn't have been, I suppose, but I found myself irritated by this comment. He was making himself sound very grand and important. Much more important than me, obviously.

'And don't forget that he's your responsibility,' Chris said, as if he could guess what I was thinking. Both he and Sir Galahad looked at me now. 'I'm just the back-up guy, remember.'

'But I've signed a contract,' I lied whingeingly. I hadn't got round to doing it yet, because it was the weekend and the office would be closed, but no way was I pulling out now. 'I have to be available when I'm required.'

'Sorry to sound unsympathetic,' he said, not sounding sorry at all, 'but you also made an agreement with Mrs Audesley. And, okay, I'll try to help out where I can, but it's very possible I won't always be available when *I* am required.'

I was getting madder by the moment. I could see that he had a point, but it was the way he was making it that I found so annoying. 'Fine,' I said coolly, 'so maybe you could let me have your itinerary for the next couple of weeks, so I'll know when not to *bother* you.'

At that moment Sirg lifted his wings and flew over to me. He perched on my shoulder and rubbed the side of his feathery head lovingly against mine, making me feel guilty for talking about him as if he was an inconvenience.

'I don't consider the old feller a bother,' Chris said, echoing my own guilty thoughts. 'But I can't do that, I'm afraid. I just don't happen to work that way. It depends as much on the weather as anything, and there is no predicting that in advance.'

I wondered meanly which kind of 'work' he meant, the indoor or outdoor variety. I don't think I'd have actually said it out loud, but I didn't get the chance anyway, because at that moment Sir Galahad made the sound of a telephone ringing in my ear.

'Do answer that blasted thing!' he shouted then, in the same imperious tones of his mistress. Which made me think about the woman, and how, despite my frustration, she was depending on me to do the right thing by her precious bird. And I also remembered that Chris would probably be speaking to her in the near future. She was bound to call him to see how I was getting on. 'Okay,' I said, struggling to sound reasonable. 'I don't want to fall out about this, so maybe I should just check with you on a daily basis.'

'Fine by me. As long as you remember that ultimately it's you that's in change of our feathered friend.'

He left shortly after that, with a friendly farewell to Sir Galahad and a cautious nod to me, and I didn't even bother to tell him about my general bird-sitting concerns. There didn't seem very much point. He'd made it quite clear that the problem was mine. So I sat and seethed for a while, until Sirg made me smile when he answered the bark of a dog in the street by a rapid shake of his head and the words, 'dratted animal!' in another excellent imitation of Mrs A.

I spent another hour with him, chatting away as I got my bearings around the house, while he perched precariously on my shoulder. I went from room to room, taking in the beautiful furnishings and exquisite pieces of silver and artwork. I was particularly drawn to several nicely framed miniature portraits that hung in a group over the dining room fireplace. I'd studied some art as part of my course, and I had a good idea that they were extremely valuable. I was increasingly glad of the intricate security system that Mrs Audesley had taken a good deal of time to explain to me before she left. I was also amazed all over again of the faith she was placing in me. What was even more extraordinary was that it was clearly all down to her African Grey, whom she seemed to endow with uncanny wisdom when it came to picking people she felt she could trust.

When we'd finished touring the house, Sirg helped me check out his food supplies, and because I'd remembered fresh fruit on the list, I looked in the fridge and found a large stock of all things exotic. He squawked in excitement, so I took out a star fruit and cut off a slice, which he proceeded to tear between beak and claws into surprisingly neat little bite-sized chunks. When we went back to his cage, he hopped into it quickly and let out a long low wolf whistle, for which I thanked him warmly as I closed the door. Then I turned on the radio, as per my instructions, and left him to listen to the six o'clock news on Radio Four.

There had been all sorts of goodies left in the fridge besides the bird's fruit, which Mrs Audesley had said were for me—to keep me going, until I got the opportunity to do some shopping. This included a packet of sumptuous-looking smoked salmon, I now discovered, and a couple of bottles of nicely chilled wine. There was also some healthy-looking wholemeal in the wooden bread bin, and as I contemplated my feast I thought about Sophie. I'd promised to ring her, and although I was tired, and would have welcomed an evening curled up with a book on one of Mrs Audesley's gorgeously comfortable sofas, my conscience got the better of me.

Only I didn't get as far as making the call, because just at that moment the doorbell sounded again. I guessed it was Chris, with some forgotten nugget about the responsibilities of my role as pet-sitter, and I prepared a smile. It had occurred to me that I was probably more likely to gain his co-operation if I remained pleasant, no matter how hard he tried to provoke me.

Maybe if I was determinedly nice he'd eventually come round and put himself out a bit for me. It was certainly worth a try, I decided.

But it wasn't Chris at the door. It was Sophie.

Sophie and *Jerome*.

Shit, I thought, imagining Chris downstairs in his basement flat. If Jerome opened his mouth he was bound to hear him and report straight back to Mrs A. So without further ado, without speaking first, I grabbed hold of Sophie and dragged her inside. And then I reached out and dragged Jerome in as well.

'Sorry about all that,' I said to an astonished Sophie, 'but Mrs Audesley said...' I looked at Jerome, who was looking amused again.

'My great-aunt said she didn't want me in the house and you were afraid that the gardener would hear me and report back to her.' He said the word 'gardener' in a derogatory way, as if it was a job to be despised.

'Precisely,' I said, as the two of them followed me through to the kitchen.

'But you said that she didn't mean it,' Sophie said to Jerome.

'She doesn't,' he replied with a dismissive shrug as he removed his jacket and hung it on the back of one of the chairs. 'She adores me, really. It's just that we had a small falling-out.'

'What about?' Sophie wanted to know.

He walked over to the fridge and opened it. 'Nothing important,' he said as he took out a bottle of Chevin Blanc. 'Just family stuff—you know how it is.'

Sophie and I looked at one another. Did we? we seemed to be asking one another. Despite the problems I had with my mother, I'd certainly never fallen out with any member of my family so badly it had resulted in a ban from their home, and I was fairly sure that Sophie hadn't either.

By now Jerome had opened the bottle and was taking glasses out of a cupboard. He certainly seemed to know where things belonged.

'Now,' he said in a businesslike manner as he poured out the wine, 'I'm sure Sophie would like to see the house, so if you show her around I'll prepare some food for us all. I take it you haven't eaten yet,' he said as he passed me a glass.

I shook my head. For some reason it didn't occur to me to object. He just seemed so at home in the place, and it didn't seem right to tell him to go now. But then I thought about Sirg. I wasn't sure how he'd react if he heard Jerome's voice. 'What about Sir Galahad?' I said.

'Do you imagine he's going to tell Aunty I've been here?' he said with a sneer.

'I just don't want him upset, that's all.'

Jerome lifted the sleeve of his pale blue cashmere sweater and glanced at his wristwatch. '*The Archers* will be coming on soon, so if you just turn up the radio he won't hear a thing. Especially if I stay here in the kitchen.'

'Okay,' I said cautiously, 'but I don't think you should stay very long.'

We left him to it and, after turning the radio up for Sirg, I showed Sophie around upstairs. There were five bedrooms in all, spread over two upper floors, but I'd guessed there had been more before rooms were altered to accomodate spacious *en-suite* bathrooms.

'I had no idea it was as incredible as this,' she said, agog at the drapes in the bedroom I'd chosen to use. There were two sets of silk curtains, one loose and plain, one gathered in cord and lightly patterned, and a toning yellow blind at the window. These dressings alone would have probably cost more than all of the furnishings put together in my parents' lounge. Especially since most of them came from junk and charity shops.

'Not bad, is it?' I said, sitting down on the edge of my bed with its mahogany scroll-edged ends. There were even flowers on the dresser beside it—yellow roses, mostly, with some sweet-smelling herb mixed in. We'd done all of the rooms now, except Mrs Audesley's, because I didn't feel it was right to nosy about in there.

Sophie's forehead crinkled into a frown as she turned to me. 'Do you think Jerome's aunt *was* serious about not wanting him here?' she said in a low voice.

'Deadly,' I said. 'And I have to be honest, I feel really bad about letting him in.' I shook my head. 'I can't let it happen again, Sophie. I'm absolutely certain she'd ask me to leave if she knew he was here.'

'She sounds like a bit of a tyrant,' she said defensively. 'I can't believe that Jerome has done anything too terrible.'

'Maybe not,' I said cautiously, 'but I have to abide by her wishes, and if Chris sees him here I'm sure he'll tell her.'

'Chris being the gardener, I suppose?'

I nodded and made a face. 'He's a bit of an old woman himself, if you ask me.' I thought about mentioning the fact that he seemed to like other old women for company too, but that would have required explanations that didn't seem very relevant at the moment.

Sophie sat down beside me on the bed. 'He really is great, you know, Tao,' she said dreamily. 'I've never known a man quite like him.'

'And what about the Cs?' I said, feeling uncomfortable. For some reason I really didn't want to hear what she had to say about Jerome Audesley. 'They seem to have hit it off with his friends as well.'

'Not in the same way, though,' she quickly replied.

'Have you seen them today?' I went on determinedly.

'No. They were still out on their picnic when I called back at the flat for a change of clothing.' She turned and smiled at me shyly. 'Jerome has asked me to move in with him.'

I felt panicky suddenly, and swallowed the remains of my wine to calm me. 'A bit soon, isn't it?' I finally managed.

She shrugged. 'Normally I would agree with you, but I think you know when you've met the right person. And what's the point in hanging around when you have?'

I couldn't tell her that she was mad, because mad people usually don't accept their condition and I was fairly sure that Sophie wouldn't. I wondered frantically if I should contact her parents, tell them that she needed forcibly rescuing, because I only had to look at her happy gleaming face to know that she had completely forfeited her personal freedom along with her sense.

Luckily Jerome called to us then, to tell us the food was ready, so I was saved from responding to the crazy woman. We went down the stairs, and although she asked to see Sirg I told her it wouldn't be a good idea. He'd been squawking as we passed through the hall, as if he knew something was amiss. And since he'd savaged two young women already that day he might have developed a taste for it.

That's what we talked about as we ate the food which Jerome had prepared—the salmon, with artichokes from a jar, along with a salad over which he'd poured a delicious honey and mustard dressing. Jerome was highly amused by the story, and Sophie, of course, laughed along with him.

We finished the bottle of wine between us and I was glad when Jerome slipped on his jacket as soon as we'd cleared the table. I made them promise to leave the house quietly, and to my relief they were as good as their word. I watched anxiously until they disappeared around the corner, where I presume Jerome had parked his car, and then, just as I was closing the door, my mobile started to ring.

It was Taylor, telling me that the first shoot was to take place in Brick Lane market at seven o'clock the following morning.

Which threw me into a mighty panic. There were just so many things to think about—not least of which was how the hell I was going to get there at such an unholy hour with all my equipment in tow.

He'd said that he liked the Brick Lane shots so much that it was where he wanted to start. If we could also manage some in Felix's café then so much the better, but he was happy to return at a later stage if it was going to prove too much in one day. What was important was the Sunday Market and, since he had a meeting at ten o'clock that he must attend, the earlier we got moving the better, as far as he was concerned. In fact he'd been all for starting at *six* o'clock if I'd have let him, but I had to remind him that the market didn't actually open till eight. On the other hand, having been a resident in the area a couple of weeks, with a certain privileged knowledge provided by one memorable all-night Saturday clubbing session to celebrate my arrival in the city,

I knew there would be things to photograph sooner than that. In fact, between seven-thirty and eight o'clock would be the ideal time for capturing the atmosphere without too many tourists and browsers to get in the way. So long as I could get there in plenty of time to set everything up, that is.

But first things first, I told myself as I remembered my agreement with Mrs Audesley. I was obviously going to be away longer than an hour, that was for sure, and if Mr Chris Ultimately-It's-Your-Responsibility wasn't available to take over from me then I might even have to cancel the shoot. Which as far as bad starts went was up there with the *Titanic* disaster. It seemed crazy to me—why couldn't the bird be left on his own for more than an hour?—but I'd already broken one important promise and I didn't dare push my luck too far.

So I took a few calming breaths, left the front door on the latch, and went down the stone steps to Chris's basement apartment. Practising my smile all the way. He answered quickly and I crossed my fingers behind my back in the earnest hope that he hadn't seen Jerome arriving at or leaving the house.

His long hair was in disarray, as if he'd been running agitated fingers through it, or—and the thought made me blush—someone else's fingers had been running through it… The important thing, however, was that he looked more surprised than guarded. And *guarded* was what I'd have expected if he *had* seen Jerome.

'I'm really sorry to trouble you,' I said, as humbly as I could manage, 'but I need your help.' Someone once told me that if you use the word 'need' when asking a favour, for some deep-seated psychological reason on the part of the would-be bestower of favours you usually got it.

He flattened his dishevelled hair with the palm of his hand. 'Go on,' he said, frowning curiously now.

The fact that he did not ask me in, that he kept his hand on the door as it stood a quarter open, as if barring the way, added to my suspicions that he had someone with him, but I thought that might work to my advantage now. It might make him more agreeable to my request if he wanted rid of me fast. 'I've just had a call, and I have to do a couple hours' work in the morning...'

He sighed lightly. 'I thought you weren't starting till Monday.'

'So did I.'

He considered this for a moment, then asked me what time I'd be leaving.

'I have to be at Brick Lane at seven.'

'And you'll be back by nine?'

I remembered what Taylor had said about his appointment. 'More like ten,' I said, pulling a face that I hoped looked both apologetic and appealing.

His raised his left eyebrow. 'That sounds like three hours, not two. And two is a "couple", isn't it?'

I got the feeling he was enjoying making this hard for me. 'Yes,' I agreed patiently. 'But according to my instructions I'm not supposed to wake Sir Galahad till eight o'clock, so it'll only be two hours actual birdsitting time required.'

'Mmm,' he said, considering this. 'And how do you intend getting there and back? I presume you don't have any personal transport?'

'I'll call a cab,' I said, getting a little bit sick of this now. It was, after all, none of his damn business how I got around.

'You could always borrow my van, I suppose—so long as you don't crash it, of course. It's insured for all drivers, but I couldn't afford to have it off the road while it was being repaired.'

I was more than a little taken aback by this surprisingly generous offer, and it occurred to me that the 'need' word was even more powerful than I'd imagined. 'Are you serious?' I said carefully, a little suspicious that he was having me on.

He shrugged. 'Only if you have a clean licence.'

I couldn't help wondering if there was a catch, but then again if this was a gift horse I really shouldn't look it in the mouth.

'And you promise to be back by ten?'

'Faithfully.'

'Hang on, then, and I'll get you the keys.' He pushed the door to on me, which I thought was pretty rude, but returned in a matter of seconds. 'I haven't had it valeted lately,' he said with a hint of sarcasm, 'but you'll just have to make do.'

'I'm really grateful,' I said as I took the keys. I looked vaguely behind me. 'Where will I…?'

'It's parked in the next street on the right. You can't miss it. It's the only vehicle there that doesn't look as if it belongs.'

'And I take it you have your own key for the house?' I said. 'So you can get in to see to Sir Galahad.'

He nodded and took a step back.

'See you tomorrow, then,' I said chirpily. Only I said it to myself, because the door had already clicked shut.

I spent the rest of the evening in a frenzy of making notes and testing my photographic equipment. Then, when that was done and I was satisfied, I panicked wildly for about ten minutes when I couldn't find any fresh rolls of film. I finally unearthed them in the place I'd looked first, only clearly not very well. Then I had what I thought was a bright idea of the killing-several-birds-with-one-stone variety, and made a couple of telephone calls. I also had a bath in my gorgeous *en-suite,* and afterwards went in to see Sirg and sang him a lullaby—'Rock-a-bye-Baby', because it was the only one that I vaguely knew—before covering him up for the night. It was on my list of instructions, and although I felt silly doing it, he seemed to like it a lot and chirruped sleepily along to my tuneless and faltering rendition.

I went to bed at eleven o'clock, fearful that I would not wake up when my alarm went off at half past five, and—as always happens at such times—I had difficulty falling asleep. I must have eventually drifted, though, because I woke with a start when the telephone on my bedside table blared in my ear soon after midnight.

It was Mrs Audesley, safely arrived at her son's home in Portugal, with anxious enquiries about her African Grey. I must have finally assured her that all was well, but it took the best part of fifteen minutes. Then came another reminder about Jerome, about not letting him into the house *under any circumstances—no matter what persuasive tactics he used,* and the guilty knowledge that he'd already been here and gone kept me awake for another hour. Maybe two. I was too afraid to look at the clock to be certain.

As it turned out I was actually awake before the alarm went off, and had everything packed into Chris's battered red van before six o'clock. I'd had to lay an old dust sheet down first, which I found in a cupboard, to protect my precious equipment from caked mud and dust, but it didn't stop me from being extremely grateful to him. I was still a bit flummoxed by the gesture. He'd seemed as curt and off-hand as he had been before, so I couldn't quite understand where all this generosity was coming from.

I went back into the house and took a quick shower, and changed into an outfit that was both comfortable and warm. It was a chilly morning, but the sky was clearing rapidly and I had high of hopes of it staying fine.

I didn't bother with food or drink. I was too concerned about driving across a city I was still so unfamiliar with. I also had to set the house alarm, which I'd only had one quick lesson with, and I was desperately fearful that I'd mess it up and the thing would go off and wake everyone within a half-mile radius. But it was easier than it looked in the end. I didn't even need to make a note of the entry code, which was 1066, and as such probably the most unimaginative and commonly used security code ever. But I wasn't knocking it and, buoyed by this minor but significant success, I breezed through the empty streets of London.

With the help of my trusty *A to Z,* I drove into Brick Lane with a good twenty minutes to spare. I parked in a side street near Sophie's flat, in a neat little spot next to a secondhand furniture store, whose goods were already displayed outside on the pavement. I'd seen them out there in pouring rain, mattresses and foam-filled sofas included, and I couldn't help wondering what state they'd be in by the time their new owners got them home.

I rang on the bell of the flat several times, until a sleepy voice eventually answered, and I told whichever C it was that I'd meet them at Felix's Place.

Which is where I went then, and found Peter already waiting for me. Peter and his heavily overmade-up mother. She looked like a pantomime character, a man playing one of the ugly sisters in *Cinderella*. I'd made the call to Peter on impulse, just after I'd phoned the Cs and told them that if they wanted to meet Taylor then this was their big and only chance. I'd agreed to let them know when I arrived, but I was still half hoping they'd fall back to sleep. And if they didn't show up—well, I'd done my bit, fulfilled my side of the bargain.

As for Mrs Parker—well, I didn't know why, but I'd had this idea that it might prove useful to keep on good terms with Peter Parker, and I was sure I could do a good job on that score by making his mother happy. And meeting Taylor Wiseman, I was quickly assured, would make her very happy indeed.

Only I wasn't so certain that it would work both ways when she enveloped me in her wrestler-like arms and clasped my head tightly against her mountainous heaving bosom.

'You didn't tell me she was a looker,' she boomed in her thirty-a-day husky voice when she thankfully let me go. She winked theatrically at her son, and he looked deeply uncomfortable.

'Don't go all shy on us, you soft ha'p'orth,' she hooted, and she pinched his cheek in what I imagine was meant to be an affectionate gesture, but which made him visibly wince.

'Nice to meet you, Mrs Parker,' I said, now that I could breathe again.

'Call me Rosie,' she bellowed cheerfully. 'Everyone else does.' She was wearing a fur coat that smelt very peculiar. I'd never smelled real mothballs before, but I had a feeling that's what it was. It had been left unbuttoned, and beneath she had on a low-cut black dress, showing crinkled neck and breasts adorned with an outrageous diamanté necklace. She looked as if she was dressed for the opera.

They'd been sitting just inside the café. There were two half-drunk mugs of tea on their table and Peter asked me now if I'd like one too. I said that I would, and I sensed his relief, that he was glad of an excuse to get away from his mother for a while. I waved at Felix and he looked at me curiously. Wondering what I was up to, no doubt. Then I remembered that we might want to get some shots in here, so I excused myself from Mrs Parker and, while he was pouring out my tea, asked Felix if it would be okay.

'Not that American feller that Angie has the hots for?' he said with a shake of his head, then he laughed. 'She'll kill me when she finds out. She went off with the two youngest to her sister's in Haringey yesterday morning, and she isn't due back till this afternoon.'

I told him we might well be making a return visit, and he shrugged. 'Well, if you don't it'll be her fault for deserting me on a busy weekend,' he said, gleefully. 'And here he is now,' he said, looking over my shoulder. 'The man himself.'

I turned and saw Taylor being engulfed by Mrs Parker's bosom, and I smiled at him apologetically over her head. My face had gone red again at the sight of him, and I hoped that he wouldn't notice.

I made some quick introductions and, apparently unfazed, Taylor shook hands politely with Peter and Felix. There wasn't anyone else in the café yet, so I excused myself from the Parkers while Taylor and I discussed a plan of action. That was the idea, anyway, until the door opened again, and a tall woman with long dark hair swept into the café and called out to Taylor.

'It's absolutely marvellous, darling,' she said to him—of the café, I think, but it was me she was looking over.

'This is Mary Deacon,' Taylor explained. 'My, er, producer.'

'Hi,' I said, feeling instantly inadequate next to this authoritative-looking older woman. I put out my hand. 'I'm Tao Tandy.'

'What an interesting name,' she said coolly to me, and then she turned to Taylor. 'Go and get me one of those scrumptious-looking pastries on the counter, will you, darling?' she ordered him, and with a slightly hesitant frown he moved to the counter. Leaving Mary and me on our own.

She asked me what I had in mind regarding the shoot, and my mind went blank. I eventually managed some nervously tentative suggestions, and she nodded without any comment. I had the feeling she had something else on her mind, and I glanced over at Taylor, who'd been waylaid again by the boisterous Mrs Parker.

'And how are you finding things generally?' I heard Mary saying, and I looked her curiously. 'Here in London, I mean. I understand you haven't been here very long.'

She had incredibly piercing blue eyes, unusual for such a dark brunette, and they seemed to be boring into me now. 'Fine,' I said. 'But I do miss my boyfriend.' I don't know where the lie came from, but the change in her was immediate.

'A boyfriend?'

I nodded. 'More like fiancé, really. He lives in Manchester, but we're both hoping he'll move down here soon.' The relief on her face was obvious, and I didn't feel nearly so nervous now. She no longer seemed the scary TV producer, just a woman who was anxious about the competition, and I was glad to put her mind at rest—even if I was doing it with a lie.

'And you…?' I dared to say, now we seemed to be getting along so well. Now we were having this girlie chat. I glanced over in Taylor's direction again. 'I heard that you and he…'

But I didn't get an answer because at that moment Taylor disentangled himself from Mrs Parker and headed our way with Mary's coffee and pastry.

'Sorry,' she said, getting up quickly. She made a pantomime gesture of looking at her watch. 'Gotta go, I'm afraid.' She glanced at me briefly. 'Tao was just telling me about her fiancé. It seems such a shame that they can't be together, doesn't it now?'

Taylor looked at me, and I felt as if my nose was growing. He murmured something I couldn't hear and then walked with Mary to the door. The café was beginning to fill up now, and I thought it was time we made a start. And, because Mrs Parker was very persuasive, we started with some shots of Taylor and her bargaining with a market trader who specialised in Second World War memorabilia, a subject upon which Mrs Parker turned out to be something of an expert. How it would fit into a cookery book was not explored, but I think Taylor just did it to keep her happy. And, whether or not he was a liar, that sort of warmed me to him.

We did some more relevant shots, with food and vegetables as the background, and by eight-thirty I was down to just two remaining rolls of film. We used them up in Felix's now crowded café, with Taylor in the queue, flanked by Peter and the ubiquitous Mrs Parker, and the genial owner smiling broadly behind the counter. Felix asked me to send him a couple of pictures when they were developed, which he would no doubt use to annoy Angie with, and I was just putting my camera away in its bag when the Cs finally made an appearance.

After some quick introductions, I apologised and announced that I had to go. I knew Taylor would have to leave soon as well, but I didn't want the Cs blaming me for that, so I left him to make his own explanations. I said that I'd ring him the following day at his restaurant, and he nodded thoughtfully as I left the café. Though not before I was once more forcibly immersed in Mrs Parker's voluminous breasts, and told how happy I'd made a poor old woman—a description that somehow defied the grip she held me in for a good thirty seconds.

I also got a thank-you from Peter, who'd been helping to haul my equipment around the market, and now helped me haul it again back to the van.

'That'll keep her off my back for a while,' he told me slyly as he loaded the stuff with surprising care into the van. 'And if you ever need any favours yourself, you know where to come.'

I said with a smile that I'd bear it in mind, never thinking for a moment that in the space of a very short time I'd be needing the kind of favour I sincerely hoped Peter Parker was uniquely equipped to provide.

I was feeling pleased with myself when I got back to the Hampstead house at ten minutes to ten. I'd made it back in very good time, so I wouldn't be in trouble from Chris, but—most importantly—I'd got my first professional shoot in the bag. And, bar a major disaster along the lines of all the film that I'd used being faulty (ha, scary, ha), I was hopeful of a few decent photographs to present to Taylor in a day or two. My only slight concern was the lie that I'd blurted out to Mary Deacon, but even then I wasn't sure why it should matter. In all probability I'd never see her again, so there was no real chance of being found out.

I frowned as I hoisted the strap of my camera bag over my shoulder and humped the accessories, including my tripod, over the front door threshold. I'd just got a clear image of Taylor Wiseman in my mind, and the way he'd looked at me when I left Felix's Place. As if...

As if *nothing,* I told myself firmly, with a self-administered mental slap of my own hand. He couldn't possibly be interested in me, foolish girl that I was. Not in *that* way, at any rate. So, okay, he had seemed a bit flirty that first day we met, but that, I was beginning to believe, was just his way. I'd seen how he operated generally now, how he'd been with the Cs—how he'd been with Mrs Parker, for God's sake—and it hadn't been any different from the way he'd been with me. He was just friendly and charming and very polite. Absolutely nothing else to it.

And then there was Mary. Who was sophisticated and worldly, and clearly nuts about him. And I knew who I'd choose if I was him and I was given the option. And, yes, I know that sounds like maybe I don't have a very good opinion of myself, but I think it's more a case of being realistic.

I didn't get the chance to take these musings any further, because at that moment, before I had time to close the front door, Chris appeared from a room further down the hall. He was frowning deeply, and the first thing I thought of was the bird.

'Has something happened?' I asked, as I dumped my stuff and closed the door with my foot.

'I'm not sure,' he said.

'Have you called the vet?' I said worriedly, and I have to admit that part of the worry was for myself. I was getting to like it there, and I wouldn't be needed if the bird kicked the bucket. And even if whatever was wrong didn't prove fatal, it wasn't going to look very good. I hadn't even been there twenty-four hours yet and the pet in my care was already ill.

'It's not the vet I've been thinking of calling,' he said. He inclined his head to the dining room. 'You better take a look for yourself.'

I moved slowly towards him, nervous about what all this

meant. When I got there I stepped past him into the room and looked about. By now I was beginning to imagine that I'd made a mistake with the burglar alarm and the place had been broken into. I was half expecting to find it stripped bare, so it was quite a relief to see that it all seemed in order. I looked at him and shrugged. 'I don't get it,' I said.

'Take a closer look above the fireplace.'

I glanced at him, and because his eyes were fixed on the spot, I moved round the table and did precisely as I was told. It took a few seconds for the penny to drop, and then I let out a tiny strangulated gasp.

I heard him sigh. 'I was hoping you were going to tell me that Adrienne had taken them with her,' he said. 'It didn't seem very likely, but I didn't want to ring her till I knew for sure.'

'Ring Mrs Audesley!' I looked in horror at him and then back at the wall. The miniatures that I'd particularly noted on my tour of the house were gone. No more. Disappeared. Departed. Absent without leave. All that remained were seven tiny accusing pins, on which they'd formally hung, and I knew without a shadow of doubt exactly who had taken them. And he'd done it when he'd sent me off to show Sophie round the house. Sneaky bastard. And I'd thought how decent he was for leaving the house so quickly after the meal, for being so obligingly quiet… When it was just about getting away with his booty as quickly and silently as he could.

And, oh, my God, I was the one who'd let him in.

All this took place in my head in a nano-second, without even a flicker on my face. I knew this because Chris turned away from me, without further comment or any funny looks, and left the room. As I guessed he was heading directly for a handy telephone, I followed my instincts and raced after him. 'But you can't,' I wailed desperately as I caught him up and grabbed hold of his arm.

His eyes narrowed suspiciously as he looked at my hand, which was squeezing him now. Tightly, if the whites of my knuckles was anything to go by. I let go quickly, as if his flesh had suddenly become very hot. 'Why can't I?' he said in measured tones, almost as if he already knew the answer.

'Because I know who's got them and I've got a plan and I'm sure I can get them back if you'll just give me some time...' It all came out in a rush, and sounded so garbled I might have been speaking a foreign language. But he seemed to understand all right.

'Don't tell me,' he said with a phonily sorrowful shake of his head, 'you let that waster of a nephew of Adrienne's into the house?'

'I couldn't help it,' I whined. 'I didn't know it was him at the door when I opened it and then he practically forced his way in.' It was an exaggeration, certainly—but excusable, I think, in the circumstances.

'Why didn't you call me, then? I'd have been happy to see him off the premises.'

I found myself sighing noisily in a desperate attempt to stall for time. I didn't know whether to tell him the full story or not. My instincts were *not,* but then I had this horrible feeling that the truth would come out anyway, and I'd only get myself in more trouble then. So I told him about Sophie, and how I'd thought it would be okay with her there as well, and that I'd made it quite clear he couldn't come back. 'And besides,' I finished, pathetically, 'I wasn't to know that he was a *thief.* Mrs A never said anything like that. If she had then of course I wouldn't have let him in.'

He shook his head again, in a genuinely despairing way

this time, and I guessed I hadn't exactly won a sympathy vote. 'Whether she chose to tell you that or not, the fact is she *did* tell you not to let him in.'

God, he could be smug when he was in the right, and I hated him as much as I hated Jerome at that very moment. But, even though I was so very upset and so very anxious, I knew it wouldn't be sensible to give way to my feelings. If I lost control for a single second I knew perfectly well that he would be on that phone before I could say *golden goose.* Which is what Sirg was to me, and I'd kill it for sure if Chris called Mrs Audesley. But it wasn't just that, to be fair to myself and my motives. There were additional complications concerning Sophie, and, I'm not sure why, but I just had the feeling that we'd never get the miniatures back if he did make the call.

'Has he done this before?' I found myself asking, on a desperate hunch. It had occurred to me that Chris hadn't mentioned the police so far, and although that was vaguely comforting it did seem a bit strange under the circumstances.

Chris nodded a bit impatiently. 'It was some valuable silver last time.'

'Was he charged?'

'No. Adrienne didn't want the police involved. Besides, there was no more proof of his involvement then than there is now. Just the fact that the silver was here before he came to the house and was gone after he left.'

'Circumstantial,' I said eagerly, sensing that I was getting somewhere.

His expression was pensive. 'I wasn't sure that I even believed Adrienne, I'm sorry to say. She's never been that fond of her great-nephew, and when she told me about it I secretly gave him the benefit of the doubt.' He shrugged. 'I thought maybe she'd mislaid the stuff, or sold it off and forgotten—she is getting forgetful—and to be perfectly honest…' he frowned at the irony '…I felt a bit sorry for Jerome.'

'But you called him a *waster*,' I reminded Chris now. I wasn't so mad with him any more, now that he was admitting his own lack of judgement.

'He certainly seems to be. He might have a job, but that's only because his father knows all the right people. I've been told that he only does the absolute minimum to survive, and that he's always in debt despite the huge salary he screws out of the bank every month. Though, to be perfectly fair, I only have Adrienne's word on that too, of course.'

I was surprised—impressed, even—by his attempt at fairness despite all the damning evidence against Jerome. 'Well, if she was right about the silver, she's probably right about that as well,' I said dismally. I was thinking about Sophie again, and what she'd got herself into, but that really wasn't the issue right now.

We moved into the living room, and after a quick check on Sirg, who was apparently engrossed in the Sunday omnibus edition of the *The Archers,* we sat down on the squashy down-filled sofas and looked gloomily off into the distance while we thought independently about what to do next.

'So what's this plan of yours, then?' he eventually said, presumably because he hadn't come up with any ideas himself.

I didn't have one, of course. I'd just said that in a panic. But for some reason, because I'd been put on the spot, I found myself mentioning Peter Parker. 'I can't promise anything,' I said cautiously, 'but he owes me a favour and I've just got a feeling he'll be able to help.'

'Sounds a bit vague and half baked, if you don't mind me saying so,' Chris replied.

I did, actually, but I had a strong vested interest in coming up with a solution that didn't involve calling Mrs A, so I pressed home my idea with slight embellishment. 'He's got underworld connections,' I said, but even to me it sounded ridiculous.

'You haven't been watching any gangster films lately, have you?' Chris said sceptically. 'This is a serious business, you know. They might not look much but those tiny little paintings are worth a great deal of money.' He shrugged lightly. 'And if we don't sort this out quickly we might even be deemed accessories—if the police ever did become involved.'

I reminded myself of the importance of staying calm. 'But that seems unlikely, from what you've said, and at least this way there's a chance that we could get the miniatures back. Besides, we might not have found out for ages. If you hadn't looked in the dining room they might not even have been missed till Mrs A got back.'

He nodded his head very slightly. 'Okay,' he said, 'I'll give you a week. But if you haven't sorted out something by then, *I'm* going to have to.'

I sighed with relief. I was not particularly hopeful of pulling it off, but at least I'd got some breathing space, and it certainly wouldn't do any harm to talk to Peter.

And then I had another horrible thought. I was going to have to have a little talk with Sophie as well, which worried me a lot more at that very moment than some valuable missing miniature works of art.

Only as it turned out it was Sophie who did most of the talking when the time came—a lot sooner than I'd expected. She turned up on my doorstep just after midday—just as I was planning to call her, in fact. I'd already tried Peter's number by then, and been waylaid by his mother while she told me again what a lovely young woman I was, and asked if I'd like to come round for tea later that day. She was very persistent, and it took a great deal of effort to excuse myself without causing offence and eventually extract a promise from her that she'd get her son to call me back the moment he came in.

I was shocked by Sophie's appearance when I opened the door to her. She looked as if she hadn't slept, or if she had then she'd done so in the clothes she was wearing while being dragged through the proverbial hedge backwards at the same time. And that wasn't like Sophie at all. She was always so neat and well—*just so*—the sort of woman who normally made me feel a mess even when I'd made an effort.

She followed me into the kitchen, and with a strong sense of foreboding I made some fresh coffee while she gathered herself. She sat at the table for a good five minutes before opening her mouth, and because I knew her so well, I knew not to push her. I also knew that it was Serious and that it had something to do with a Man, and I didn't need to ask which one, of course.

'What is it about me?' she finally said as I poured the coffee into a couple of mugs. 'I mean, why do men always think they can treat me like shit?'

They didn't, of course, not usually. But she'd never been out with an arrogant wanker like Jerome Audesley before.

'What's happened?' I said, as I sat down opposite her.

'He's dumped me,' she answered miserably.

I was all for raising a marauding mob, seeking out the shyster and lynching him there and then. But, since I guessed marauding mobs weren't nearly so easy to raise as you'd think,

I put that idea on hold for a while. Besides, when I thought about it for a moment it made perfect sense. Of course he would dump her once he got what he wanted. He couldn't possibly have carried on seeing her because sooner or later she was bound to find out the truth: that he'd used her simply to get into the house.

I made comforting noises while she told me what a fool she felt, how she'd never trust a man again, and I wondered if it would make her feel better or worse when I told her the facts. It was a hard call, but I decided it had to be marginally better to know he at least had a good reason for dumping her. So I took a deep breath and blurted everything out.

'My God!' she said, when it finally sunk home. 'Are you saying he planned the whole thing in advance?'

Her face was so pale I wondered if I'd made a mistake. But it was too late to worry about that now.

'I imagine he got the idea when he picked up your e-mail asking about accommodation,' I said. 'Although I wouldn't be surprised if some of the other applicants for the parrot-sitting job were sent by him.' Hopefully the ones who'd come off badly from their interview with Sirg, I thought...

'I can't believe I fell for it,' she groaned, and then shook her head hopelessly. 'That I really believed all those lies of his.'

'You can't blame yourself for that,' I told her firmly. 'He's a very good bullshitter and you were just, well...unlucky.'

'*Unlucky,* or just plain stupid?' She put her hands over her face and groaned again. 'Oh God, I even told the two Cs I was moving in with him...'

Now that was unfortunate, but it couldn't be helped. 'Never mind about them,' I said briskly. 'The important thing now is that he isn't allowed to get away with it. We've got to get those miniatures back.'

She parted her hands and looked at me. 'Isn't that a job for the police?' she said unhappily.

I shook my head and explained the problem. 'But with your help I think we can do it,' I said with a confidence I didn't really feel.

Sophie put her hands on the table and looked at me long and hard. And slowly, very slowly, I saw her expression change from defeat to grim determination.

'Just tell me what you want me to do,' she said, with a coolness that was now bordering on the sinister.

9

'My big worry is that he may already have sold the minia-tures on,' I told this new Sophie, but she shook her head with surprising firmness.

'If we think like that we may as well give up now,' she said. She cupped her chin in her hands and planted her elbows on the table. 'And I don't think he can have sold them on yet. Not if the whole thing was as opportunistic as it seems to have been.' She was quiet for a moment as she thought about it, then she nodded her head confidently. 'My bet is that he's stashed them away somewhere, with the intention of unloading them just as soon as he possibly can.'

It seemed likely, and so I asked her what his movements had been after they left the previous evening. 'Did he disap-pear from your sight any time before you left here and…?' I paused for a moment, trying to think of a nice way to put it.

'…and *dumping me* this morning?' Sophie said. 'Is that what you're so delicately trying to say?' But she said it with humour, thank goodness.

'Precisely,' I said, and she even managed rueful smile.

'Not until this morning,' she told me, then she shook her head in ironic dismay. 'Seems he was up for one last shag before relieving me of my girlfriend-stroke-ruse-to-get-inside-this-house duties. We went straight back to his flat last night, did the business, went to sleep—and, no,' she put in when I looked at her questioningly, 'he didn't slip off somewhere during the night. You know what a light sleeper I am. I'd have noticed, and besides, I know exactly when he got rid of his stash,' she said in disgust. 'That was this morning, first thing. He left the flat at about nine o'clock to get some things for breakfast, or so he said, but he didn't come back till nearly eleven. And it was then he told me that it was over.'

'What? Just like that?'

'More or less. He just sauntered in, said he was sorry, that he'd had a great time and everything, but that he *didn't do* long-term relationships.' She still seemed bewildered at the memory. 'And this from the man who'd asked me to move in with him the day before!'

'Are you saying he didn't even give you any breakfast after making you wait all that time?' I said it with a wry smile on my face, and she made a sound which I took to be a bitter little laugh.

'The bastard had come back empty-handed! He didn't even offer me a lift back to the flat. Not that I'd have taken it.' She shook her head and looked horrified. 'No way was I going back to that place to face the Cs. They probably already know I've been dumped through those revolting cronies of his.'

I would have liked to go down along this road, put in my own two-penn'orth about Jerome's friends, but I needed to stick to the business in hand. 'So, if we assume he got rid of the stuff at that time,' I said, 'we can also sort of assume he didn't go very far. Not if he was back in a couple of hours.'

Sophie frowned at me deeply. 'Which isn't much help, really, is it? That still leaves most of London.'

'What we need is a list of all his friends and contacts,' I said, trying to stay positive. 'Which reminds me—there's something I haven't mentioned yet.'

She sat up to attention and I told her about my plan to call on the assistance of Peter Parker, and now she actually laughed. 'You can't really be serious,' she guffawed. 'What could *he* do? And why would he help us anyway?'

I loved that word 'us'. It made me feel less alone with a problem that really was mine. 'I'm his new best friend,' I announced proudly, 'and if he knew that you were involved he'd be there like a shot.'

She didn't seem keen on the implications of that, but I pressed home his potential usefulness and she eventually agreed that it wasn't such a bad idea after all. 'So long as you don't offer to swap my favours for any services he agrees to provide. In fact, I'd sooner you kept my name out of it.'

'Fine,' I said, 'but you could help by asking round at the bank. You know—discreetly. I've heard that Jerome is a well-paid slacker, and if that's true then he's bound to have the odd enemy.'

She didn't seem to like that idea either much, but she half-heartedly agreed on the strict proviso that she didn't have to make any direct contact with the slimeball ever again.

Since there didn't seem much else we could do until Peter made contact, we traded offensive language to describe Jerome Audesley for a while, outdoing each other with the grossest possible insults, until we ended up laughing like drains. Then we stopped laughing suddenly and Sophie became very serious.

'I've got a favour to ask you,' she said.

'Name it,' I said.

'Since I still don't feel like facing the Cs, I wondered if I could stay with you tonight.'

Of course she could stay the night. The were several empty bedrooms upstairs, and quite honestly I was glad of the company. But if she was to be a guest it seemed only right to introduce her to the bird of the house, which would be a nerve-racking affair, bearing in mind how he'd treated the Cs. I spent a few minutes advising Sophie on how to conduct herself in the Sirg's presence, and to my surprise, Sir Galahad behaved...well, if not exactly like a gentleman, he certainly didn't bite her, or flap his wings in a threatening manner. In fact he behaved with perfect in-difference, almost as if she wasn't there.

'It seems I really have lost my touch,' Sophie said wryly, and as if to prove it Sir Galahad turned his back on her and barked like a dog.

I found myself quite relieved. Not just because he'd failed to attack her, as I'd feared he might, but because this was proof positive that I really was special to him.

The call came from Peter at a quarter to eight that evening. He sounded surprised to hear from me so soon, but when I told I needed some advice he seemed pretty chuffed. 'Can we meet?' I said. 'I'm afraid it's a bit involved for talk-ing about over the phone.'

He offered to come right over, but I didn't think that was a great idea. I believed I could trust him, though I've no idea why, but I didn't think it was very sensible to bring him into the house just yet. Besides, I doubted that Sophie would care for the idea very much.

So I agreed to meet him at Liverpool Street Station in forty-five minutes. I probably wouldn't be away much more than an hour, though even if I was I felt it was perfectly safe to leave Sirg in the care of Sophie. She didn't seem very keen herself, but I assured her that being there was all that was required of her. So I did what I had to where the bird was concerned, topped up his seeds and chatted to him for ten minutes or so, and then left the house to keep my appointment.

I'd taken a few details from Sophie about Jerome. His address, his telephone numbers, home and mobile, the names of any friends she'd heard him mention, and I already knew his place of employment. It wasn't much to go on, but Peter, when we met outside the station's W H Smith outlet, nodded with confidence when I passed the information to him. The really weird thing was how easily he took the whole thing in his stride, as if he received requests of the like on a daily basis.

'So let's get this clear,' he said as we wandered up and down the concourse. 'You want me to find where he's stashed the stuff?'

I nodded, pleased with his positive no-nonsense attitude. 'And then what?'

I shrugged. I hadn't thought any further than that. 'Maybe we could talk again at that stage and decide what to do then.' I'd been deliberately vague about details. I certainly hadn't mentioned the Sophie connection—a) because she asked me not to, and b) because I just had the feeling he might want to punch Jerome if he knew how she had been treated. And, much as I'd have liked to punch him myself, I could see the sense in keeping all this on a less personal basis. Basically, I just wanted to get those miniatures back where they belonged before the week was up and Chris carried out his threat to contact Mrs A. To be honest, I wasn't that hopeful. I didn't have very great faith in Peter Parker's ability to track them down, but it was all I had and it was better than sitting around doing nothing.

He was looking surprisingly thoughtful for someone with a spider's web tattoo on his cheek. 'I reckon that might be the wrong way round,' he said.

'What do you mean?'

'I think we might be talking needles and haystacks here.'
He stopped walking suddenly and looked at me. 'I reckon
I'd spend the time better by putting out feelers to dealers.
He's got to dispose of the goods somewhere.'

'Yes,' I said, 'but the sort of dealers you're talking about
are bound to be dodgy, and if so why would they want to
co-operate? Why would they want the, er, *goods* returned to
their rightful owner when they could make a fast buck by
selling them on?'

'Don't you worry about that,' he said. 'It's as much about
favours in certain types of business as it is about filthy lucre.'
He was beginning to sound like a comic strip character and
I wondered if I was making a big mistake here. But what option did I have?

'Well, you know best about this sort of thing, so I'll leave
it to you.' Along with the compliment I offered what I
hoped was an engaging smile. Then I remembered the *need*
word. 'I know it's a lot to ask, Peter, but I really do need to
get those miniatures back.'

We started walking again.

'Have you got any descriptions to go on?' he asked. 'Of
the miniatures, I mean.' It seemed a sensible enquiry, but of
course I hadn't. They were all portraits, that much I did
know, but then miniatures invariably were.

'I'll have to come back to you on that one,' I said,
wondering if Chris might he able to help. 'But there are
seven of them, and as far as I remember they were all of
women.'

'It's a start, I suppose. But the names of the artists would
help.'

'I suppose so.' I was actually beginning to feel quite impressed by his assured manner and the type of questions he
was asking, and I found my hopes rising a little.

He glanced at his wristwatch now, and then looked me
in the face again. 'Just one last question before I head off.'

I looked back at him enquiringly.

'What's in this for me?'

I was stunned for a moment, then I gathered myself. 'I thought you said that you owed me a favour,' I said, putting emphasis on the word he seemed to set so much store by.

He looked at me long and hard, and then his pudgy features broke into a grin. 'Nice one,' he said. He nodded and told me he'd be in touch, and then he turned away and set off towards the upward-moving staircase.

When I got back to the house Sophie came out the hall to meet me.

'You've had a visitor,' she said.

'What did he want?' I said, assuming that it was Chris who'd called, and wondering what he would make of me leaving Sirg with a stranger.

'It wasn't a *him,*' she replied with a frown as I followed her through to the kitchen. She'd prepared some food and the table was prettily laid with some flowers in a vase at the centre.

I looked at her curiously. 'Who, then?'

'Someone called Alina. Apparently you told her you were moving in here and she popped round to see how you were getting along.'

It took a while for the penny to drop. 'Oh, *Alina,*' I said, picturing the elfin-like creature I'd met at the gift shop. 'That was nice of her. I must give her a call some time.'

Sophie was getting something out of the oven, and she brought it over to the table. It looked like a pasta concoction, with tomatoey sauce, and because I was starving I couldn't wait to tuck in. 'That's another reason she came round tonight, apparently. She said that she'd got a small part in a TV drama set in Scotland, and she'd be away for a fortnight filming.'

'Good for her,' I said, spooning quills of luscious sauce-covered pasta onto my plate.

'She also said that she knew the gardener chap who lives in the basement.'

I looked up with interest now. 'Oh, yes?' I said cautiously.

Sophie took the seat opposite mine and spooned a tiny amount of the pasta onto her own plate. 'Apparently he does some work for Alina's mother and her mother's friends, and they all think he's wonderful.'

'That figures,' I said, a bit sourly. 'He seems to have a way with older women.' I told her about the one I'd seen going down to his flat, and about my theory that he was some sort of gigolo. And although Sophie usually likes a juicy tale as much of the rest of us she looked at me sceptically across the table.

'That's not the impression I got from Alina, but, hey—' she shrugged '—what do I know?' She popped a single quill into her mouth and chewed on it thoughtfully. 'Though you will have to introduce me, of course, so I can make my own mind up.'

I was surprised at her interest. 'Haven't you had enough of men for a while?'

'As a matter of fact I have,' she said seriously, 'but that isn't the reason I want to meet him. I'd just like to check out his potential for you.'

'Hah! Well, don't bother. He isn't my type.' And then, without meaning to, I started talking about Taylor and Mary Deacon.

'And you think he's lying,' she said when I mentioned what Amber had said.

I shrugged. 'Maybe. But, then again, why *should* he lie?'

'That's obvious I would have thought,' she said cynically.

'I don't think he's like that,' I said, with a certainty I had no right to feel on such a short acquaintance. I'd cleared my plate and I was debating whether to go for a second helping. I thought about what I'd eaten already that day, and decided my calorie count would just about allow for it.

'Well, maybe it's just wishful thinking on Mary's part,' Sophie suggested.

'That's what I've been beginning to think. And maybe he finds it difficult, you know, what with her effectively being his boss and everything.'

'Could be, I suppose.' Sophie had stopped eating now and was watching me fill up my plate again. 'Do I take it you fancy the arse off the bloke yourself?'

I shrugged. 'Well, I wouldn't go that far, but I do find him kind of attractive,' I said, recalling the tingle factor when I touched his hand. 'Not that he'd look at me twice, of course,' I added, and even to me it sounded as if I was fishing for compliments.

'You're probably right,' Sophie said, and she sounded serious. 'Why would he look at a minger like you when he's surrounded by gorgeous, adoring women…?'

'Precisely,' I answered quickly, then there was a long pause and her words slowly sank home. 'Did you call me a *minger?*'

Sophie started to laugh. 'Yes, you silly cow, and you know perfectly well you're not that—far from it, in fact—so why *wouldn't* he look at you?'

'Do you really think that he might be interested then?'

Sophie rolled her eyes at the ceiling. 'From what you've told me he *clearly* is.'

Which was all very cheering until I remembered something else. The fact that during our discussion about whether or not Taylor Wiseman was a liar, I'd failed to mention a pretty big fib of my own.

'Just be careful, that's all,' she added with the wisdom of someone who'd learnt by her mistakes.

'Of course I will,' I replied with the ignorance of someone who hadn't.

10

The next morning Sophie borrowed one of my least tatty skirts and a just about okay sweater—that looked a lot better on her than it did on me—because she hadn't brought a change of clothes with her for work. By now we'd agreed that she should stay a few days, till the fuss about Jerome died down a bit—and the Cs, we were sure, would make plenty of fuss in the phoney sympathy department. The idea now was for her to leave work early that afternoon and pick up some stuff from the flat while they were out. She would also drop off a note explaining where she was so that they didn't think she'd jumped in the river or something.

The plan made sense for more than just the obvious reason. If the Cs interrogated her—and it was hard to imagine that they could resist doing so—then it might be hard not to give away the fact that there was a lot more to Jerome Audesley than a bastard who dumped her. And, as we wouldn't be able to trust them to keep anything to themselves, we decided the best thing would be to simply avoid them. They were bound ring her, of course. Their curiosity would be just too much to bear, but it would be far easier to fob them off on the telephone than it would face to face.

She left the house at eight o'clock, and after I'd woken Sirg with a nice slice of mango, I went down to the basement and knocked at the door of Chris's flat. I'd forgotten to return the keys for his van, and I wanted to ask him something.

I'd clearly got him out of bed, and he didn't seem at all pleased to see me. He'd thrown on a T-shirt and a pair of old jeans and looked distinctly rumpled.

'I was wondering if you happened to know the names of any of the miniature artists,' I said as I handed over his keys.

He looked at me with bleary-eyed lack of comprehension. 'You'd better come in,' he said, 'and I'll make some coffee.'

The flat was surprisingly spacious and swish. The sitting room, which the outside door led straight into, was sparsely but tastefully furnished, with two red sofas, a couple of occasional tables, some shelves containing books and CDs, but not a lot else. Just a desk with an Apple Mac computer and a pile of handwritten notes next to it.

'Writing your memoirs?' I asked him wryly as we passed through the room on the way to the kitchen. That was small and narrow, but neat as well, with shiny white kitchen units that looked very expensive and new.

He didn't bother to reply to my question, but instead indicated a tall stool with a slight wave, and I hoisted myself up onto it.

'Want some?' he said, as he spooned freshly ground coffee into a cafetière.

I nodded and he added an extra spoonful. He switched on an electric kettle and then parked himself on a matching stool right next to me.

'What's this about artists?' he said, rubbing his hands over his face. He seemed to be coming round a bit now.

'I need some names so my contact knows exactly what he is looking for.'

Chris smiled at me slightly. He hadn't shaved yet and there was heavy dark stubble on his chin. 'Ah, yes,' he scoffed, 'your *contact*.'

'Yes,' I said, refusing to take the bait. 'He seems quite confident of getting the miniatures back, but if you have any additional information it could be helpful.'

The kettle clicked off and he dragged himself off the stool. He didn't speak until the coffee was made and he'd poured out two steaming mugs. Then he shrugged. 'I think Adrienne has some documentation somewhere—you know, for insurance purposes. I suppose I could see if I can locate it.'

'That would be great,' I said, keeping my tone upbeat. 'When do you think you could manage that?'

He glanced at his watch. 'Not this morning. I've got someone coming here in half an hour, and I'll be out all day after that.'

My God, I thought, this bloke is insatiable. No wonder he looked so whacked. 'Heavy night?' I said casually.

'You could say that. I was working on something till gone three o'clock.'

I'll bet you were, I thought with disdain. I imagined it must be very hard work keeping all his women happy. Which reminded me. 'I understand that we have a mutual acquaintance,' I said.

He looked at me curiously. 'We have?'

'Yes, Alina.' I didn't know her surname, unfortunately. 'You know—the actress. Apparently you do some work for her mother.'

He looked a bit cagey. 'That's right. Nice woman. Nice family.'

'She didn't call on you last night, then?' I said. I thought that she might have done if she'd come round to see me.

'May have done,' he said with a shrug. 'Someone did ring the bell but I wasn't home to visitors last night.' He looked at his watch again, pointedly this time. 'I'm going to have to…'

'It's okay,' I said, 'I'll let you get on.' I looked at my untouched coffee as I got down from the stool. 'I'm afraid I'm going to have to leave that. Too hot to knock back, unfortunately.'

'Take it with you,' he said. 'I'll pick the mug up when I come round later.' He walked with me to the door. 'Are you planning on going out today?' he asked as he opened it for me.

'I have got some film that needs developing,' I said, concentrating on my full coffee mug to make sure none of it spilled, 'but I shouldn't be out for more than an hour.'

'Why don't you do it yourself?' he said. 'I'm sure you could black out one of the bathrooms.'

I didn't particularly like being told what to do by him, but it didn't actually seem such a bad idea. 'Maybe,' I said.

'I'll call up around six this evening,' he said, just before he closed the door on me.

And, call me nosy, but I ended up sipping the coffee at the sitting room window. I stayed there until I witnessed the arrival of the same smart middle-aged woman I'd seen before. It would be hard to be sure which of us looked most furtive at that moment—me, as I slipped behind the curtain, or her, as she glanced quickly around before disappearing down the steps which led to the basement flat.

As it turned out, I ended up doing exactly as Chris had suggested. I actually used one of the *en-suite* bathrooms that had been created from part of the main bedroom, without the benefit of an actual window. It took me the best part of the day, on and off—a lot longer than it would have taken to drop the film off with Miss Chilli-Pepper—but at least I had the opportunity to fine-tune the prints to my own particular liking—a little less colour here, a little lighter there. In fact the end result was very pleasing indeed, and at about three o'clock I got on the phone to Taylor Wiseman to pass on the good news.

He'd just finished serving lunches and asked if I could meet him somewhere to show him the results. I almost said yes, and then I remembered that I was effectively housebound.

I told him my situation, and he suggested coming to me. 'If that's okay with you, of course?'

Darn right it was okay, so I gave him the address and he said he'd be round at about five o'clock.

Then, because I'd kept my mobile turned off while I was developing the rolls of film, I checked for messages and found two from my mother and one from Peter.

I decided to get my mother out of the way first. She'd certainly be the one who gave me most grief for leaving it too long before calling back, so the quicker I rang her the better.

'Hi, sweetie,' she said, sounding worryingly cheery. 'Thanks for calling back so quickly.'

This wasn't like her at all, and I immediately sensed that

she was after something. She went through the motions of asking me how things were working out at my new address and I kept my responses brief.

'And it's a big house, you say?'

'I did say that, yes,' I said cautiously, wondering what was coming next.

'Well, that's excellent news because I'm coming down to London on Friday night and I'd like you to put me up for the night.'

My mother, in London. God help me. 'Why are you coming down here?' I asked.

'There's an exhibition of Native American art that I'd like to attend. I'd like to see some authentic dreamcatchers to get a few tips—you know the sort of thing.'

I didn't, not really. 'I don't think you'll find any dream-catchers there,' I said, not to stop her coming, although that would be a bonus, but because I believed it to be true.

There was a sneer in the laugh she let out. 'Of course I will. What nonsense you talk at times, Tao.'

'I doubt it,' I persisted. 'I think they only make them for the tourists—you know, on the reservations. I don't think they're really part of an artistic tradition.'

But of course she wouldn't have that. She got all huffy because I'd challenged her knowledge of Native American culture. Not that she had very much, knowledge, that is, but there was no arguing with her when she was in this sort of mood.

Neither was there any stopping her when she made up her mind, so I resigned myself to putting her up on Friday night. 'So what time will you get here?' I said, interrupting her indignant flow.

'About seven,' she said, cooling down quickly, now that she'd got what she wanted.

I gave her the details on how to get across London, and directions from the tube station to the house, and she wrote them down with painful slowness.

'I take it that Dad's not coming with you?' I said when she'd finished, and she let out little snort of derision.

'I don't know what's the matter with your father lately, I really don't. He spends more and more time at work these days, and seems to have completely lost interest in what's important.'

'Like *the environment?*' I said.

'Exactly!' she replied, apparently oblivious to my sarcasm. 'Which is much more important than the welfare of abused children, of course.'

Now she picked up the irony in my tone and snorted again. 'There might not be any children at all in the future, abused or otherwise, if we don't take care of the planet,' she snapped.

She had a point, I supposed, but her argument might have been a little more valid if she really did do anything seriously useful for the planet herself, as opposed to just talking about it.

'Well, see you on Friday, then,' I said, winding up quickly before we ended up falling out. 'And give Dad my love when you do see him next.'

I called Peter back after that, and he told me he was on the case and asked if I had any more information for him yet. I said that I didn't but might later on, and promised to call him again later.

Then I had a shower, ironed my favourite shirt and jeans, subtly tarted myself up, and chatted to Sirg while I waited for Taylor to arrive.

He did so at ten to five, ten minutes early, and now that

I'd admitted the fact that I fancied him—not only to my-self, but Sophie as well—I felt oddly shy in his presence.

He was duly impressed with the house, and I liked him all the more for that—for not playing the celebrity and pre-tending that he was used to this sort of luxury. I gave him some tea in the kitchen, and because he was curious I told him the story of how I'd come to be there. He expressed a desire to meet Sir Galahad when I'd finished, but since I didn't want to risk him falling victim to an unprovoked at-tack, I explained that he had a very strict routine and that right now he was taking his afternoon nap. Besides, it was time to show him the results of my recent labours, so I got out the best of the prints I'd developed and felt a warm glow envelop me as he heaped on the praise. We also laughed a little at the amount of pictures in which Mrs Parker appeared alongside Taylor, and I made a mental note to send her a few of the best.

'I knew that I'd chosen well,' he said, beaming up at me as I stood next to him at the kitchen table. He looked back at the photographs and shook his head in what I took to be delighted disbelief. 'You know, Tao, I think we already have enough to go with here,' he said, and I got a sinking feeling in my stomach. He looked up at me again. 'But it seems a shame not to make the most of the two weeks that you've been booked for.'

I couldn't have agreed more, and so I smiled and told him that if he thought *these* were good, then he should just wait till he saw the next batch. 'I've been thinking,' I said, busi-ness-like now. 'Since the market shots turned out so well, I thought maybe we could try some others. There are quite a few all over London, and if we did some more shots of food stalls, say, it would all fit in very well with the book.'

'I like it,' he said, and he looked up into my eyes, making me squirm like a teenager who fancies her teacher.

'Why don't you sit down?' he said, and I did. Right next to him. And because that made direct conversation awkward, he pushed back his chair a little and turned to me.

'It's my night off tonight, Tao, and I was wondering if you'd like to go out somewhere.'

'What?' I said, before I had time to think. 'Like a date, you mean?'

He grinned at me and I felt extremely stupid, using words like 'date' to a sophisticated man-of-the-world like Taylor. My face must have coloured revoltingly. It certainly felt very hot. 'You could say that, but since you're engaged...' he glanced at my ringless left hand as he spoke '...we could call it a celebratory dinner to mark our collaboration.'

I preferred my version, even if it did sound daft. I was tempted to tell him there was no fiancé, but that would mean having to admit that I'd lied to Mary. Besides, it could wait, I decided. I could tell him when we were out together later, by which time I would hopefully have come up with a plausible reason for the lie. Then I remembered that it wasn't quite as easy as that, and found myself groaning out loud. 'I'm not sure I can,' I said when he looked at me questioningly. 'The terms of my agreement mean that I have to get someone in to sit with Sir Galahad if I go out.'

'Then get them,' he said, which sounded so simple put like that, and my first thought was Sophie. But it didn't seem fair to burden her with the long list of evening duties that must be complied with. Besides which, although Sirg had appeared indifferent to her when I was around, I wasn't sure how he'd react if I wasn't. Which left me with Chris. But the thought of asking him yet another favour didn't exactly fill me with joy.

'Can I ring you in about an hour?' I suggested. 'I'll know then whether the reserve sitter is free or not.'

'I'll ring you,' he said, getting up now from his seat. 'And I'll be keeping my fingers crossed.'

Mine were already, behind my back, as I showed him out. I watched till he disappeared out of sight and then, just as I was about to close the door, Chris suddenly appeared at the end of the path. I stayed where I was so I could ask him the favour, but it was he who spoke to me first.

'Was that Taylor Wiseman I just saw leaving?' he as good as demanded.

I nodded, somewhat taken aback by his tone.

He stood at the bottom of the short flight of steps and glared at me. 'What the hell was he doing here?'

'He's the person I'm working for,' I said. 'I'm doing some shots for his cookery book.'

'Oh, really?' he scoffed.

'Yes, *really.*'

'Well, you and your friend certainly aren't too choosy about the company you keep,' he said, shaking his head and rolling his eyes at the same time.

I presumed he was referring to Sophie, but I didn't see how he could compare Taylor to that parasitic slimeball Jerome Audesley. 'He's a perfectly decent man, and a very talented chef,' I said defensively, but I could see by the look on Chris's face that he was far from convinced.

'Is that what *he* told you?'

'He didn't need to. He wouldn't have his own TV show if he wasn't talented.'

'I'm not questioning his culinary skills,' Chris replied. 'It's the *decent man* bit I'm taking issue with.'

I was getting mad now. I couldn't believe this conversation was even taking place. 'How could *you* possibly know what kind of man he is?'

'What?' said Chris. 'You mean because he's a celebrity chef and I'm just a gardener?'

I did, actually, but bearing in mind that I needed the gardener to help me out here, I didn't come right out with it. 'I just mean that you don't even know him.'

'Well, you're right about that, I suppose. But I do know someone who unfortunately does.'

I felt uneasy suddenly. 'What do you mean, exactly?' I said.

He started to open his mouth and then closed it again. He shook his head. 'Look,' he said, 'you're right. It's none of my business.' He shrugged. 'And so long as it's only a job of work...'

He looked up at me, right into my eyes, making me feel deeply uncomfortable. And I couldn't do it. I couldn't possibly ask him now if he'd birdsit for me while I went out for a celebratory meal with a man he clearly detested.

'Well, if that's all...' I said, stepping back into the hallway.

'It is if you've changed your mind about looking for those insurance documents.'

Ah, yes, the *insurance documents.* And, with luck, the names of the artists who painted the miniatures. I managed a sort of smile. 'Do you want to come in now?' I said.

He was still poking around in Mrs Audesley's desk in the drawing room when Sophie got home about half an hour later, dragging a loaded suitcase with her. I hadn't come to any decisions yet as to what to do regarding Taylor. It wasn't what Chris had said about him that was worrying me, just what I was going to say to him when he rang. It just seemed too good an opportunity to miss, a possibly never to be repeated one at that. I'd been wondering again whether to leave Sophie in charge, but my conscience wouldn't allow it.

When she came in I met her in the hall, and with finger to my lips, to shush her up, I ushered her into the kitchen. 'The gardener is looking for something that will hopefully tell us more about the missing miniatures,' I said in a lowered voice. I shut the door then, to make sure he couldn't hear us, and told her briefly about my predicament.

'So what's he got against Taylor?' Sophie said with a frown.

'God knows. He went all secretive suddenly. But I'm sure it's nothing. He's probably just jealous because Taylor is so successful.'

Sophie looked unconvinced about this. 'Men don't usually take so strongly against people for just being successful,' she said.

I was annoyed with her for missing the point. And the point was that I had to ring Taylor soon and I wanted to be able to say I could go out with him that evening. 'Whatever,' I said irritably. 'But I can't ask him to sit for Sir Galahad under the circumstances.'

'But didn't you say that the bird goes to sleep at eight o'clock? Why can't you just go out once you've done whatever you have to do at bedtime—or *perchtime,* in his case. I'm sure it would be okay if I'm here in the house.'

'But I'll still have to tell Chris. It's part of the agreement I made with Mrs A. And I daren't break any more rules.'

'Yeah, but does he have to know that it's Taylor you'll be going out with?'

'No, but…' Then it clicked that she had a good point. I

didn't have to tell him where I was going or who I was going with. It was none of his damn business.

I let out a grateful sigh. 'You're a genius,' I said, and gave her a hug. Then I remembered to ask her how things had gone today.

'Fine. I didn't bump into Jerome, thank God, but I did put some feelers out about him.'

'Anything interesting transpire?'

'Just the fact that he's a notorious bastard.' I frowned at this, and she smiled back at me wanly. 'I just wish I'd done the asking around before I agreed to go out with him in the first place.'

'I wouldn't like you nearly so much if you were that sensible,' I said, and just as I said it we both turned when we heard someone knock at the kitchen door.

'Come in,' I called, and Chris opened the door and popped his head around it.

'I thought I heard someone with you,' he said, smiling at Sophie warmly. The sort of smile he'd used on me the first time we met, but which I hadn't seen since.

'This is my friend Sophie,' I said, remembering my manners.

'Ah,' he said coolly now, 'the Trojan horse?'

I was furious about this remark, but Sophie just laughed. 'I've been called lots of things in my time,' she said, 'but that is a first.'

He came into the kitchen properly. 'No offence,' he said.

'None taken,' she replied. 'And you're right, anyway. He did use me to get into the house, and I very much regret being such a fool.'

'Do I get the impression things are over with you and our thief now then?'

'Very much so,' she agreed vehemently.

I noticed he was holding a sheet of paper, and now he turned his attention on me. 'I found this,' he said. 'I think it's what you were looking for.'

I took it from him and saw it was part of an insurance inventory, with items described along with their estimated value. My heart sank. Not only did I recognise one or two of the artists whose names were listed, which meant they were famous, but they were also worth a great deal more than I dared believe.

'Are you still sure you don't want me to call Adrienne yet?' he said when he saw the sick expression on my face.

I didn't know what to say for a moment. This was a very scary situation, but the thought of Mrs A coming back was scarier still. I thought quickly. Despite the shock, the situation remained the same. It still seemed to me that our best chance of getting the miniatures back was by finding a way of outwitting Jerome. So I shook my head and looked at him pleadingly. 'Just one week,' I said. 'After that you can do what you like.'

He shrugged. 'I think I should remind you that one day of that week has already passed. Which leaves only six days, I'm afraid.'

'Fair enough,' I said gloomily. And although I knew I should have been concentrating my mind strictly on the problem in hand, I found that it had drifted back to Taylor. 'I've got to go out tonight, by the way.' I quickly explained that I wouldn't be going till after eight, and Sophie would be staying in the house.

He looked me up and down as I spoke. 'I wondered why you were all scrubbed up,' he said wryly. Then he shrugged.

'Should be okay,' he said, surprisingly reasonable. 'And I'll be downstairs if you need me,' he added, addressing Sophie now.

I called Peter the moment he left, and gave him the information he had been waiting for.

And then I rang Taylor Wiseman.

11

I'd arranged to meet him at a local restaurant, which looked very smart, with its tasteful furnishings and fine linen napkins, but although we got lots of attention, due to the fact that Taylor was famous, he insisted it wasn't much cop in the actual food department. He was very apologetic, saying it was all he could find at such short notice, but he needn't have been. The food tasted brilliant to me, though I didn't actually say so because I didn't want him thinking that I was a pleb. Clearly I did not have the sophistication to distinguish what he said was merely okay food from excellent.

I passed on a starter because I was so nervous, and I didn't eat much of the main course either—slivers of duck with a plummy sauce—even though it really did taste great. We had champagne, of course, because this was supposed to be a celebration, and I didn't like to say that I hated the stuff. I can never understand what all the fuss is about. To me, champagne is just like not very nice wine with an Alka-Seltzer added for fizz. And it always goes to my head straight away, and makes me feel vile the next day.

But I went through the motions of pretending to like it, drinking a lot more of it than I should have done in an attempt to settle my rattled nerves. And by the end of my second glass my tongue had loosened considerably.

'So,' I said, looking right into his molasses-coloured eyes, 'any chance of you solving a mystery for me?' He was dressed all in black, and I marvelled at the fact that he wasn't covered in bits of hair and fluff, which I always seemed to be when I wore black.

'I'd be delighted to, if I possibly can,' he said with a pleasant grin.

I took another sip of my noxious drink for added courage.

'Well,' I began, 'the first time we met I thought you made it quite clear to me that you were single.'

His expression became very slightly guarded, but the smile remained.

'And you're not mistaken,' he said. 'That's exactly what I did say.'

I nodded. So far so good. 'But since then I've…' I paused for a moment to find the right words. Although she didn't deserve it, I had just enough of the sisterhood thing left in me to not want to drop Amber in it. '…been told by someone that you and Mary—'

'Did Mary say that?' he interrupted sharply.

'Well, no, as a matter of fact.' Which was perfectly true, but I had seen the look on her face. And, okay, so she hadn't exactly got as far as telling me that she and Taylor were more than just colleagues, but I'd had the very distinct feeling she was about to.

'Then whoever did tell you was misinformed.'

'But…'

'But nothing,' he said with exaggerated patience. Then he shrugged. 'We did go out once or twice, it's true, but it was nothing special.'

'That's not the impression I got from her,' I said, unable to let it go quite as easily as that.

He put his fork down and let out a sigh. 'I know,' he said, 'and to be honest with you, Tao, it's been kinda awkward.'

And of course I pressed him, and eventually heard the whole sorry tale. He'd been very flattered when she'd approached him about doing a series for TV, but right from the start he'd been concerned that her interest in him was more than strictly professional. He liked her well enough— thought she was a great woman, in fact—but he had never been remotely attracted to her. His big mistake, though, had been accepting a couple of invitations for dinner with some of her friends. She'd obviously thought there was more to it than he ever did, and when he realised what was going on he had to put on the brakes. He told her he was worried about mixing business with pleasure, and although she appeared to accept it she'd made it clear that she wasn't happy about him seeing anyone else.

'But of course that hasn't really been an issue,' he said, in conclusion. He looked at me over the rim of his glass, and I could see his dark eyes twinkle. 'Until recently, that is. And then I go and find out that the *someone* I might have wanted to see is already engaged to somebody else.'

I knew he knew that this was a lie, so I shrugged. 'I just said that because, well… I'm not sure why, really.'

'Because Mary interrogated you and you felt it was the safest thing to say?'

I didn't admit that she hadn't needed to interrogate me.

'Stupid, I know, but it wasn't entirely a lie. I *was* engaged until just over a year ago. We even shared a mortgage together. But then I suddenly, well…let's just say that I had a change of heart.'

I was about to give him a quick rundown on my life in Manchester, before I'd started the photography course, but I noticed that he was looking around. For the waiter, I imagined. We'd both finished our food and I sensed he was a little impatient with the staff for not taking our plates the moment we'd put our knives and forks down. Either that or he wasn't interested in my boring past, and I preferred the first scenario.

Fortunately he caught someone's eye at that moment, and because neither of us opted for a pudding or coffee he paid the bill, and we didn't really speak again until we were outside.

'I'm sorry about all that,' he said to me then.

'Sorry for what?' I wanted to know. Despite the impatience he'd shown near the end of the meal, I was feeling pretty happy myself. Now everything was out in the open and a few loose ends had been cleared up. And, since Taylor had made it perfectly clear that he was interested in me, what did I have to complain about? Only the champagne, and it wasn't his fault that I was a Philistine.

'For putting you in a position where you felt you had to lie.'

'That's not *your* fault,' I said. And then, because this was getting unnecessarily serious, 'You're not to blame just because women find you so irresistible they come on all possessive…'

He managed a smile as we stood beneath the dim overhead lights of the bookshop adjoining the restaurant, and then he reached out and took me into his arms. 'I'm going to kiss you in a moment, Tao Tandy,' he said, 'and I'm very worried.'

The whole of my innards were turning flips at that moment, and I couldn't make sense of what he was saying. 'Worried?' I managed hoarsely.

'The first kiss is very important, and if we don't get it right it could spoil everything.'

'Well, let's risk it,' I said, just a tad impatient as I stretched my neck up to him and puckered my lips. Then I closed my eyes and waited expectantly. For what seemed like a very long time. And then, when he finally did it, his lips touched mine so lightly I thought I was just imagining it. But I couldn't have been because the effect was explosive, like little charges going off all over my body.

His lips continued to touch mine softly this way for a good ten seconds, and, my God, it was good. Then the pressure increased and it got even better. I don't know how long it went on, but when he finally let go I was a jellified heap.

'Can we go back to your place?' I heard him whisper.

'Yes,' I croaked back, already dragging him along the pavement in the general direction of the place I currently called my home. For a couple of yards, anyway, until the awful realisation dawned that I couldn't do it.

It was only just after ten o'clock. Chris would almost certainly still be up, and, although I was now utterly confident that he could have nothing unpleasant on this lovely man who kissed like a dream, I just didn't want any more trouble with him. And then there was Sophie. I could hardly take a man back when she was there. Could I? Well, even if I could there was still the Chris problem. It would be just my luck if he happened to be taking an evening constitutional as we turned up.

So I told Taylor that it wasn't a *yes,* after all, but a *no*—for a very good reason, of course, which I didn't go into. 'But we could always go back to your place,' I said breathlessly.

He looked at me sadly, though. 'I'm sorry, sweetheart, but I've got the decorators in at the moment, and apart from the fact that the place is upside down I'm afraid it stinks of toxic paint. I couldn't possibly subject you to that.'

I wouldn't have minded one little bit, and although I was touched at his obvious concern for my comfort I couldn't help feeling deeply disappointed.

'Not to worry, though,' he said, kissing my forehead tenderly. 'We've got all the time in the world ahead of us.'

That wasn't how I saw it though. And since I had to blame someone for spoiling things, I blamed it on Chris.

'How about we do this again on Wednesday night at my place? And do it properly this time,' he said.

'But won't you be working?' I said, coming round to the fact that I really would have to put my lust on hold.

'Yes, but I can probably get away by nine. And if I give you the address we could save some time if we met there.'

Of course I saw no sign whatever of Chris when I got back, although I did see light coming up from his sitting room, and I was sure he'd have been out like a shot if he'd heard any voices.

Sophie was waiting up—agog, I supposed, for news of my night out with Taylor. And although she'd seen him on TV it was hard to describe what he was actually like in the flesh. So I concentrated on the kiss, and when I noticed the far-off look in her eyes I wondered if she was thinking about Jerome. He might be an old-fashioned cad of the very first order, but he clearly had something going for him or she'd never have fallen for him so hard.

'And I'm seeing him again on Wednesday,' I concluded, 'and I can't bloody wait.'

As I spoke I thought about clothes. I'd worn my only decent dress tonight. It wasn't too bad, but it was three years old, and I could hardly wear it again on Wednesday.

'I must remember to take in my contract tomorrow,' I said out loud to myself. 'The quicker I do that, the quicker I get some money.' I was practically down to my last ten quid by now, and that wouldn't get me very far.

'I'll lend you some, if you like,' Sophie said. 'You can pay me back when the money comes in.'

I almost refused, but I wasn't really in a position to do so when I thought about it, so I thanked her heartily and promised to take her to the Caribbean when I was rich and famous.

'Chris called round, by the way,' she said, instead of responding to my generous offer.

'Oh, yes?' I replied, not really interested. 'What did he want?'

'Just checking that everything was okay with Sir Galahad.' When I didn't respond, she said, 'He seems really nice.'

'Well, he's not very nice to me.'

'Maybe you weren't very nice to him.'

'That's not true,' I said defensively. 'I even asked him to go out for a drink—you know, just to get to know each other better as we'd be sharing pet-sitting duties—but he turned me down flat.'

I think Sophie must have got the message at last, because she didn't pursue it any longer. In fact she changed the subject to one that I liked a lot better.

'So, when will you be working with Taylor again?' she asked, and I realised that work had not been discussed all evening.

'Probably not till the weekend, I don't suppose, because that's when all the markets seem to be open.' I told her about my idea to stick to markets, especially food ones, and she told me about the one at Brixton.

'That's mostly food,' she said, 'and it's open every day except Sunday.'

I made a mental note of this information, and then, when I was wondering if I should ring Taylor now, to set up a shoot later in the week, I remembered that my mother would be arriving on Friday. I mentioned this troubling news to Sophie, and she rolled her eyes and said she thought that Thursday might be a good day to move back to her flat.

'Thanks for the support,' I said, but I couldn't blame her. My mother had that effect on all my friends. And then, because I suddenly realised I'd been talking about myself for an hour, I asked her if the Cs had rung. I was certain they would have.

'Several times,' she confirmed. 'I've had my mobile switched off all evening, but I just checked for messages before you came in. They're full of false pity for me, of course. They seem to know everything.'

'Not *everything,* I don't suppose.'

'They said they're coming over tomorrow, to see me.'

I scrunched up my face sympathetically. 'You could always be out,' I said.

'I'll have to face them some time, and if you don't mind I'd rather do it here.'

'Fine by me,' I said with a shrug, and then we talked some more about the miniatures, and our chances of getting the damn things back before the week was out. I didn't really think that Sophie was any more hopeful than I was.

I felt even worse at a quarter past one that following morning, when Peter Parker called and woke me from a very deep sleep. The champagne had done its worst by now, and I was suffering the after-effects keenly.

'Got some news,' he said, cutting straight to the chase, and I wondered who he could possibly have been talking to at such an ungodly hour.

'Which is?' I asked him drowsily.

'Seems there's no way that wanker could unload them pictures in this country. Not if he wants to get anywhere close to their actual value.'

I thought about this for a moment, but the fog in my head refused to lift. 'What does that mean, exactly?' I said.

'It means that he'll probably have to take them abroad.'

'Abroad?'

'Yeah, the States, the Far East—most likely Japan.'

I sat up in bed now, and rolled my neck to try and increase the blood circulation to my addled brain. 'When you say *take,* do you mean that? Or will he just send them somewhere?'

'He'll have to take them himself, I'd say. It's too risky sending something as valuable as that by post, and if he's got any sense he won't let them out of his sight till he gets the readies in his hand.'

My brain was beginning to function again, and I thought about this for a moment. 'So it looks like we might have some time,' I said, trying to take some comfort from this. 'I mean, he'll have to set things up in advance, won't he? It can't be that easy to find a buyer, can it?'

'Maybe—maybe not. You did say that he'd already pulled a similar stroke, though, didn't you?'

'Uh?'

'That he'd liberated some of the old lady's silver in the recent past?'

Oh, that. I agreed that I had. 'But what's that got to do with the price of eggs?' I was getting confused again now.

'Well, I can't find anyone who handled the goods, so he may have unloaded that abroad too, and if so then maybe he already has his contact set up.'

'Shit!' I managed, but nothing more helpful.

'I'm not saying he's airborne as we speak, precisely, but my bet is that he'll be making the trip pretty soon. He probably assumes you haven't noticed anything's missing yet, but he knows that he can't afford to hang around. My bet is he'll be booking his ticket pretty darn quick.'

And, having left that cheery thought in my head, he ended the call without even wishing me goodnight.

12

I told Sophie about Peter's call when I struggled out of bed at seven-thirty the following morning. I wanted to catch her before she left for work because I'd decided I badly needed the money that she'd offered to lend me. Apart from something to wear tomorrow, food was running low, and now that I had a guest I felt I really should replenish the stocks.

As it turned out she had remembered, and because she tends to carry a fair amount of cash around she was able to give me a hundred pounds, with the promise of more later if that wasn't enough. I doubted it would be, with what I had in mind, but at least I had my overworked credit card to fall back on as a temporary measure.

She said that she would try and find out if Jerome was planning to take any time off, and reminded me—as if I could forget—that the Cs would be coming round to the house straight after work. She really wasn't looking forward to their gloating dressed up as concern, but at least I'd be there to lend some support.

When she'd gone I showered, dressed, put on jeans and a T-shirt, and then attended to Sir Galahad, who was swearing a lot and flapping his wings in what I took to be agitation. He calmed down a bit when I chatted with him, but I sensed that something wasn't quite right that morning. And just when I'd left him, to make a second cup of tea, I heard the front doorbell ring.

It was Chris, and beside him was an unsmiling middle-aged woman in an oversized raincoat whom he introduced as Olive and informed me that she was the cleaner. Which was something I'd completely forgotten about. She nodded a greeting but didn't speak, and when she'd brushed past me to get into the house Chris asked me if I was planning on going out today.

'As a matter of fact, yes,' I said. 'I was going to come down and see if you could spare me an hour. But maybe if Olive is here it would be okay to leave Sirg with her for a while.'

''Fraid not,' he said, lowering his voice. 'Olive is not one of our friend's favourite people. He hates her, as a matter of fact, and gets quite, well…excitable on her cleaning day.'

'Ah,' I said. 'So that's what's wrong.' I told him that he'd been a bit strange that morning, and Chris nodded his head knowingly.

'He always seems to know when she's coming.'

'So does that mean I'm housebound?' I said, and I think I must have sounded sulky.

'Not necessarily. I have to do some work in Adrienne's garden this morning, so if you make it quick I suppose I could keep an eye on things.'

I wasn't so keen on the *make it quick* bit, but since he was doing me a favour I accepted the offer graciously.

I gathered my belongings within five minutes, including my recently signed contract, and headed off to the tube station. I got to the agency just before ten, and handed the contract over to Amber. She didn't have much to say for herself, but I noticed the snooty, disapproving way she looked at my jeans and the ageing fleece I'd put on over my T-shirt. I was very tempted to rub her nose in the fact that I'd been out with Taylor and would be seeing him again tomorrow night, but I didn't want the contract 'going astray', like my telephone number, so I just wished her a cheery good morning and left without further comment.

I headed straight for a nice little clothes shop I'd spotted on my last visit to Covent Garden, and spent a happy half-hour trying on dresses I couldn't really afford. I ended up with a flowery, gypsy-style, off-the-shoulder number, that fitted where it touched and would not allow for any meal above and beyond five hundred calories.

When I got back to the house Sirg was in a major sulk, the kitchen was shiny clean and the sink was filled with freshly cut garden flowers. Olive was still working upstairs, but there was no sign of Chris. I presumed I hadn't been as quick as I should have been, and that he'd already set off for wherever he had to be next, but I'd just found a couple of vases in a cupboard when his head appeared round the kitchen door.

'Just keeping up the old routines,' he said of the flowers, presumably in case I'd begun to suspect that he'd brought them in especially for me.

He came into the room and leaned against the huge pine dresser that took up half of one the walls. I was busy trying to squeeze too many flowers into one of the vases and he shook his head. 'You're making a complete pig's ear of that. Why don't you let me do it?'

He was right, so I could hardly take offence. I stood aside and eyed him wryly. 'So you arrange them as well as grow them, do you?'

He shrugged. 'Not really. I just have a little more patience than you seem to have.'

I made a childish face behind his back and he turned round quickly, as if he'd guessed what I was up to.

'Any more news from your *contact?*' he said, in that maddeningly cynical tone of his.

'Yes, as a matter of fact.' Which was entirely true. 'And he's making good progress.' Which wasn't.

'Well, you're down to five days now, so I hope you're right.' He turned around further and looked at the bags I'd left on the table. A couple had food in them, but it was the pink bag with the dress in it that seemed to interest him most. 'Glad to see that you have time for frivolities, at any rate.'

I couldn't think of anything to say to that, so I gave him a mild evil eye and he grinned and turned his attention back on the flowers. He had them sorted in a couple of minutes, and I had to admit to myself, if not to him, that they looked pretty good when he'd finished.

'I'll leave you to put them where you want to,' he said, and then he looked at me directly again. 'Olive has been paid in advance, so you don't have to worry about that, but you will need to give Sir Galahad some extra attention today, to calm him down. I've already turned his radio up to drown out the sound of the Hoover.'

'How does Olive manage to clean his room out?' I asked him then. It was something that had not been discussed with Mrs Audesley.

'She doesn't. She won't go anywhere near him now. Not since he took a chunk out of her arm.'

I made a face, not because of the injury inflicted on the cleaner—I was becoming immune to accounts of his violent behaviour—but because his room was getting in quite a state, with his feathers and bedding strewn far and wide. 'Will he let *me* do it later?'

'Much later, maybe. Tomorrow, perhaps, when he's forgotten about Olive. And it might be an idea to move him somewhere while you're doing it. He has been known to attack the Hoover as well.'

And then, because we seemed to be getting along okay, even if we were just talking about a neurotic African Grey parrot, I was tempted to ask him again what he had against Taylor. Not that I believed that there was anything valid, of course, but I couldn't help being interested in why Chris seemed so opposed to someone who, by his own admission, he didn't even know directly.

But just then Olive came into the kitchen to boil some water for a cup of tea, and he told us both that he would have to get on his way.

I rang Taylor at the Tulip later, and suggested a shoot at Brixton Market whenever suited him. He told me that he'd get back to me. I was a bit miffed because he sounded quite cool and distracted, and I found myself asking if it was still okay for tomorrow night.

'Should be,' he said. 'I'll ring to confirm later, though.'

He might have been talking about a dental appointment for all the enthusiasm and warmth in his voice, and I felt a rush of unease. 'You sound a bit strange,' I said. 'Are you okay?'

'Talk to you later then,' he said, ignoring my question, and then the phone went dead.

My immediate reaction was to ring him straight back and tell him what to do with himself, but then I remembered the contract I'd signed and delivered that morning, and the importance of behaving in a professional manner. And I also remembered that kiss.

'He was probably just busy,' I said to Sirg, as he chomped on a fresh piece of paw-paw that I'd picked up on my way home.

'Wanker!' he screeched when he'd finished the fruit, and then he flew from the top of the cage and landed delicately on my shoulder. Because I couldn't imagine Mrs A using that particular word, I guessed that he'd definitely learnt it from Jerome.

'Who's a wanker?' I wanted to know as I scratched his chin.

'Who's a wanker?' the bird repeated, and I realised I wasn't going to get very much sense from him on the subject.

He'd quietened down quite a lot now, now that Olive had left the building, and I couldn't help wondering what went on in his tiny mind, and why, out of all the people he'd met over time, and mostly detested, he'd taken such a liking to me. To me and to Chris. Two people who certainly didn't like one another.

I took him for a stroll round the house, and when he treated me to a number of choice new phrases I threatened to wash his mouth out with soap if he didn't clean up his act a bit. He rewarded me for that threat with a gentle nip of my earlobe and a tender request of 'kisses for Mummy', which made me smile and think about Mrs Audesley again. I found it hard to imagine her talking that way to a bird, but since he'd spoken in a perfect imitation of her voice I knew that it had to have come from her.

I was grateful that she hadn't called again—yet—and I was hoping very much that she wouldn't until those miniatures were hanging back on the dining room wall where they be-longed. I kept running hot and cold about our chances of getting them back. One minute I was in despair, then next I was hopeful and confident. At that moment my optimism had taken a dip, but that probably had a lot to do with my current mood and the fact that I was worrying about Taylor.

I went on worrying for another half an hour, until my mobile rang and he said he was sorry. 'I had a client with me,' he said, and I forgave him instantly. He rattled on a bit about the said client, and some plans for an important book-ing in the restaurant, and if I didn't know better I'd think he was covering something up. But I was just glad that he'd put matters right and now sounded again like the person I knew and lusted after.

'Would Thursday afternoon suit you for Brixton?' he wanted to know, and I said that it would. I also suggested a couple of other venues for the following week, now that I'd picked up a leaflet from the station which listed all the mar-kets and their times of opening. And he said that we'd talk more about that when we met.

'So we are on for tomorrow, then?' I said. 'Only you didn't seem so sure earlier.'

'Didn't I? Well, I am. I've fixed everything up here at the restaurant. My second will be covering for me, so I'll be home at nine sharp and I've got a surprise planned for you.'

At which point I got some very unladylike thoughts in my head, but I wisely kept them to myself. 'I'll look forward to it,' I said instead.

Sophie got back to the house ten minutes before the Cs showed up. She just had time to tell me the news she'd picked up at work. The fact that Jerome Audesley had arranged to take Friday off work. Which effectively meant that we might only have two and a half days left, in all, since it was quite possible that he might leave the country any time after finishing work on Thursday evening.

Feeling flat and depressed, it was even more of an onerous chore to play the happy hostesses to the dreadful Cs, but we knew that we'd have to carry it off if we were going to disappoint them. And we were determined that we would. They were coming here to rub Sophie's nose in the fact that she had been dumped, no doubt about it, and for the sake of her pride it was very important that she must be seen not to give a damn. That she couldn't care less about Jerome. They might not entirely believe it, of course, but if she could just put on a very good act, it would spoil a lot of their pleasure.

That was the plan anyway, but as it turned out the act wasn't necessary because the Cs were only interested in their own particular grievances. Which were plenty. They'd worked themselves up into such a froth that it took ages to work out that they too had been dumped, by Simon and Lawrence.

'And the worst bit is that we'd arranged to take them home this weekend,' Fiona groaned. 'To meet our parents.'

'Imagine what fools we're going to look now,' Jemima shuddered.

'I wouldn't worry about it,' I said. 'I'm sure you've done stupider things in your time.'

The two Cs looked at me across the kitchen table with narrow-eyed disdain. 'It's okay for you,' Fiona said. 'But our parents have high expectations for us, and this will come as a bitter blow.'

'I don't see how, for God's sake. You've only been seeing those twats a few days.'

They both shook their heads, as if I was some greatly to be pitied simpleton. 'I don't know why we're wasting our time,' Jemima said. 'It's obvious that you would never understand.'

'Then why *are* you wasting your time?' I said, getting a little bit sick of being talked to as if I was from another planet.

'When did this happen?' Sophie asked then, with a sideways glance in my direction. I got the impression she was trying to tell me to shut up.

'This morning,' Fiona answered glumly. 'I rang up Lawrence to ask him round for a meal this evening—you know, with Simon as well—and he told me then. Just like that, without any prior warning whatever.' She looked over at Jemima. 'And when I told Jem she called Simon and he announced that it was over with them as well.'

They both shook their heads in a mirrored display of bewildered despair.

'How odd,' said Sophie.

'How wicked and cruel, more like,' said Jemima.

'And no explanations either,' said Fiona. 'Not even any expression of regret.'

I shrugged. I was getting a bit bored with their self-pity now, and I had more pressing matters to think about.

'Do you suppose they did it because Jerome dumped me?'

The two Cs looked at one another and then at Sophie. 'We wondered that, as a matter of fact,' said Fiona, almost accusingly.

Sophie nodded. 'I wouldn't be surprised,' she said. 'I've heard that Simon and Lawrence tend to dance to Jerome's tune, and he probably didn't think you could be of any more use.'

I looked as sharply at Sophie as the Cs did, but for a different reason. I was very afraid that she was just about to tell them everything, while they were probably just confused.

'What *use* could we possibly have been to Jerome?' Fiona wanted to know.

Sophie turned and looked directly at me when I kicked her under the table. 'Maybe they can help,' she said. 'And what harm can it do anyway?'

I knew what she was talking about, of course, and I thought about it for a moment. And the answer I came up with was, What harm indeed? Things were so bad that we really didn't have all that much to lose. So I nodded to tell her she had my permission to say what she wanted.

'Before I say anything,' she began, 'I must stress that it really is very important that you don't repeat what I'm going to tell you.'

They were agog, of course, now, and would have agreed to anything to hear what Sophie had to say.

'Promise,' she said, and they eagerly repeated the word as if it had magical qualities.

So she told them everything—about the miniatures, about Peter's involvement, about Jerome's probable trip abroad. 'And so you see,' she said in conclusion, 'it's essential that we find those miniatures before he leaves the bank on Thursday.'

The Cs were clearly thrilled with the whole thing, and were full of annoyingly irrelevant questions. I shushed them eventually and cut to the chase. Because I'd suddenly realised something important. Something that made perfect sense.

'The point is that he's obviously hidden the miniatures somewhere,' I said with a meaningful glance at Sophie. 'And my guess is that they are probably with one of his two faithful cohorts.'

There was a bewildered silence as the Cs looked at me gormlessly for a good few seconds, then the penny seemed to drop and Fiona's eyes widened.

'My God,' she spluttered. 'I think they must be at Lawrence's place!'

We all looked at her and she clamped her mouth shut for a moment while she thought about it. Then she nodded. 'I think I'm right, you know.'

'Go on,' Sophie said encouragingly.

'Well, I went round to Lawrence's place on Monday evening, and—well…' she looked a bit embarrassed '…he went out for a while to get some wine, and of course I mooched around a bit.' She shrugged. 'Everyone does that, though, don't they?'

We all nodded in breathless agreement, and she seemed relieved.

'Well, anyway, so I eventually looked in his wardrobe and I found a locked briefcase—which was very annoying at the time. I even tried prising it open with my nail file, but the clasp wouldn't budge.' Sophie and I were frowning now. Sure, we'd mooched around boyfriends' flats with the best of them, but I don't think either of us had ever gone quite so far as trying to break into a briefcase.

'Are you saying you think it was Jerome's briefcase?' asked Sophie.

'It had to be. I thought it was odd at the time, but you see it actually had his initials on it. A *J* and an *A!*' she said triumphantly. 'I nearly asked Lawrence about it, as a matter of fact, but then I realised I'd be giving myself away.' She grinned like a naughty schoolgirl who'd just stuck chewing gum on somebody's chair.

I felt like kissing her. This was brilliant news, but then the downside struck me. It was one thing knowing where the miniatures were, but it was quite another getting our hands on them.

'Do you think there's any chance we could break into the flat?' I asked desperately.

Fiona and Jemima exchanged a smirk.

'That won't be necessary,' Fiona said proudly.

'You're going to have to explain that,' I said after a while, when she didn't continue and no one else spoke.

'We have a little collection,' Jemima informed us slyly.

'I hope this is relevant,' I said irritably.

Jemima giggled. 'You know the way some men mark up notches on their bedpost…?'

'I didn't really believe anyone *actually* did that,' I said. I was getting annoyed with all their coyness but I shut up when Sophie gave me a warning look.

'Well, we get keys cut,' Fiona said. 'You know, for the flats of our boyfriends.'

'Do they know about this?' I said, so shocked that I missed the point for a moment.

'Of course not,' said Fiona. 'We make an excuse to borrow them for a while, and—well—' she shrugged '—that's more or less it, really.'

'And what do you do with them afterwards?'

'Nothing,' piped in Jemima brightly. 'We just add them to the collection. We've got over twenty between us now.'

Just then Sophie nudged me. 'Aren't you missing something here?'

It took a moment, but then it clicked. 'Oh, my God,' I said. 'We won't have to break in!'

'Precisely,' she said. 'We can just put the key in the lock and open the door.'

It all sounded worryingly easy, and then I thought of a major problem. 'How will we know that it's safe to go in the flat? I mean, what would happen if we just trundled on in and Lawrence was there?'

'He has to go to work, doesn't he?' Fiona said sensibly. 'You could do it during the day.'

I didn't like the sound of that much, though. I was the only person who didn't have regular working hours, and I really didn't fancy going into a flat I had no right to enter all on my own.

The Cs left the house a lot more cheerful than they'd been when they arrived. They seemed to be on a high, in fact, now that they could smell the sweet scent of revenge in the air.

They promised to drop the key round later that evening, and I braced myself well in advance for the job that I knew with dread I would have to carry out the following day. And then I thought about Peter, and I cheered up a bit and decided to call him. It was expecting a lot to ask him to join me, but then I did have some very nice photographs of his mother and Taylor...

13

After a quiet night with Sophie and early to bed, I got up soon after she left for work and moved Sirg's cage into the main drawing room, with him inside it. Then I thoroughly cleaned his room out, and despite the fact that I turned the radio up really loud he squawked for the whole of the time I was at it.

He was a bit off with me when I put him back. He even nipped me ever so lightly when I opened the cage and offered him my finger as a perch. 'Wanker!' he said out loud again. I reminded him firmly about washing his mouth out and he responded to that with the sound of a whistling kettle.

I would have had to do it all anyway—clean out his room—but I was glad of the task to keep my mind off the day ahead. Peter, God bless him, had agreed to meet me at Lawrence's Docklands apartment at two-thirty that afternoon. It was his suggestion that we did it then because that was, according to Peter, the time when we were least likely to encounter nosy neighbours. I had the key now, along with the address, duly supplied by an eager Fiona, who'd made me promise to ring her at work the moment the deed was done.

But I still had several hours to kill, and with the rest of the house already sparkling clean, thanks to Olive, I decided to ring my mother. I was half hoping that she might have changed her plans, and forgotten to tell me, but unfortunately that wasn't the case.

'I'm thinking of staying over for a day or two, if that's okay with you,' she said, in a way that told me it didn't much matter if it was okay with me or not. 'I thought we could see some of the sights together. It's ages since we had a girlie day out.'

I told her that was impossible—firmly. That I had to look after Sirg all day, and when I wasn't doing that I would be working.

'Didn't you say there was someone else to look after the parrot when you went out?' she went on, regardless.

'African Grey. Yes, but—'

'But nothing, darling. Don't worry, I'll speak to whoever it is if you're too shy. I'm sure they'll be only to happy to help out when they understand the situation.'

There was no stopping her when she was on a mission, so I didn't even try. I would sort her out when she got here, when all this business with Jerome and the miniatures was over and done with.

'How's Dad?' I asked, as usual, and she got a bit sniffy.

'You'll never believe this, Tao, but he's taken up *golf.*' She might have been saying that he'd taken up pornography as a hobby by the tone of her voice. 'I mean, how utterly *bourgeois* is that?'

I had to admit it didn't sound much like my dad, but I didn't imagine it would do him much harm. 'Maybe he just wants some exercise,' I said.

'That's what he said, as a matter of fact, but to me it's the thin end of the wedge. Next he'll be joining the Conservative Party and having cocktail parties…' I heard her shudder theatrically at the thought, and I wondered if anything was wrong between them. What with Dad acting out of character and her wanting to stay longer in London. But I wasn't in the mood for parent problems. I had enough of my own at the moment, so I told her that someone was at the door and I'd have to go.

It was then that I remembered I hadn't checked with Chris to see if it was okay to go out. I didn't expect to be very much more than an hour, fingers crossed, but I still thought I should let him know. But when I went down to his flat I found it was empty, so I went back to the house, scribbled a note to cover myself, and slipped it through his letterbox.

Because I'd used plastic to purchase the dress, I had cash enough left to pay for a taxi. I didn't like wasting so much precious money on a ride across London, but if I really was going to get back in the hour I didn't really have much choice.

I arrived outside the swishy block of flats with ten minutes to spare and spotted Peter almost once. It was hard to miss him. He looked completely out of place, and I couldn't help wondering if I'd made a mistake. If anyone saw us they'd be on the phone to the police before you could say *Spider-Man*.

'Have you got the photos?' he asked me quickly, and I felt like a spy doing a secret trade-off.

I patted the giant-size shopping bag I had slung over my shoulder, which I'd found in the kitchen and looked about the right size to hold a briefcase.

'I'll give them to you later,' I said in hushed tones as I scanned the clothes he was wearing. He had on a hooded zip-up jacket, and with that and the spider's web tattoo he looked like something from a public information film to warn householders against afternoon sneak thieves. Not that I looked all that much better, come to think of it. I was wearing a pair of old jeans and the same elderly fleece that Amber had looked down her nose at. It being the colour of a satsuma, I wasn't that easy to miss either.

But there wasn't any going back now, and whether or not Peter looked like a villain I decided I'd still rather have him there than be on my own.

Somehow we managed to get to the right front door without seeing a single living soul, and I took heart in what Peter had said about the timing. My hands were sweating so much, however, that the key slipped from my grasp as I took it out of my pocket. It made such a racket when it hit the tiled floor that I stood frozen for a good ten seconds before I bent to retrieve it.

Then Peter rang the bell of the apartment and I glared at him in horror. 'What if someone answers?' I said in a whisper, and then I realised what a stupid remark that was and prepared a lie in my head if by some horrible chance somebody did open the door.

I'd decided on playing the part of a Jehovah's Witness, even though with Peter beside me I doubted that we'd get away with it. I stood there for a whole minute with my heart beating wildly, having prepared my opening gambit: *When did you last feel really happy?* Which was precisely what the last

Jehovah's Witnesses who called at my door put to me. I couldn't remember the answer I'd given, but it must have been the wrong one because I'd spent the following half-hour desperately trying to get rid of them without appearing too rude. In the end they'd only departed when I promised to read the three leaflets they left and pick up the discussion next time they called. I was afraid to answer the door after that, and made all my friends call me first when they were coming round.

'Get the key in the lock,' I heard Peter say, and with trembling hands I attempted to comply with his order.

Until he got fed up with the way I kept missing the lock and snatched it out of my hand. And then the door suddenly opened. When my feet wouldn't move of their own accord I felt myself being shoved inside.

'Pull yourself together,' I heard Peter hiss with disgust, so I took a deep breath and tried to focus on what I was there for.

Fortunately, it was not a big flat. Just a sitting room with a small kitchen off it, plus one bedroom and bathroom. Nevertheless, bearing in mind its situation, I guessed it would still have cost about double the price of my parents' four-bedroom detached house in Manchester, and possibly ten times as much as the starter home I'd briefly shared with poor Malcolm.

And the bedroom only had one wardrobe, so unless Jerome had been there in the last twenty-four hours and taken the briefcase away again, the miniatures, I realised with an incredible thrill, were almost within my grasp.

I opened the wardrobe door very slowly—almost as if I expected Jerome to leap out and grab me—until it was gaping wide and a row of neatly pressed office shirts were colourfully revealed. There were some trousers and jackets as well, and some shoes on the base, but no bloody briefcase...

I think I must have let out a small cry of dismay, and I rather expected a comment from Peter, but when I turned round he wasn't with me. I moved some of the clothes, in the unlikely event that the briefcase was hanging behind them somehow, but when I could see that it wasn't I closed the door and did quick general search of the bedroom. Under the bed, in a chest of drawers, behind the same chest of drawers. And nothing.

So I went and found Peter, who was in the kitchen, and told him my miserable news. He was trying to open a Dairylea cheese triangle, and clearly finding it difficult by the look of concentration on his face. He was certainly too busy to respond to me.

I wasn't sure this was a good idea, stealing Lawrence's food as well as gaining unauthorised entry into his flat, and I was just about to say so when I glanced at the opened fridge and saw something strangely foreign at the bottom of it. It was black, and leather, and it had a handle attached to it...

'My God!' I squealed, as I tore across the room and grabbed hold of the handle. 'Didn't you see it there when you were raiding the fridge?'

'Of course I saw it,' Peter said. 'I just thought it wouldn't do any harm to let you sweat a bit.'

'Thanks a million,' I said as I dragged the briefcase out of the fridge, being careful not to upset the food on the shelf above.

I put it down on the counter next to the fridge, noted the initials on a metal disc—the *J* and the *A*—and wondered what to do next. 'I suppose I should just put it in this big bag of mine and take it,' I said uncertainly.

Peter finally managed to separate the cheese from the wrapper, and as it squished around in his mouth he shook his head. 'Better we open it and remove the contents,' he finally said, when his mouth was empty again.

'But we haven't got the key,' I replied as I rubbed my fingers over the lock.

'No problem,' he said as he reached into his jogging pants pocket and took out a bunch of very small keys. 'I keep these for just such emergencies,' he said, and I decided not to pursue the matter. I was getting very edgy. It was all going a bit too well presently, and I was fearful that Lawrence would burst through the door with a posse of policemen in his wake.

But Peter was completely unperturbed as he coolly tried one key after another, until, at long last, the lock made the happiest sound in the world as it softly clicked open.

'Hallelujah!' I cried as I lifted the lid and found a package on the inside. It was a padded brown envelope, A4 in size, and on further examination I discovered it was loosely sealed. I opened it and carefully removed each of the precious miniatures in turn. They were wrapped in bubble-wrap plastic, and I suddenly had a bright idea. I opened the cupboards overhead and hunted about until I found something suitable. Not perfect, by any means, but not bad considering the current urgency of the situation.

It was a packet of Bath Oliver biscuits, and as I opened it up Peter looked over at me curiously. I didn't bother to explain, though. He could see perfectly well what I was doing, and as I undid the bubble-wrap around the pictures and slipped three biscuits in each wrapping instead he nodded his head approvingly.

The biscuits were roughly the same size as the miniatures,

and although they were lighter in weight, I figured that they might well not be noticed so long as Jerome didn't decide to check them closely. I wasn't sure what I wanted to achieve, but the pleasure I got was enough for the moment.

When the envelope was sealed again, and the case returned to the fridge, I slipped the miniatures into my bag and, far less nervous than I had been before, quietly nipped out of the flat.

I was laughing aloud by the time we departed from the building, and Peter had to warn me to be quiet. 'We don't want to be noticed now,' he hissed, 'not now we've got this far.'

I was so happy and elated that I was seriously tempted to throw my arms around him and kiss him. But luckily I managed to resist the temptation, and after I'd handed over the pictures of his mother and Taylor we went our separate ways.

I got back to the Hampstead house fifteen minutes later than I should have done, and didn't Chris let me know it when he met me at the front door with a very sour look on his face.

'I'm sorry,' I said, before he could speak, 'but when you see what I've got I think you'll let me off.' I slapped my bag as I spoke, and nudged by him on my way to the kitchen.

He followed me in and I triumphantly lifted the bag onto the table. I didn't speak as I took the miniatures out of the bag and carefully placed them down in a row. The whole glorious seven of them. Then I looked up at him and waited to hear him congratulate me on a job well done.

Only that didn't happen—I should have guessed, really.

'If you're looking for praise—well, I'm sorry, but the way I see it they should never have been removed in the first place. And they wouldn't have been if you'd followed Adrienne's instructions.'

I didn't know whether to laugh or cry. Okay, so I didn't exactly deserve a medal, but the bastard could have at least acknowledged that I'd done something right. Just thinking that made me angry, and I didn't cry *or* laugh, I just let him have it instead. Big time…

'What is it with you?' I demanded to know. 'Why can't you just say something nice for a change? It's obvious that you don't like me, but since we're stuck with each other for the next few weeks you could at least try making an effort.'

There was a short silence, and then he let out a sigh. 'I never said I didn't like you. I just think that you haven't taken your responsibilities as seriously as you should have.'

'That's bollocks! What do you call this?' I yelled as I stabbed my finger in the general direction of the miniatures. 'I've done things today that made me sick with fear, because I *knew* it was my fault they went missing in the first place.'

'But you could have let me know what you were doing,' he said. 'What if you'd been delayed? What if whatever made you so *sick with fear* had gone wrong? And I'm not going to ask about it because I don't want to know.' He sighed again. 'The point is that Sir Galahad *could* have been left for hours, and believe me he's a lot more important to Adrienne than these miniatures here.'

I could see that he had some sort of a point, but I wasn't ready to admit it. 'Well, he wasn't left for hours,' I said sulkily. 'And at least I left you a note.'

'Yeah, but I might not have found it till this evening. It was only luck that I happened to call in a while ago because I needed something from the flat.'

I opened my mouth to speak again, but he wasn't finished.

'*And* you forgot to set the alarm,' he said.

Oh, dear. I couldn't think of what to say about that, because now that I thought about it I knew he was right. 'Okay, okay,' I said. 'I'm sorry about that and it won't happen again.'

Suddenly the fight had gone out of me. I couldn't see any sense in arguing any further. He had his point of view and I had mine, and the twain were never very likely to meet. 'Thanks for stepping in like that,' I added grudgingly, and he shrugged and left me alone with the results of my first ever dalliance with crime.

At least Sophie was proud of me when I called to tell her the news. She was very excited, as a matter of fact, and so was Fiona when I phoned her next. They were all for getting together that night to hear the details and drink some champagne (no, thank you...), but I couldn't make it myself because I already had plans of my own.

As it turned out Sophie called by her flat when she finished work, and decided to stay and have a drink with the Cs, so she didn't get back to the house till it was almost time for me to leave. I'd sorted Sirg out by then, sung him his goodnight lullaby and got myself ready, and Sophie, the angel, was full of compliments about the way I looked.

I really didn't have time to go over my afternoon adventure, however, so I agreed to get together with her and the Cs the following evening.

I borrowed some more money from her, and a short while later climbed into a taxi for the third time that day. I got to the address I'd been given in Primrose Hill at ten past nine, which seemed just about right. Not so early that I'd seem too eager (although I was, of course), and not so late that I appeared too casual.

I was surprised to find that the address was a house and

not a flat. It was a nice little terraced place, with a pair of bay trees, one on either side of the door, just like at the door of the Tulip.

I took a deep breath and rang the bell, and waited excitedly for Taylor to answer. Only he didn't—not then, and not the second and third time I rang the bell either. At which point I decided that he must have been held up at the restaurant, and checked in my bag to see if I'd switched my mobile off. I hadn't.

By now I was beginning to feel self-conscious. Several people had passed by the house and looked at me curiously. I thought about calling the Tulip, but I couldn't help thinking that he *must* be on his way by now. Rather than hang around like a lemon, I decided to take a little walk. I went as far as a row of shops a few hundred yards away, and when I saw that one was an off-licence decided to buy a bottle of wine. I should have thought of it earlier, but I'd been so busy, and besides I couldn't have left the house again—not after the tongue-lashing I'd received from Chris.

I bought a special offer Chevin Blanc, and then headed back to the house again. It was half past nine by now, and dark, and I felt a bit of a fool in my off-the-shoulder dress. Because I'd expected to go straight into the house when I got out of the taxi, I hadn't bothered with a coat, and as well as feeling underdressed for that time of night, now I was getting cold as well.

There were still no lights on in the house, but I tried the doorbell again. And again. I kept on trying for another ten minutes, and then I reached into my bag for my mobile and made up my mind to call the restaurant.

I'd just got through, in fact, when I heard a car on the road behind me. As I turned around I saw a new black Mini Cooper slip into a nearby space, and I recognised the driver as Taylor.

I should have been mad with him, I suppose, but he was *so* very apologetic for keeping me waiting. He was carrying a bag with him, one of those containers for keeping food hot, and as he kissed me lightly on the cheek and told me how gorgeous I looked the heavenly scent of suet pastry wafted up under my nose.

All was revealed when he led me inside, to a pretty little kitchen at the back of the house. It was surprisingly girlie, as a matter of fact, with flouncy blinds at the window and a matching cloth on the tiny table. But then he probably hadn't lived here long and if, as he said, the decorators were in, then maybe the kitchen was next on his list. Not that there was any sign of work going on, and I certainly couldn't smell any fresh paint.

'This is the real reason I was so late,' he said as he put the bag down on the table.

He turned and switched the oven on, and with the kind of aplomb usually employed by a magician's assistant un-zipped the bag and brought forth the most beautiful-look-ing pie I'd ever laid eyes on. It was golden and glistening and heavily decorated with petals made from more gorgeous pastry, and if there had been any residue of annoyance for being kept waiting so long outside in the cold, then now it melted entirely away.

He smiled at me widely and transferred it to the oven. 'It's still pretty hot, but I thought we could have a drink before we eat.' He took a couple of foil-covered bowls out of the bag as well now, and added them to the oven. 'No chips, I'm afraid, but Angie has included some vegetables.'

'Angie?' I said, confused.

He nodded. 'You told me how much you liked the food at Felix's Place, so I rang there this morning. I know it sounds bad for a professional chef to admit it, but I was never that great with pastry, so I asked them to create something special for us.'

I'd never had anyone do anything like that for me, and frankly I was quite overcome.

He went to the fridge then and took out a bottle of *wine,* thank goodness, and not more champagne. Which reminded me that I'd brought some myself, and I handed it over to him. He thanked me, looked at the label, and then put it down on the counter—not in the fridge, as I'd expected him to. At which point it occurred to me that it probably wasn't very good wine and would end up consigned to the back of some cupboard, or even the bin.

He opened the bottle of better stuff and poured me a glass, and then apologised all over again. 'I didn't have your number with me,' he said, 'or I'd have rung you, of course, when I realised how late I was running.'

He joined me at the table and I assured him that I was fine. How could I be anything other than fine when someone had gone to so much trouble? 'I was very late myself,' I lied, to make him feel better.

'Well, that is a relief,' he said, and then he raised his glass in a toast. 'To suet pastry and cholesterol!'

Which made me think about my tightly fitting dress, and the five hundred calories I'd allowed myself, and whether or not I dared do the meal justice.

Except I need not have worried, as it turned out, because I didn't even get a single mouthful of that pie. I didn't even find out what the filling was. Not then, anyway, because just as we took the first sip of wine it all went a little bit crazy.

14

It started with a telephone call. The phone rang in the kitchen, and for a moment I didn't think Taylor was going to answer it. Then he must have changed his mind, but instead of taking it there he excused himself with an apologetic sigh and left the room. I heard a door open, then close, and assumed he was taking the call in what I supposed was the living room at the front of the house. I didn't hear his voice, so either he spoke very quietly or the house was extremely well soundproofed.

So I just took another sip of wine and bathed in the pleasurable knowledge that someone as gorgeous and famous as Taylor thought enough about me to drive halfway across London after a day's hard work to provide me with such a wonderful treat.

I think the pleasure-bathing lasted all of thirty seconds, until Taylor suddenly burst into the kitchen again and announced in a panic that I'd have to go.

I looked up at him startled. 'Go? But I've only just got here!' I stared stupidly at the oven. 'And what about the pie?'

'Take it with you,' he said, moving quickly towards the oven. He flicked it off and with the help of a teatowel transferred the three containers back into the bag he'd brought them in.

Next he went to the telephone extension in the kitchen, and after checking a card pinned to a board next to the phone dialled a firm of mini-cabs. 'As quick as you can,' he said at the end of the call, and then he put down the phone and finally looked at me.

'I'm so sorry,' he said. 'There's been…a fire! A fire at the restaurant.'

Which galvanised me a lot quicker than anything else he had said.

'My God,' I exclaimed, getting up quickly from my seat. 'Is there anything I can do?'

'No, no,' he said quickly. 'But I need to go straight over there, so…' He was zipping up the bag with the food in it, which I took as my cue.

'Of course,' I said. 'I'll leave at once.'

He looked relieved, and I felt a bit miffed suddenly. It was selfish, I know, but it had occurred to me that there was no real need for him to send me on my way. I could have stayed where I was and waited until he'd sorted things out, and maybe…well, maybe been a comfort to him. 'Are you sure you don't want me to hang on here till you come back?' I offered.

'I could be gone all night,' he replied in a rush, and as he said it he glanced distractedly at his watch. 'It wouldn't be fair on you.'

Clearly the mini-cab firm was a local one, because just

then I heard a car horn beep outside. Taylor grabbed the bag and headed at speed towards the front door. I was in the cab in seconds, with a twenty-pound note thrust into my hand and a promise to ring me later. When he had some news to report.

Which had been almost exactly twelve hours ago, and I still hadn't heard from him. I'd tried ringing his mobile several times, but it was always switched off, and I was getting quite worried now. I had this image of him leaping into the flames to save a precious piece of kitchen equipment, and not coming out.

I'd spoken to Sophie about it, of course. She'd obviously been surprised by my early return the night before, but she hadn't seemed nearly as concerned for Taylor's safety as I was. Which was only natural, I suppose, since she hadn't even met the man, let alone been kissed by him. But I couldn't help thinking that she could have been a little more sympathetic.

'If you're so worried why don't you take a taxi over to Covent Garden and see what's happening?' was the best that she could suggest.

'Because I'd probably only get in the way,' I said. 'I'm not very good in a crisis.'

'Well, then, stop whingeing and wait till you hear from him.'

That was last night. This morning, before she left for work, she'd said I should call the restaurant.

Which had seemed a mad idea, because if the place had burnt down the telephones would hardly have survived, but since I couldn't think of anything else to do I decided to give it a shot.

I picked up my mobile and pressed in the number, and then, before it started to ring, switched it off again. I knew

I had every right to ring, that if nothing else we were sup-posed to be doing a shoot today, but my unexplained reluc-tance seemed a great deal stronger than any good reason I could give myself for making the call.

And in the end I didn't need to make it. Because half an hour later *he* called me.

'I've been so worried,' I blurted out, and he sighed and said he was sorry.

'Are you okay?' I asked him quickly, picturing him a hos-pital bed swathed in bandages.

'I'm perfectly fine.'

I sighed with relief. 'And the restaurant? Did it burn down?'

'The restaurant's fine too,' he said. There was a pause, then, 'Things weren't nearly as bad as I was led to believe. Just un-necessary panic, as it turned out. The fire was out by the time I got there. I'm sorry I didn't ring you sooner,' he went on, having clearly anticipated my next question, 'but I didn't get back to the house till way after midnight and I figured that you'd be asleep.'

Which was thoughtful of him, I supposed, not wanting to wake me. He wasn't to know that I'd lain awake for most of the night inventing catastrophic scenarios.

'How was the pie?' he said with a smile in his voice, and I let out a sigh.

'Still *looking* good, though I never got round to eating it. Maybe we could give it another try tonight?' I hadn't for-gotten that I'd already arranged to see the Cs and Sophie, but this had to be more important.

'I'm sorry,' he said, and I was beginning to weary of his apologies, 'but I have to work late tonight.'

'And the shoot?' I reminded him. 'We were supposed to

be going to Brixton this afternoon.' Even as I said it I knew that it wasn't going to happen, but I needed to hear it from the horse's mouth.

'Gonna have to take a rain check on that as well,' he said. 'I'll have to stay here at the restaurant all afternoon and get things straight.'

Although I was tempted to press him, to set up another time for the shoot at the very least, I knew it was not the right thing to do or the right time to do it. There are few things more likely to send a man to his cave than a pushy, persistent woman—or so I've been told—so I left it loose.

'I understand,' I said. 'Just give me a call when you're ready and we'll fix up a new time.' It sounded formal, but I sensed it was the right tone to take. Above and beyond anything else that had happened—or *might* happen—between Taylor and me, it was our professional relationship that took precedence. At least until I got my fee in my hand. After that I could be as emotionally neurotic as anyone else in my position.

'You've been great, you know, Tao,' he said then, and I melted a bit. 'And I really will make it up to you, I promise. Just give me a few days to sort everything out and we'll do something really special next time.'

I was tempted to tell him that he couldn't do anything more special than what he'd done last night, but I was doing so well and I didn't want to risk sounding soppy. So I simply said I'd look forward to it and left it at that.

I did a fair bit of restless thumb-twiddling the rest of that day, but I found that Sirg was a very good listener. It was just his occasional responses that could be disconcerting. For example, when I told him what had happened last night, when I mentioned the fire, he let out one almighty, brain-numbing screech that might well have been a fire alarm.

Then, when I told him what a great guy Taylor was, how he'd gone to so much trouble for me, he laughed like banshee and squawked the word 'Sucker!' on several occasions.

At which point I decided I'd had enough of his cynicism and phoned Sophie at work. Since it looked like the arrangement was still on with her and the Cs, I wanted to firm things up now. I asked her if she'd ring the others and suggested that they came round to the house straight after work. I offered to share my pie with them all. It might not be exactly the Cs' kind of food, but I thought they might be amused to try out the culinary fare of ordinary northern folk.

She phoned me back ten minutes later and said it was on, and I nipped down to the local shops and topped up again on essentials. Making sure to set the security system first, of course. Sirg was running short of exotic fruit, so I bought him a mango and a star fruit and gave him a slice of the latter when I got back.

And then, at about five o'clock, my mobile rang, and Amber informed me that she was putting a call through from Jerry Marlin. I couldn't help thinking that she sounded smug.

'Hi, Tao,' Jerry said brightly, 'how are things going?'

I didn't know whether he meant work-wise or in general, but I took a stab at the former. 'Slowly,' I said. 'Taylor had to cancel a shoot we'd planned for this afternoon.' I didn't know whether he'd heard about the fire and I wasn't sure if it was my place to tell him.

'Um, that's the reason I'm calling, as a matter of fact,' he said, and he didn't sound so bright any more. 'I spoke to Mary a while ago—you know, the producer woman—and I'm afraid I've got some bad news for you.'

Oh, God, how I hated those two little words, especially

when they were put together. What sort of *bad news?* My first thought was for Taylor, of course. He'd been underplaying his injuries when I spoke to him, and the truth was that he was seriously ill. Dead, even... 'Go on,' I managed to croak.

'She's decided not to use any extra shots for the book. She doesn't think they are necessary.'

Several other scenarios had flashed through my head in the couple of seconds it took him to respond, but this had not been one of them. 'You mean I've been fired!'

'It's not as bad as it sounds,' he said soothingly. 'It often happens, unfortunately.'

But it *was* as bad as it sounded, whatever he said. My brilliant career had been cut short in its prime—or rather before it even had chance to get going. Then something else struck me.

'What's Taylor got to say about this?'

There was a slight hesitation. 'I don't know what he's got to say. I tried calling him but he wasn't available, and I'm not even sure that his opinion matters. Our Ms Deacon is the one in control, and I'm sorry to say that she's refusing to sign her part of the contract.'

It was getting worse and worse.

'Does that mean I won't even get paid for the work I've already done?' It wasn't the most important thing on my mind—that was Taylor, and the fact that he'd said nothing to me about all this when we'd spoken earlier and he must have known—but it mattered. I'd been borrowing from Sophie and I owed so much on my credit card that I was in serious danger of having to sell my body to make up the deficiency.

'As it stands the answer, sadly, is no, but since she has no complaints about your actual work, I don't think we should give up on it yet. I'm going to try working on her conscience.'

'If she has one,' I said dryly.

'Cheer up,' Jerry said, 'there'll be other work. But if you'll take a tip from an old pro, you'll avoid getting involved with clients in the future.'

Shit! So he knew about Taylor and me—or what bit there was to know. And he obviously believed that it was the reason I had been sacked. I was tempted to protest, explain to Jerry that nothing had actually *happened*. To tell him that it didn't make any real sense, that as far as I knew Mary had accepted my story about being engaged, but I only had to think about it for a moment to see the great holes in that particular line of defence. Clearly she *hadn't* accepted my story, and it wasn't Jerry's fault (or mine, either, for that matter) that she'd turned out to have some sort of Glenn Close complex as far as Taylor was concerned.

So I didn't say anything at all, and Jerry told me that he had to go now, but that he'd be in touch soon.

I groaned aloud when he ended the call, as I thought of all the people I'd told about the brilliant start to my new career, people from the photography school who'd be looking for my name in the credits of Taylor's cookery book… Oh, God. What a bloody mess.

I badly wanted to ring Taylor again, and hear what he had to say on the matter, but to be honest I didn't dare. My instincts told me that this would not be a good move, but what I really needed was some friendly advice on the matter.

As it turned out I got more than I bargained for when Sophie turned up with the Cs that evening.

Jemima was all for calling Mary directly.

'The woman is clearly a psycho and should be told where to get off.'

'But if she is a psycho she might not take too kindly to that,' I said—quite reasonably, I thought.

'Well, I think you should call *him*,' offered Fiona. 'When he hears what she's done he'll be so appalled that he'll probably tell her what to do with her rotten little TV show.'

'But I don't want that either,' I said, and besides, I didn't believe deep down that he *would* tell her what to do with her rotten little TV show.

'Well, if you want my opinion,' Sophie said at last, when I looked to her in desperation for a casting vote, 'I think you should leave well alone. If his career is more important to him than you are—and we can't really blame him for that— then he's going to toe the line with his boss. You could just end up making a fool of yourself.'

I could see that the words were heartfelt, that she was still feeling a bit of a fool herself.

'Let's face it,' she added, 'he must know what's happened by now, and he'd have called you if he gave a damn.'

'But he must give a damn,' I said, and I looked at what was left of the pie as if that was proof positive.

'It was a nice gesture, certainly, but it's not gestures that count in the long run, it's positive action, and nothing he's done over the last twenty-four hours could be regarded as that.'

The Cs protested, of course. They would hear no word against Taylor since meeting the man, and seemed to regard him as some sort of demi-god. I thought how strange it was that I could talk to them now about my misfortune and actually have their sympathy instead of their scorn. And that,

I supposed, was due to the fact that in some slight way our fortunes had become entangled.

We'd eaten most of the pie by now, which I'd served with salad instead of the vegetables that Angie had kindly prepared but were well past their best now. I'd rung her just before the Cs and Sophie arrived, to thank her, and she'd gone on and on about Taylor—what a wonderful man he was, etc., etc. In the end I'd had to make an excuse to get off the line. I hadn't mentioned the fact that Taylor and I never got round to eating the pie (which turned out to be steak and stout, by the way) because that would only have led to questions I really didn't feel in the mood to answer.

The Cs had brought the promised champagne with them, but I was sticking firmly to water. I could have done with a drink, but I didn't have anything else in the house that actually belonged to me, and I didn't even have the promise of money now to buy anything.

I listened to the Cs defending Taylor for a while—but, galling as it was, I knew perfectly well that Sophie was right. I still didn't want to admit it, though, so I changed the subject, brought it back to Jerome and the fact that he obviously hadn't yet discovered that the miniatures had been returned to their rightful owner.

We'd eaten the pie in the kitchen, and I suggested now that we all go into the dining room and look at the miniatures, where we laughed at the thought of Jerome opening his briefcase in front of his would-be Japanese fence and discovering the Bath Oliver biscuits.

Sophie laughed as loud as the rest of us, but it was her words that eventually sobered me up.

'But *he's* not going to see the funny side, is he?' she said. 'And he's bound to work out who was responsible…'

'We'll worry about that when it happens,' I said, with more confidence than I actually felt. 'Besides,' I added to reassure myself, 'there's not much he can do about it now.'

Jemima had turned away from the miniatures now, and was looking at a picture on the back wall. It was another family portrait, or at least I guessed it must be, because why have a portrait of someone who wasn't a family member?

'I think that's a genuine *Reynolds,*' she said, and Sophie and I looked at her in surprise. It wasn't so much what she'd said—at first—but the fact that it was Jemima who'd said it. I'd had no idea she knew anything about art, and Sophie clearly hadn't either.

'I did an art history degree,' she explained with a modest shrug that didn't really become her, and I found myself looking at her with new interest, maybe even respect. Then it sank home—the exact meaning of her words.

'You mean as in *Sir Joshua* Reynolds?' I said, dumbfounded.

She smiled and nodded. 'Indeed. And if I'm right, then the miniatures pale into insignificance in terms of monetary value.'

We were all a bit stunned, I think, but Sophie was quick on the uptake.

'And what you're wondering is why Jerome didn't take this instead of the miniatures?' she said.

'Precisely.'

I was coming around now, out of my daze, and I managed to find my voice.

'It's obvious, though, isn't it?' I said, as I looked at the life-size portrait of a delicate-looking woman who bore no resemblance whatever to Mrs Audesley. 'He could hardly have slipped that under his jacket, now, could he?'

'Maybe not,' said Jemima darkly. 'But let's just hope he didn't have plans to come back for it later.'

15

I didn't have a lot to do the next day, apart from looking after Sirg and preparing for my mother's arrival, which didn't involve much more than changing the sheets in Sophie's room and putting the used ones in the washing machine. The Cs had taken most of her stuff back to the flat in the car the night before, and she'd cleared the rest out of her room before she left in the morning. I'd tried to persuade her to stay over the weekend, but she didn't even bother to make an excuse. 'I'm sorry,' she'd said, 'but I don't fancy any lectures from your mother on how I should conduct my life.' And I could hardly blame her for that.

And because I didn't have much to do, and because I was still upset and bewildered about what had happened with my job, and because I hadn't heard any more from Taylor and was still pretty wary of calling him, I spent the hour between ten and eleven o'clock composing a letter instead.

I read out what I was writing to Sirg, and whether I kept

what I'd written or not depended on his responses. To be perfectly precise, I judged his approval or otherwise on whether or not he swore at me. And, since he swore quite a lot, the end result was a very pared-down version of the long and drawn out original.

In the end, I wrote, in my spidery handwriting that I'm not very proud of:

Dear Taylor,
I presume you know that I've been sacked, and although I think I know why I would like to hear what you have to say about it.
I hope all is well at the restaurant now.
Tao

When I read out the finished version to Sirg he snorted rather rudely at me, but at least he didn't use foul language, so I took the snort as approval.

I'd used a sheet of Mrs Audesley's quality writing paper for the final draft, and swiped one of her envelopes as well. And because now that I'd done it I couldn't bear to wait a whole day for him to receive it through the post, I decided to take it to his house right away. I hesitated briefly before I left wondering whether I should see if Chris was free to keep an eye on Sir Galahad, but since I knew I couldn't possibly be away more than an hour, even if I used public transport, I decided not to bother.

I made good time to Taylor's house, well within the half-hour I'd allowed either way, and dropped the envelope off through his door just after eleven-thirty. I knew he'd be at the restaurant, so I wasn't concerned about rattling the letterbox. If I had been I might not have disturbed the person who was inside the house, and I might never have learned the truth, the whole truth and nothing but the truth.

But of course it didn't feel like that at the time. All I was aware of was the deep and excruciating embarrassment I felt when I heard the door open and looked round to see Mary Deacon holding the letter that was meant for Taylor. Then I thought how lucky it was that I'd had Sirg to censor the worst of my ramblings, because even if she chose to open it now there wasn't much in it to incriminate me.

'Why don't you come in for a minute?' she said with a sigh, and images of Glenn Close in *Fatal Attraction* flashed through my mind again. Glenn Close with the knife near the end of the film… 'I won't bite,' she added, and although I didn't know whether to believe her or not I ended up going into the house anyway.

'I knew you'd been here,' she said as I followed her into the kitchen. She opened a cupboard and took out a bottle of wine that I immediately recognised as my cut-price bargain. 'He carelessly forgot to dispose of it.'

I looked at her and the wine blankly, and she smiled at me. Not a friendly sort of smile, but not a scary one either. 'He wouldn't touch something like this with a bargepole,' she said. 'He's a real wine snob, so I guessed that someone else had brought it, and since I'm not aware of any other dalliances at the moment I knew it had to be you.'

I didn't like being referred to as a *dalliance, or* being thought of as a wine Philistine (even though it was true), but since I was the one at a disadvantage I didn't bother complaining.

'Why don't you sit down,' she said, as she put the bottle away again, and because my knees were a bit weak at that moment I took up the offer.

'I take it you haven't really got a fiancé,' she said when she'd sat down as well.

'Not as such,' I admitted.

'But you thought I'd be happier if I believed you had?'

'Well, it's true, isn't it?'

'You must think I'm a very sad woman,' she said, and I didn't respond. Of course I thought she was a very sad woman. A very sad woman who felt it necessary to search her client's house for evidence of other women. And the fact that it was Taylor's house suddenly made me feel braver.

'Does Taylor know that you're here?' I asked her then.

She looked at me for a moment, and then laughed without any obvious humour. 'Of course,' she said, shaking her head, 'he probably told you that this was *his* place, didn't he?'

'Well, yes…' I began, and then I saw the look on her face. 'Are you trying to say that it isn't?'

'I'm not *trying* to say anything,' Mary sighed. 'This is most definitely *my* house, although Taylor has been sharing it with me for the past few months.'

Ahh… I couldn't think what to say for a moment, although now that she'd said it I didn't doubt her for a second. The house was just so feminine that I should have guessed the minute I walked into the place. But it was what she'd said about Taylor and her living together for the past few months that was uppermost in my mind.

'And I suppose you were here the night before last,' she said.

I nodded. 'The night of the fire at the restaurant,' I said ruefully, realising what a sucker I'd been.

She almost laughed. 'My call must have really alarmed him to come up with a story like that.'

'And I fell for it hook, line and sinker,' I said more to my-self than to her. 'I don't expect there was a fire at the restaurant...?'

She shrugged her shoulders unsympathetically, then fell silent for a moment as she pondered something.

'I thought he sounded strange when I rang to say I was coming home. I'd been away for the day, and had planned on staying overnight, but then I changed my mind. I tried the restaurant first, and when they said he'd left early I got a bit suspicious.'

I breathed an unconscious sigh of relief when I thought what she might have found if she hadn't bothered to make that call. Maybe she guessed what I was thinking, because then she frowned.

'I always like to give him fair warning in case he's up to something.'

I think that shocked me more than anything, but not so much that I lost my sense of irony.

'I take it you mean that I'm not the first?' I said, with the hint of a smile.

'Not by a long shot.'

I was about to ask her why she put up with it, but then I felt suddenly angry. Just because she couldn't control the man she was living with, I had been sacked. And, even though I knew it was cruel, I let her have it. 'He made it seem that you were little more than a pest he had to be nice to because you're his boss.'

I saw her face flush, but I hadn't finished with her yet. 'You might have been able to get rid of me, but that isn't the an-swer, surely. You can't spend the rest of your life sacking the competition. Where's your pride, for God's sake?'

'That left the house when he moved in,' she said flatly, but I didn't feel sorry for her in the least.

'If you believe that then you really are a sad woman,' I said, getting up from my seat. Then I noticed the letter that I'd brought on the table and grabbed it up.

'I won't bother leaving this after all. And if he does ring me, you needn't worry. I wouldn't dream of seeing him again. He's a loser as far as I am concerned.' With that I turned and left the place in a hurry, just in case I'd gone a bit too far and Glenn Close really did make an appearance.

And of course I was late getting back to the house. And of course Chris was waiting for me when I got there...

And worse, a lot worse than that, he was waiting for me with my mother.

I heard her raucous laughter before I saw her, and I didn't know what to apologise for first—the fact that I was late again, or the fact that he'd apparently had to entertain my mother in my absence. He'd made tea for her, and was just pouring it out when I lumbered into the kitchen.

'I'm sorry,' I said to Chris—in general, to cover it all.

'What for?' he asked, and I realised that he might not even have known that I *was* late.

'For not being here when my mother arrived, of course,' I said. Then I looked at her. 'Though she wasn't expected till this evening,' I added pointedly.

'Chris and I have been getting along just great,' she gushed, 'and for goodness' sake stop referring to me as your *mother.*' She looked at Chris and shook her head sadly. 'I've been asking her to call me by my first name for years, but she's just so stubborn.'

She could call it what she liked, but to me it was just a small act of rebellion. Another attempt at being as normal as possible, and not the daughter of a wacky throwback from the Sixties who liked to be called *Stella* by her only child. It might not even be so bad if Stella really was her name. In fact it was Doreen, and I was so tempted at that very moment to remind her of this. But she looked ridiculous enough, in her flowing Indian dress and matching scarf wrapped round her head, so I let it go this time.

'He's been telling me about his travels,' she said now of Chris. 'Did you know that he's been everywhere? South America, India—you name it, he's been there.'

I should have guessed, I thought grimly. Now that I thought about it, he certainly looked the travelling type, and in my experience all travelling types are a little bit odd—full of strange notions they've picked up along the way. And my mother was bound to like someone like that.

'Not *everywhere,*' Chris corrected her mildly, 'and I didn't stay long anywhere. Not as long as I'd have liked to, anyway.'

'Ah, yes, Chris, but you *did* it,' she said. 'You walked the talk—unlike a lot of people I know.' She looked at me then, and I glared back.

'I've never *talked* about going anywhere,' I said defensively. 'I've never particularly wanted to travel, and I don't feel that I'm a lesser person for not ever having been any further than the Costa del Sol.'

My mother rolled her eyes in despair at me, and I was sorely tempted to remind her that she'd never been anywhere of particular note either. I wasn't even sure that she'd been as far as Spain. But I didn't want to embarrass her, even if she was hell-bent on shaming me.

'Anyway,' I said, 'I don't think we should be holding Chris up. He has got a job to do, you know.'

'Talking of which,' Chris said, not making any signs of a

move, 'I'm having a few days off, starting tomorrow, so you'll be free to come and go a bit more if you need to.'

'That's great,' said Mum, before I could reply. 'I was hoping to drag Tao out with me, and now she's got no excuse.'

'Except that she might be working,' Chris said, looking at me.

I didn't want to tell either of them that I'd been sacked from my job, because that would inevitably lead to questions like *Why?* and I certainly didn't want to get into that.

'I'm not sure about that yet,' I said, then, remembering my manners, added a thank-you. 'I'll let you know as soon as I do, though.'

Chris lifted his cup and swallowed the contents. 'I really should go,' he said, 'but I'll see you at seven,' he added to my mother, and then he glanced a bit sheepishly at me. 'If it's okay with Tao, that is?'

I looked at my mother in dismay. What the hell had she been up to now?

'I've invited Chris up for a meal,' she explained. 'I thought I'd do my Cashew Special.'

Her Cashew *Special* was not very special at all, and the last thing I needed tonight was having to share it with the gardener. But what could I say when they were both looking at me? When he'd been so nice to my mother?

'Of course it's okay,' I said. 'Only I don't have any cashews,' I added hopefully, 'so it might have to be something else.'

'Don't worry,' said my annoying mother, 'I've brought some with me.'

I spent the remainder of the day keeping her and Sirg apart—because he took an instant dislike to her and the feeling seemed to be mutual—and fending off questions about Chris. To *him* she'd taken a very strong liking. In fact, if the thought didn't make me feel slightly queasy, I might almost have entertained the idea that she fancied him rotten.

'Why on earth didn't you mention him when you phoned?' she wanted to know. And then, 'I can see why you were so keen to move in here, though.'

'I didn't mention him because it didn't even cross my mind,' I responded stiffly, 'and he had nothing whatever to do with me moving here. In fact, I'm not even sure that I like the bloke,' I said, even though that felt a bit unfair now, after his offer to free me up for a couple of days. Not to mention the fact that he'd looked after my mother, and seemed unperturbed by her loud voice and pushy manner.

'You really should get that bug seen to,' she said, and I looked at her suspiciously.

'The one you have firmly planted up your bottom,' she enlightened me, and then burst into more raucous laughter. 'I sometimes think you don't know how to enjoy yourself. But don't worry, because it's never too late. And we can start by having a really good time tonight.'

Which made me dread the whole thing even more, and long for the evening to be over and done with. So I could get off to bed and be tragic about my failed career and love-life all on my own.

It was just as bad as I had feared it would be. With knobs on. My mother's Cashew Special was even more awful than it usually was (although Chris was very polite about it), and her flirting—especially after imbibing several glasses of wine—was deeply, grievously embarrassing.

I looked at her over the kitchen table and wondered what she thought she looked like. This overweight, middle-aged woman with a turkey neck, dressed like teenager at a Sixties love-in, making goo-goo eyes at a man young enough to be her son.

To be fair to him, he handled the situation well. I noticed that whenever she went a bit far—like the cringe-making time when she told him what a nice little bottom he had—he would just laugh pleasantly and ask her something about her own life. He showed a particular interest in her dream catchers, for example, and insisted she explain exactly what materials were used and how they were put together.

This was the high point of the evening, however, a short period when I was almost able to relax. Then, for some reason I cannot recall, she started on my father, mocking him again for taking up golf, and I think that's what did it for me. I think that's what sent me over the edge.

'Maybe he's taken it up so he can get away from you,' I heard myself saying, and before I knew what was happening I found I was yelling at her, fishwife-style.

It must have been the timing, I think. Well, that and the free-flowing wine. At any other stage in my life I'd have done what I always do—buttoned my lip and seethed inside. But that night, with my future as a photographer on the line, with the unhappy knowledge that I'd been taken for a ride by a man I'd been stupid enough to trust, and now with my mother unfairly criticising my dad, I let it all out.

All the stuff that had been getting to me for years—the way she'd made me feel so different from everyone else, all the bullying I'd had to endure at school because of the clothes she'd made me wear…and she just sat there and took it.

I think she was just too stunned to respond, at least until I'd said everything I wanted to say, and then she just let out a long quivering sigh and burst into a fit of noisy, heaving sobs.

I was so shocked by this that I did the only thing I could think of. I bolted. Leaving Chris to deal with my hysterical mother. And I didn't go back either. I just went to my room, got into bed and covered my head with pillow. In a feeble, cowardly attempt at blocking everything out.

16

But as well as feeble and cowardly, it was also a vain attempt. Although I didn't see either of them again that night—which was a small mercy—I lay awake for the whole of it. At least until four o'clock, anyway, because I remember looking at the clock and noting the time. But I don't remember much after that.

Of course I pretty soon regretted my outburst, and most of all the fact that it had happened in front of a witness. I'd often fantasised about telling my mother just what I thought, but the aftermath of those fantasies was very different indeed from the aftermath of the real thing. It all seemed so empty and pointless now. What purpose had it served, after all? My mother would just go on her own annoying way, only now she'd be a *victim* as well. Of her cruel and ungrateful only daughter's venomous tongue.

In fact, when I forced my eyes open at some unspecified stage of the following morning, I briefly prayed for a debilitating illness that would divert attention completely away from the horrors of the previous night. I prayed a bit harder when I realised that I had a hangover to boot, and the thought of facing my mother in that particular state became almost unbearable.

But then something quite unexpected happened. About ten minutes later, when I was still lying inert under my goose-down duvet, I heard a gentle knock at my bedroom door.

'Come in,' I croaked like a consumptive invalid, already into debilitating illness mode.

The door opened—not quite with a creak, but slowly, very slowly. I held my breath until eventually a colourful turban appeared round the door, with my mother's head underneath it.

'Hello, darling,' she said, and I held onto my breath even longer. Her voice was light and pleasant. *Too* light, *too* pleasant, and I waited for the act to drop and the real Stella/Doreen Tandy to come to the fore.

Only it didn't happen. Instead, this contrite-looking creature, that seemed familiar and yet strange as well, was creeping into the room with a laden tray in her hands.

'I thought you might like breakfast in bed this morning,' the alien body-snatcher said.

I sat up nervously in bed and covered my mouth with the duvet.

'What's this?' I asked suspiciously, my voice muffled by the goose down as she lifted a soup dish off my plate to reveal three bacon rashers and scrambled egg. My mother had been a vegetarian for thirty years and claimed disgust at the very thought of *seeing* bacon, let alone actually cooking it.

'Chris cooked it for me,' she said solemnly. 'I couldn't quite bring myself to do it, but I know how much you like a full English breakfast.'

She hovered there next to the bed for a moment, waiting for me to co-operate by adjusting the duvet so she could put the tray down. Which I eventually did, despite residue misgivings about the true identity of this scarily amiable and thoughtful woman.

'I've made some fresh coffee as well,' she said, 'but I couldn't find any juice, I'm afraid.'

'There isn't any juice,' I said, and looked at the rashers with interest. They did look very appetising, and there is nothing better than bacon and eggs, in my humble opinion, to cure a hangover. Then I remembered who she'd said had cooked the breakfast...

'What on earth is he doing cooking bacon for me?' An unpleasant possibility flashed through my brain before she could reply. That he had stayed the night with my mother in order to *comfort* her. He did, after all, have a penchant for older women. Was this, therefore, the real explanation for her personality change?

'I was worried about the parrot squawking when I got back from the shop,' she said, 'so I went down to the his flat to ask his advice.'

'Oh, God,' I groaned. I'd forgotten all about Sirg in my misery. 'Is he okay?'

'He's fine. Chris came up and saw to him, and then, when I mentioned the bacon and my problems in handling it, he offered to cook it for me. He's downstairs now, tucking into the rest.'

Despite my relief that they probably hadn't spent the night together, I still felt uncomfortable. It occurred to me that I ought to get up straight away and apologise to him.

Not only for sorting Sir Galahad out, but for the awful scene I'd created last night. Not to mention just getting up from the table and leaving him to cope with a hysterical woman. But my mother suddenly did an oddly motherly thing at that moment, and insisted I ate every bit on my plate before I did anything else. Almost as if she'd guessed what was going on in my mind. And, since I wasn't exactly looking forward to seeing Chris, I did precisely as I was told.

And it was a very good fry-up, very good indeed, and I did feel loads better by the time I'd swallowed the last piece of heavily buttered toast with a light spreading of orange marmalade.

My mother sat at the end of the bed throughout and watched me without saying a word, which must have been some kind of record for her. Then, when I'd wiped my mouth on the piece of kitchen roll that she'd neatly folded into a triangle, she got up and removed the tray from my lap.

'There,' she said, 'you're looking better already. Now, if you don't mind, I'd better get off and see how Chris is doing.'

I wanted to say something about the previous night, but I just got the feeling that it wasn't the right thing to do. Besides which, I didn't want to break whatever magical spell had been cast on her, so I just murmured my thanks and allowed her to leave.

I took my time getting ready. I'd gone completely off the idea of speaking to Chris by now, so I wanted to be certain that he'd left the house by the time I went down. In fact, I'd reached the stage where I was rather hoping I might never meet up with him again, that I could somehow keep my head down for the next few weeks, until Mrs A came back, and thereby avoid him completely.

I spent a long time in the shower, therefore, creating heaps of lather with some expensive gel that was already there in the cubicle, and I'd just got out and wrapped a towel around me when I heard the front doorbell ring.

If I'd been on my own I wouldn't have answered it. I didn't feel like facing anyone yet. But I knew that my mother would open the door without a second thought, so I braced myself. I expected to hear her yelling up to me from the foot of the stairs, with news of whoever it was at the door, but although I stood perfectly still for at least two minutes I didn't hear a single sound.

So I went quietly to the window and peered out of it, down to the spot just outside the front door, to see if I could see anyone there. Only the angle wasn't quite right. I would have needed to open the window to get a full view, but that would only have drawn attention to myself. I could sense that there *was* someone there, however and I couldn't help being rather curious now.

My wait lasted another few seconds, and then I saw a figure appear below as it moved away from the house and then down the steps. It was a female form, no doubt about that, but she'd got as far as the gate before I realised just who it was.

I stepped back from the window quickly then, before she had chance to turn and look up, which was precisely what she did next. I don't think she saw me, though. She seemed to be very deep in thought, and despite what had happened I couldn't help feeling a little bit sorry for her.

Since my mother didn't come up to the room, as I'd expected her to, I got dressed quickly then, in jeans and a sweater because it had turned quite cold, and went downstairs rather nervously.

I found my mother in the kitchen—on her own, thank

goodness. She was busying herself with the dishwashing machine, making piles of clean plates on the work surface, but she turned and smiled at me when I entered.

'What did *she* want?' I said.

My mother looked a bit blank for a moment, and then realised what I was talking about. 'Oh, you mean *Mary?*'

I rolled my eyes slightly at this—the fact that she was already on first-name terms with my enemy.

'She asked me to give you this,' she said, picking up a white envelope from the table.

I took it suspiciously. 'So what kept her at the door so long?' I wanted to know. 'She must have been talking to you for a good five minutes.'

My mother shrugged her chubby shoulders. 'We were just chatting, you know. Passing the time of day. She wanted to speak to you directly, of course, but I said that you weren't feeling well…' She looked slightly alarmed suddenly. 'I hope that's okay?'

I nodded, bewildered again at all this concern for my feelings and well-being.

'She seemed quite concerned, as a matter of fact,' my mother went on, 'and she asked me to pass on her best wishes to you for a speedy recovery. Nice woman, I thought.'

This was really weird. Spooky, in fact. What with my own mother acting as if she'd had a personality transplant, and now Mary apparently behaving like a caring human being, it was almost too much to cope with. But then it occurred to me that it was probably all a front. That she was up to no good, really, and her concern for my health was a cunning ruse to allay any suspicions my mother might have had. That this was, in fact, just the beginning of some nasty get-even-with-Tao-for-coming-on-to-my-man plan.

I frowned at the envelope I was holding, and wondered whether it might be best if I ran it under the tap first. I'd heard somewhere that this was the thing to do with suspicious mail that might contain an explosive device. But it seemed a bit slim for that, so I decided it was probably just old-fashioned hate mail. I was tempted to chuck it straight in the bin, but if this really was the beginning of a long drawn-out harassment campaign I would need it as evidence to pass on to the police.

For once in her life my mother didn't seem all that curious about something that was none of her business, and to my surprise returned to the job she'd been doing when I came in, which involved opening cupboards and putting dishes away.

I paused for a moment before slipping my finger into a small gap on the envelope fold, preparing myself for its abusive contents. I'd never received hate mail before, and oddly enough part of me was excited. It was making me feel kind of important.

I was almost disappointed, therefore, when I eventually removed the contents and discovered a very short message indeed.

Dear Tao,
Thanks to our little talk yesterday, I think I've finally come to my senses.
Please accept the enclosed, as well as my apologies for any inconvenience. I will be sending the agency's placement fee directly to Jerry Marlin.
All best wishes,
Mary Deacon.

And then of course I looked at the 'enclosed' and my mouth fell open in astonishment.

She'd written out a company cheque for the entire fee I

had been promised, for the whole two weeks' work that I hadn't even done. It was like an instant cure for my mental anguish regarding Taylor. In fact I was so cock-a-hoop that I didn't even wonder what she meant about coming to her senses and suchlike. Not just then, anyway.

I let out a whoop of joy and my mother turned around in surprise.

'Whatever's happened?' she wanted to know.

But it was too long and complicated a story, so I just said that my cheque for the job had arrived sooner than expected. And because she seemed so happy for me, and not sniffy any more for earning so much for so little work (if only she knew *just* how little work…) I amazed myself by suggesting that we went out for the day.

'If it's okay with Chris, that is.'

'I'm sure it will be,' she said, and she sounded pleased—excited, almost. 'He told me to remind you that he was free for the next few days. He's just doing some writing, or something, and he said he could as easily do that here as in his own place.'

Which was very nice of him, I supposed, but I still didn't feel like facing him.

'Would you mind asking him, then?' I said. 'While I go and see Sirg. He'll be wondering what has happened to me.'

And that seemed to be perfectly true, because I'd never received a welcome from him quite like it before. The moment I walked into his room he let out a joyous squawk and glided gracefully onto my shoulder. And then he started on the sweet-nothings, straight into my ear. It wasn't the words he used, of course, which were fairly offensive, but I knew by the way he was saying them that he'd missed me a lot.

It seemed a shame, therefore, to leave him again, but I gave him an hour of quality time, by the end of which he was getting distinctly bored with me. It was time for the one o'clock news, and I left him chirping happily along with the announcer.

I had to face Chris, of course, when he came into the house to take over with Sirg, but by then I was feeling so much better, and since he didn't show any signs of reproach I left the house with a fairly clear conscience.

It was only then, as my mother and I were heading towards the tube station, with me trying to work out where to go for what was left of the day, that I suddenly remembered something.

'Your exhibition!' I exclaimed. 'Shouldn't you be there by now?'

'I decided to give it a miss,' she said a bit sheepishly. 'I thought it would be a lot nicer if we spent the time together, and I don't expect it's your sort of thing anyway.'

I stopped in my tracks and let out a long exaggerated sigh. It had been okay for a while, but I was beginning to tire of this obliging, thoughtful new version of my mother.

'Look, Mum… *Stella,* this is getting silly now. You came down specially for that exhibition and I'm determined that you are going to see it.' I glanced at my wristwatch. 'Whereabouts is it?' I asked.

'Near Spitalfields Market,' she said, and I could tell by the hopeful look on her face that she really wanted to go. I think she was pleased about the 'Stella' bit too. And suddenly I realised that it was no real hardship to call her that if she liked it so much.

'Well, that's great,' I said, 'because it's not far from where I was staying with Sophie, and I could take you to my favourite café for a meal afterwards. It will save us cooking later.' Besides which, I could be flash now that I had some money.

Okay, so it wasn't exactly in cash form yet, but it soon would be, and meanwhile there was always my trusty credit card.

She nodded happily and the pair of us set off together again, as if we did this kind of thing every week. Mother and daughter out on a jaunt.

We made it back to the Hampstead house at eight-fifteen, by which time Sirg was already in the land of nod and Chris was in the kitchen. When we joined him there he was just in the process of closing down his laptop computer which he'd had set up on the table.

'Good day?' he enquired of us casually.

'Pretty good, I'd say,' I replied, and glanced round at my mother.

She smiled back at me wryly, and because she looked tired I asked if she wanted a cup of tea. I threw out the offer out to Chris as well, but while he accepted my mother declined.

'I'm pooped,' she said with a theatrical sigh. She moved over to the sink and began running the tap. 'I'm just going to take a glass of water upstairs with me and hit the sack.'

Chris closed the lid of the laptop and turned to her. 'Will I see you again before you leave?'

''Fraid not,' she said. 'I've decided to head back north to-morrow.' She looked as if she was going to give him one of her bear hugs, but then she glanced briefly at me and seemed to change her mind. Instead she kissed the end of her fore-finger and touched his cheek with it softly. 'You're a nice bloke,' she said, 'and a very good listener.'

I felt my cheeks flame. During our time together that day, my mother had told me that she'd talked for hours to Chris the night before, and that he'd helped her understand the rea-sons for some of the problems in our relationship. Indeed, as far as I could make out, he was single-handedly responsible for this remarkable change in my mother, and while I was grateful, I was acutely embarrassed as well.

'And you're a very nice woman, Stella,' Chris said in response to her unusually restrained gesture of physical affection, and then he did what I'd been expecting *her* to do. He got up and put his arms right around her bulky body and squeezed her tightly.

She was flushed with pleasure when he let her go, and for some reason this made me feel guilty. We'd got along fine during the day, but I realised now that she'd been the one who'd made most of the effort. Okay, so I'd attended the exhibition with her, bought her egg and chips at Felix's Place, but there had still been a lot of holding back on my part. My only real concession to all her endeavours was to use the name that she preferred to be called.

'I'll come in and see you later,' was all I could manage at that moment, and then I turned away to attend to the kettle.

When I looked back she was gone, and Chris was looking at me curiously.

I guessed he was waiting for some kind of report on how things had gone, but I wasn't sure that I wanted to discuss the matter with him. But, then again, I was kind of intrigued about something.

'So,' I said, trying to sound casual as I sat down at the table, 'are you going to tell me how you did it?'

He sat down too, and his expression was puzzled. 'I'm not sure what you mean,' he said.

'How you managed to make my mother behave like one.'

'I didn't do anything,' he said. 'I just listened, mostly.'

'But you must have said *something*…'

He moved the computer an inch, so that he could put his elbows on the table, which made me feel like I was getting his full and undivided attention.

'I may have mentioned that I knew what it was like to feel different from the rest of my family,' he said, and he joined his hands as if in a prayer.

I looked him directly in the eye and waited for him to go on.

'I grew up in a tough environment, amongst several brothers—and sisters, for that matter—who did proper jobs for a living.' He smiled a bit grimly then, and I didn't interrupt.

'I was regarded as an odd-bod for wanting to travel, and for showing an interest in gardening. You know, a bit of a soft lad,' he said in a strong northern accent. 'I took a lot of stick from my siblings, but especially my father.'

'That's not really the same, though, is it? I was the only one, and it was *me* who was embarrassed by my parents… well, my mother, anyway.'

'Yeah, but it's really just about feeling different, not fitting in with the people around you. The people who are supposed to matter most.'

'And you solved it by moving south?'

'I suppose so,' he said. 'Though I still *want* to belong. Or at least be approved of.'

I thought about this for a moment and found myself in agreement. I still wanted that as well. I knew I was okay as far as my dad was concerned, but I'd never really felt my mother's approval. To quite a big degree I'd gone out of my way to ensure that I didn't get it, by choosing to work in a bank and shack up with Malcolm, but I'd still longed for it, that sense of it all being unconditional.

'Do you think it will last?' I said ruefully. 'This change you've miraculously brought about?'

'That's up to you, I'd say. It might not continue if she doesn't get anything back for her efforts.' He looked a bit thoughtful for a moment. 'I think she's pretty vulnerable at the moment, so perhaps it's time for you to think about her for a while.'

'I am,' I said defensively. 'I was the one who suggested she went home tomorrow to try and patch things up with my dad.' She'd told me how really worried she was. How he'd been snappy and impatient with her, and how he'd been staying out late. 'She said she thought that he might even be interested in someone else.' I didn't really believe it though. It just seemed inconceivable that my dad, who'd put up with so much for so many years, should start looking elsewhere at this stage of his life.

Chris nodded. 'That's what she told me as well. She thinks the golf might just be a cover—which is why she was so disparaging about it, I suspect.'

I shook my head in despair with her. 'I just wish she would be a little more honest about her feelings to him. I can just imagine her laying into him about the golf, when all the time she's frightened stiff that he's preparing to leave her.'

'Yeah, but we all do that at times, don't we?' Chris said. 'You know—skirt around the truth…because we're too afraid of getting hurt if we risk honesty.'

I couldn't help thinking that there was some hidden meaning in this statement, but I didn't pursue it because just then I noticed that the kettle was boiling.

'I think I'll give tea a miss,' he said when I went over to make it. 'I've still got some work to do and I really should get on with it.'

He got up from his seat and I wondered if this 'work' of his was just an excuse, that maybe he was just fed up with listening to me and my parent problems.

I couldn't blame him for that, of course, but it didn't stop me feeling just a little bit disappointed.

17

I saw my mother off on the train the following day, and she promised to ring me soon and let me know what was happening. Perhaps because she was so anxious about going back and having to face my dad about their problems, she forgot to be her new self. Well, the full-blown version of her new self. I was quite glad about it, really. It had been an interesting novelty, but I couldn't help smiling when she said I looked pasty and that I should seriously consider giving up meat.

Nevertheless, she was obviously still thinking about the heart-to-heart she'd had with Chris, because she told me, for the first time ever, that she was proud of how well I was doing. Which made me feel bad because I still hadn't told her that I had been sacked.

I thought about that note from Mary on the tube journey back to the house, and only then did it occur to me to wonder what she'd meant about coming to her senses. By the time I got in I was bursting with curiosity, and couldn't resist calling her to try and find out.

Luckily, she had used headed notepaper, and her home telephone number was printed on it.

I was nervous, of course. I was afraid that Taylor might answer the phone, which would be very awkward for both of us, but it was not enough to make me ignore such over-whelming temptation.

In fact, as it turned out no one picked up at all. I got Mary's answer-machine—with *her* instructions, not his, thankfully—so I left a somewhat garbled message asking her to call me back. I regretted it immediately, though, as a pic-ture of Taylor came into my mind, picking up the message and laughing at me. I entertained several more similarly cringe-making scenarios, in which laughter at my expense was the central feature.

But it was too late to do anything about it, I eventually concluded, so I would just have grin and bear whatever fate flung at me now.

I felt very much on my own that day, despite having Sirg around. It was actually the first day I'd had on my own in the house, and I was conscious for the first time how big it was. As lovely and luxurious as it happened to be, I didn't particularly envy Mrs A, rattling around every day in it, with only an African Grey for company. Clever as he was, and af-fectionate as he certainly could be to those that he loved, I decided that human companionship still took some beating.

It was funny I should have been thinking like that about Mrs A, because a short while later the house telephone rang and it turned out to be the woman herself.

'How is my boy doing?' she wanted to know, without any fluffy preamble.

'He's fine,' I said, looking over at Sirg as I spoke. He was performing acrobatics on his cage, and was currently upside down.

'He's fine,' repeated Sir Galahad, and with the aid of his very strong beak did a little flip into an upright position and stared at me.

'He's looking at me as we speak.'

'Can I have a word with him?'

I got up from the seat and lifted the telephone over to the cage. Luckily it had a very long cord, so I was able to put the receiver right next to his head. I wasn't quite sure where his ears were, but I assumed they were in that general direction.

I heard Mrs Audesley murmuring something to the bird, and I watched as he cocked his head on one side. Then he pecked at the handset and made his favourite whistling kettle sound. Then, for the first time ever, he surprised me by referring directly to the wayward great-nephew. 'Do smarten yourself up, Jerome!' he squawked out of the blue, and I felt suddenly guilty, as if he was trying to tell his mistress something.

I put the phone back against my own ear and spoke nervously into the receiver. 'I'm sure he's missing you, though,' I said, because I thought that was what she'd want to hear and I wanted to divert attention away from what he'd just said.

But she was very much on the ball, unfortunately.

'Did I hear Sir Galahad just mention Jerome?' she demanded to know, and I responded with a nervous little laugh.

'I don't think so,' I lied. 'But then he does say the oddest things at times. He told me to put the dustbins out a moment ago...'

'Well, that's because it's Sunday today and the bin men are due in the morning! I made a note of that in the instructions I left you, so I hope you remembered to put the bin out last week.'

I hadn't, as a matter of fact, though fortunately Chris had done it for me. And if I doubted if Sirg could differentiate between days of the week, I only had to think about the cleaner...

'How's Portugal?' I enquired, trying to change the subject. 'I expect the weather's a lot better there.' I was babbling now, and embarrassing myself in the process.

'As a matter of fact it's pouring with rain at this very moment,' she responded stiffly, 'but that is quite beside the point. What I want to know is why Sir Galahad mentioned Jerome's name. He hasn't done that in a very long time, and—'

I interrupted her in a panic. 'He came to the house the other day,' I found myself saying, 'but I didn't let him in...'

'I thought so!' she exclaimed loudly into my ear. 'Sir Galahad never says anything just for the sake of it. There's always a reason.' There was a pause, then, 'You're positive that he didn't get into the house?'

I closed my eyes in despair at myself. There was absolutely no need to have said anything at all. I could have put her mind at rest by simply denying everything—so far as I knew Sir Galahad hadn't even heard Jerome, so it must be coincidence—but now I'd told her half a story, and then lied about it into the bargain. I hesitated, wondering if I should just get it all off my chest. But then what was the point in worrying her unnecessarily? Especially since I'd got back the stuff that Jerome had stolen.

'Absolutely,' I said.

'I hope not, Tao,' she said grimly. 'And if he does return, you must call Chris at once. Promise me that, now, won't you?'

'I promise,' I said, 'and don't worry. I haven't seen him for over a week, and I'm sure he's given up any ideas that he might have had.'

'I wish I could share your certainty, Tao, but so long as you keep your word if he does come again, I suppose that will just have to do.'

If I hadn't known what Jerome was capable of, if I hadn't witnessed it with my very own eyes, I'd just have thought that she was being an old fusspot. But the fact was that her words had made me very uneasy. What Sophie had said came back to me as well now, about his reaction when he found those Bath Olivers in his briefcase instead of the miniatures…

Of course he would guess who was responsible, and to say he wouldn't be pleased about it was probably a big understatement.

I got a bit jumpy after that. If he'd gone out on Thursday evening to Japan it was not unreasonable to suppose that he might already be back in the country.

I shot up at that point of my thinking and ran round the house, making sure that all the doors and windows were locked. And as I was doing it I thought about phoning Chris, to put him on some sort of alert. I got as far as picking up the phone, but I couldn't bring myself to go through with it because it felt dangerously like an excuse just to talk to him. And if that was how it felt to me, then maybe he'd think the same thing too.

And so, in an attempt to distract myself, I went to the music centre that Mrs A kept in Sirg's room and put on one of her CDs. It was a classical piece, like all the others, and Sir Galahad, who was clearly a lot more highbrow than me in his musical tastes, bobbed his head appreciatively to a recording of Mozart's 'Don Giovanni.'

I was so into the rhythm of his bobbing head—to the point of mild hypnosis, probably—that I wasn't immediately conscious of a new sound. It was Sirg who made me aware of it, when he stopped bobbing his head and echoed the *bing-bong* of the front doorbell. Which startled me so much that I practically jumped out of my seat.

After all that worrying about Jerome appearing, I was absolutely convinced it was him. Especially when the bell *bing-bonged* again, more insistently now.

'*Bing-bong,*' Sirg repeated, and then he looked at me closely, as if to enquire what was keeping me from my door-answering duties. So I turned down the music and left the room obediently, making sure that the door was closed so that Sir Galahad couldn't follow me out. I moved nervously to the window of the main sitting room. Only I couldn't see who it was from there, so I had to go into the hall, where I approached the spyhole in the door with considerable caution. The bell rang yet again, so I took a deep breath and peered through the spyhole.

I was relieved that it wasn't who I'd feared it might be, of course, but it was certainly not a welcome caller. In fact he was probably second from the top of my list of people I'd least like to see, or ever expected to meet up with again. And maybe that was it—maybe I was just intrigued—but for whatever reason I went against my better instincts and opened the front door.

'Thank God you're here,' he said, as if it were a matter of life and death. 'Can we talk?'

I was going to keep him on the doorstep, but then I remembered that Chris was downstairs and might overhear, so I stood to one side and with a curt gesture of my head indicated that he should come in.

I closed the door and didn't speak until we were both in the kitchen, where I asked him what the hell he was doing here.

'I know what you must be thinking,' Taylor said with look of despair that was darn near theatrical, 'but if you'll just hear me out...'

I glanced at my wristwatch meaningfully, although I didn't actually notice the time. 'I'll give you five minutes,' I said.

He looked relieved and then magicked a bottle from behind his back.

'There's a corkscrew in the drawer by the sink,' I told him coolly. Some part of me said that this wasn't right. That it was a big mistake to share wine with him. But another part—the biggest part, clearly—was deeply curious. 'The glasses are in the cupboard to the left.'

He opened the bottle and poured the wine before he spoke, and then he sighed as he slumped into the chair opposite mine.

'Mary told me that you two had spoken,' he said miserably, 'and I know how it must look to you, but the situation is very complicated.'

'I'd agree with that,' I said sarcastically. 'The fact that you are living with Mary *is* quite a big complication.'

'*Was* living with her.' He corrected me. 'It's all over now, and that really is the truth.'

I thought about what Mary had said in her note again and it all clicked into place. 'You mean that she's come to her senses and thrown you out.'

'It wasn't like that,' he said, shaking his head. 'It hadn't been right between us for ages. And when I told you there wasn't anyone special, that was true in a way. She hasn't been special to me for a very long time.' He sighed again, deeply now.

'I'd been trying to work out a way to tell her, but then you came along and made everything a lot more urgent.'

He took a long slurp of wine and waited for me to say something.

'And what are you saying, exactly? That now it's over between you two we can sail happily into the sunset?'

'Of course not,' he said tragically. 'I know it won't be as simple as that.'

'But you still think there's half a chance of me coming good, or why else would you be here?'

I took a long sip from my own glass, and noted that it was a very good wine. Of course.

'Look,' he said, in an exaggeratedly patient tone, 'I can understand that you must feel angry, but—'

'Darn right I feel angry,' I interrupted. 'You invited me into someone else's home—your *partner's home*—where you presumably planned to seduce me.' This sounded very prim when I said it, but he didn't seem to notice. 'And then, when you discovered to your horror that she was coming back unexpectedly, you invented a fire at your restaurant in order to get rid of me.'

'I know,' he said with almost convincing despair. 'It was a terrible thing to do but I was just so afraid of losing you.'

'But you never even had me to start with,' I told him bluntly. 'Christ, we hardly knew one another, so please spare me the baloney.'

'It's not baloney,' he said, searching my green eyes with his melancholy brown ones. 'I might not have known you long but I wanted you to be part of my life. Why else do you think I asked you to take those photographs?'

'I thought it was because you liked my work,' I said, and then took another big swig of the excellent wine.

'I do,' he said. 'I think you've got a great talent. But I was also attracted to you from the start.'

Maybe it was the flattery, or perhaps the wine on an empty stomach, but I could feel myself lightening up. I let him top up my glass anyway, and when he continued to gaze into my eyes, I felt the blood rush to my face. He might be a cheat and a liar, but I still seemed to find him attractive. At least in the physical sense, and besides, didn't we have some unfinished business?

I emptied the contents of the glass in one and held it out for a refill. And as I watched him pour wine from the bottle I wondered what harm it would do to give in to my feelings. What was wrong with sex for its own sake, after all? Especially since there hadn't been sex of any old kind for a very long time.

'Why don't we take these into the living room?' I heard the wilder side of myself suggesting now, and even when I saw the smirk of victory on his face, I let it go. Just so long as I knew what this was really about, and that I was a willing participant, what was the problem?

Then I thought of one, something I couldn't let go quite as easily as the smirk. 'The thing that really annoyed me was losing my job,' I said, as he followed me through with the wine.

'You and me both,' he said in a sorry-for-himself whingeing tone.

I turned round and looked at him, and when I saw the bitterness in his expression I couldn't help smiling.

'So she's sacked you as well?' I said.

'It isn't like that,' he said defensively, as we sat down side by side on the sofa. 'She's just not renewing my contract.'

It occurred to me that there wasn't much difference, but I chose not to point this out. 'I shouldn't think you'll have any problems being picked up elsewhere,' I said as I slipped my shoes off. 'You're a celebrity now, after all.'

'That depends,' he said, gloomily. 'She could make things very difficult for me. According to her, TV chefs are ten a penny.'

And she was probably right, I thought. But he'd got himself into this mess and it most certainly wasn't my problem.

I wasn't well practised in the art of seduction, but I sensed that a little encouragement might help to get him in the right mood. So I put my glass down and moved in a little closer.

'You've got a lot of fans, though,' I reminded him.

'I suppose so,' he replied with a slightly smug sigh, but he didn't seem to notice my hand on his knee. 'Maybe I should be pro-active and contact a few producers myself.'

'Maybe,' I said, gently caressing his thigh. 'And the book will help when it comes out.'

'*If* it comes out…' he said, and was back into whinge-mode straight away. 'The bitch has threatened to halt its publication.'

I found myself quite admiring Mary's style. Despite what she said to me about her feelings for Taylor, she obviously wasn't as wet as she seemed. Either that or she'd just reached breaking point as far as he was concerned, and, if so, then I felt quite proud of the small part I'd played. As I considered this my mind was rapidly going off the seduction thing, but then I looked up at the petulant set of Taylor's mouth, remembered that explosive kiss he'd delivered with it and my body took over again.

'Ah, well,' I said, snuggling up, my hand on his black cashmere sweater now, 'there'll be other opportunities.'

I felt his body stiffen under my hand suddenly, and looked up at him.

'You really don't get it, do you, Tao?'

'Get what?'

'The fact that my career is on the line, thanks to you and that God-awful embittered woman.'

Which dampened my ardour somewhat.

'Thanks to *me?*' I squawked. And Sirg, who'd been quiet until now, squawked back in response from the adjoining room.

'Thanks to *me!*' he repeated perfectly, including the accent, and Taylor looked distinctly alarmed.

'It's an African Grey parrot,' I said in mild disgust as I got up on my feet. 'And as for Mary, what the hell do you expect, you…you *user,* you?'

And while I was wondering what I had ever seen in the man, how close I'd come to making a complete arse of myself—again—my mobile phone started ringing.

I grabbed at it angrily.

'It's Mary,' Mary said in hushed tones that seemed a bit melodramatic. 'Is he there?'

'Is *who*…?' Then I realised who she meant, of course. 'That is a correct assumption,' I said cryptically, because he was looking at me and I didn't want him to know who I was talking to.

'Well, then I think you should know that he's looking for somewhere to shack up for a while.'

It could have sounded like sour grapes, but I sensed that there was more to it than that.

'Oh, yes?' I said, looking over at him. He wasn't taking much notice of me now, though. He was too busy feeling sorry for himself.

'Yes,' she said. 'I was going to return your call anyway, but I've just been speaking to another *friend* of his, or rather an *ex*-friend. And she told me that he'd been to her first, looking for sympathy and somewhere to stay.'

I could feel the blood in my face, and I turned away so that he couldn't see what was going on.

'That's very interesting,' I told her quietly, 'and I'm grateful for the tip-off.'

'I'll ring you again later,' she said, 'because there's something else that I'd like to speak to you about.'

'I'll look forward to it,' I said.

Then I ended the call and turned back to Taylor. And, my goodness me, I was ready for him.

'As for it being *my* fault,' I said, picking up where I'd left off, only cooler and calmer now, 'all I can say is that I'm glad to have been of service.'

He looked at me as if I was mad.

'To all the women you've probably used in your time to get where you seem to want to be.'

When he looked shocked and confused, I enlightened him further.

'I've just been speaking to Mary,' I couldn't resist explaining, 'and she told me that I'm not the first person you've called on today.'

He looked alarmed, and then, like a rat in a trap, his expression turned suddenly nasty. He was about to say something not very nice, I was sure of that, but I wasn't finished with *him* yet.

'And, just so you know, my only interest in you was physical. Furthermore, I couldn't care less about your brilliant career—or *lack* of it, as it's looking now. So I suggest you take whatever's left in that expensive bottle of wine and sling your hook.'

When he looked confused again, I realised this was probably an English phrase he was not yet familiar with.

'Which loosely translates as *fuck off*,' I said coolly—and quietly, I thought. But not quietly enough for Sirg.

'*Fuck off!*' he repeated, loud and clear, and with a nervous expression and a shake of his head, Taylor did so without another word.

It was almost Sirg's bedtime by now, so I did all the usual stuff, wished him goodnight, and when I'd closed the door I rang Mary back.

I told her that I'd sent Taylor packing, and she sounded pleased about that.

'I hope you didn't mind me calling,' she said, 'but I thought you'd be next on his list and you don't deserve to be used by that wanker.'

I didn't bother telling her that I'd planned on a spot of *using* myself, because it would have sounded smug, and it didn't get away from the fact that I'd been number *two* on his list. 'So who was his first choice?' I found myself asking.

'Oh, just some woman he tried to mess up along the way. She doesn't live too far from you, as a matter of fact. She's older, though, and he probably thought she'd be a bit more desperate, so don't feel too bad about being the reserve. She's also richer, so that would have been an added attraction.'

I wanted to ask some more about this mysterious woman, but it somehow didn't feel appropriate.

'You said that you had something else to talk to me about,' I reminded her instead.

'I have. A couple of things, as a matter of fact, but you haven't told me why you rang me yet.'

'To thank you for the cheque,' I fibbed. There didn't seem

much point in asking her what the note had meant, because I knew the answer now.

'No problem,' she said. 'I'm just sorry that you got drawn into my messy love-life, and that you didn't get to put your undoubted skills into practice.'

Mary Deacon was growing on me by the moment. 'He told me that you're not renewing his contract,' I said.

'I'm surprised he ever imagined I would. How he thought we could work together after what he's done…'

It seemed to me at that moment that Jerry's advice was excellent. Getting involved with people you work with is a big mistake. 'But aren't you cutting your nose off to spite your face, in a way?' I said. 'I mean, he *is* very popular with the viewers.'

'You win some, you lose some,' Mary said philosophically. 'Which brings me to one of the reasons I wanted to speak to you… I understand that you are a neighbour of Chris Harris?' she said.

I went blank for a moment. I didn't have a clue what she was talking about.

'He lives in the basement flat below you, or so I've been told.'

'Oh,' I said, '*that* Chris. I'm sorry, I didn't know his surname.' But I was still none the wiser. Why could she possibly want to know about him?

'My contact tells me that he's a very talented young garden designer, and that's exactly what I am looking for.'

'I don't know about the *talented designer* bit,' I said, thinking she must be mistaken. 'I thought he just—well, you know, did some *gardening*…but he's certainly young, and if that's all you want I could ask him to call you, if you like.'

'Looks like he's been hiding his light under a bushel,'

Mary said. 'According to my contact, he's brilliant. And it's not for my garden I'm interested in him. I think some new blood is required to challenge the likes of Alan Titchmarsh… Gardening's the new rock 'n' roll,' she went on enthusiastically, 'and what's needed is someone young and good-looking to bring in a whole new audience.'

It clicked what she meant, and I was astonished.

'You mean you're interested in him doing a show or something?'

'A series of shows, if he's as good as I hope, and what I wanted to know from you is whether or not you think he's good-looking. I know looks shouldn't matter as much as talent, but in my business they do, I'm afraid.'

I was still struggling with the idea of Chris on TV, and I didn't really think before I replied. 'Yes,' I replied without hesitation. 'He's very good-looking.'

'Yeah. That's what my contact said. But she could have just been partial to his sort of looks, I suppose. And what about his voice and manner? Could you imagine him on the small screen?'

'I suppose so,' I said, thinking of his clear speaking voice. 'Though he does have a slight northern accent.'

'Even better!' she said. 'And his manner?'

I thought about the way he had charmed my mother. 'I suppose he can be quite…' I searched for the right word '…well, *engaging,* when he chooses to be.' He could also be bossy and difficult, of course, but I kept that bit to myself.

'Good word,' Mary said. 'Engaging is exactly what is required. Great,' she added, 'he's beginning to sound pretty perfect to me, and I understand he's writing a book.'

'Your "contact" seems pretty well informed,' I said, thinking now about the laptop computer and the piles of paper I'd seen on his desk. I felt a bit miffed because he hadn't told me what he was up to. But then come to think of it I never asked.

'He works for her,' Mary said, and then paused for a moment. 'As a matter of fact, she's the very same woman who was number one on Taylor's list of would-be suckers. He was seeing her as well on the side for a while, until I found out and put a stop to it.'

I didn't respond to this, and she sighed.

'I know,' she said. 'I was bloody mad, but I'm sane again now, I assure you.'

'Then how did you two become acquainted?' I asked curiously. 'You and Taylor's ex-friend?'

'I went round to see her when I'd spoken to you, and it was meeting her that clinched everything. I'd let myself believe that she was a wicked woman, but it turns out she isn't. Taylor used her as much as he used me. He even borrowed money from her to buy his car, but she's never going to get it back, of course.'

I couldn't help wondering what he imagined he'd have got from me, but apart from sex and maybe a bed for a couple of nights I couldn't think of anything. I wasn't influential, like Mary, or rich, like…

Then I had a sudden thought. 'Is she early to mid-forties, blonde, wealthy-looking?'

'I'd say she was older than that—getting on for fifty. But apart from that it sounds about right,' Mary replied. 'Do you know her, then?'

'No, but I think I've seen her.' I pictured her again, hobbling down the steps in her ridiculous high heels to Chris's flat, and it all made sense suddenly. The fact that she'd moved on to Chris now, which no doubt explained why she was so interested in advancing his career.

'Well, it certainly is a small world,' I said wryly.

'I guess it is,' Mary replied with a sad sigh, and I wondered if I should ask if she was feeling okay about everything. I decided against it. We weren't that close, and it sounded to me as if she was dealing with the situation pretty well. And if finding a new star would help even more, then good luck to her—and to Chris as well.

'You said there were two things you wanted to talk about,' I said then. As I spoke I moved over to the window and drew the curtains. It was dark now, and it had suddenly occurred to me that people outside could see into the room. Although there was only one person I was really bothered about.

'Yes,' she said. 'I just wanted to say that if this works out— with Chris Harris, I mean—that there might be some work in it for you.'

'Oh?' I said, very surprised.

'Well, I might be jumping the gun a bit here, because I don't know how far he's on with his book, but if he needs any photos maybe we can bring you into the project.'

It did seem a long shot. There was no guarantee that he'd even be interested in working for Mary—although I couldn't imagine anyone turning down such a great opportunity. And even if he did need some photographs for his book, I doubted very much that he'd want me to take them. We were on better terms now than we had been, but I still had the impression he was wary of me. And then I thought of another problem.

'You do know that I'm supposed to be a *food* photographer, don't you?'

'Food, gardens—what's the difference, when all's said and done?'

'Quite a lot, actually,' I said, though I realised I might be talking myself out of a possible job here. 'Most food work is done in a studio, for starters.'

'Maybe, but you've done all those outside market shots, so what's the problem?'

She had a point, I supposed, though it still all seemed a bit pie in the sky. And yet it seemed rude to keep putting up objections when she was being so nice.

'Well, we'll see,' I said. 'But it's definitely a very nice thought and I'm grateful.'

'You've done me a great personal favour, Tao, and I still feel I owe you.'

'There's no need,' I said. 'I'm more than happy with the cheque.'

'Like you said, Tao, we'll see.' And with that she ended the call.

18

Despite all my fears about Jerome, I had an uneventful few days following Taylor's visit and Mary's phone call. The highlight was Olive's cleaning day, which Sirg responded to in the usual let-me-at-her way. I didn't even see Chris, because I didn't have to go out anywhere and he, presumably, was indoors working hard on his opus.

I was still rather dazed by the fact that he wasn't quite what I'd taken him for. That he was not just a jobbing gardener who'd struck lucky when he found Mrs Audesley but something a little bit special in the world of horticulture. Special enough to be writing a book on the subject, and now being considered for his own television show. I was dying to find out if there had been any contact between him and Mary yet, but I couldn't bring myself to call her again. Because, despite the fact that we seemed to be getting on pretty well, the circumstances of our acquaintance still made me feel a bit weird at times.

And, since he hadn't bothered to make contact with me, I most certainly wasn't going to ask Chris.

I didn't know why, really. It would have been the natural thing to have done, after all, given my small involvement. And Mary hadn't asked me *not* to say anything. Maybe I just thought that if he had anything to tell me—or, more importantly, if he'd *wanted* to tell me—he would almost certainly have done it by now.

Which left me with the inescapable conclusion that he didn't want me in on the act.

It was hardly surprising, really, since by now he would probably know that I had been sacked from my only other professional job so far. Mary would hardly have withheld that little nugget of information from him, and if she'd told him that she might also have told him the circumstances of my sacking... What an idiot he must think I was. And a liar, as well, bearing in mind my claim that my relationship with Taylor had been strictly professional.

The fact that it *had* been strictly professional when I'd told him that was probably irrelevant in the scheme of things.

I'd worked out by now why Chris had taken so badly against Taylor Wiseman. It was obvious, really. Taylor's former bit on the side must have laid it on pretty thick about what a bastard he was. And the fact that Chris seemed so very aggrieved on her behalf was a pretty good indicator that she meant a lot to him. A *lot* more than the rich, middle-aged, looking-for-kicks-with-a-bit-of-rough woman I'd believed her to be.

He was probably madly in love with her, in fact, and she with him. And soon he would be a TV celeb, which would make him a rich woman's equal, more or less, and wasn't that just fine and dandy?

I felt a bit jealous as a matter of fact, but that was only because everything seemed to be going so well for Chris and so wrong for me.

Okay, so I had a nice cheque that would keep me going for a couple of months, but what then? The work wasn't exactly pouring in. It was Wednesday now, I'd been on the phone to the agency every day since Monday, and nothing had come up at all.

It was hard phoning bloody Amber, when she must have known what had happened to me. That I had been fired and *why*… She never actually said as much, but I could tell by the sneer in her voice that she definitely knew something.

The call that morning had been particularly trying. Once she'd told me that there was no work for me, with a great deal of relish, the cow had actually asked me if I'd seen Taylor lately.

'No,' I answered tartly, before I had chance to think about it, 'and I don't expect to either.'

'I didn't think so,' she said.

'What's that supposed to mean?' I couldn't help asking.

'Oh, nothing,' she said in a saccharine voice, and with that she put the phone down on me.

And because that exchange had left me even more restless, and because I was feeling a bit trapped in the house, I called Sophie at work and asked if she fancied coming over that evening.

She said she was tired, that she'd been working long hours—which I believed, because that's what she does when she's troubled. She throws herself into work and usually ends up with a promotion, but I pressed her nevertheless.

'Oh, go on, Soph,' I whinged. 'I'm going crazy here on my own.' I'd already rung to tell her the news about Taylor,

and Mary, and of course she hadn't been surprised because
she'd had her doubts about Taylor all along. But at least she
didn't say that she'd told me so. What I hadn't done—so far,
anyway—was mention Chris and the possibility that he
might be the next big thing in the gardening world, but I
added a hint now that I had some additional news in the
hope of luring her over.

'Okay,' she sighed, 'but don't blame me if I fall asleep.'

'I don't care if you fall asleep,' I said, relieved. 'I just need
your physical presence.'

And, because her visit was to be the highlight of several
very dull days, I decided to make an event of it. I made a list
of things I would need, informed Sirg that I was popping
out for a while, with the promise of a treat for him if he was
good, and headed off to the local shops. If things had gone
according to plan, my cheque from Mary should have been
processed by now, and I would be in funds again. So I called
at the bank first, found that I was indeed financially viable,
and made my purchases with a clearer conscience.

I bought two wild salmon steaks from the fishmonger, and
the ingredients to make a hollandaise sauce, which was my
one and only culinary specialty. Then I chose the best vegetables I could find, *mange tout,* baby carrots and new pota-
toes. And because it all seemed a bit sensible and healthy to
me, I balanced things out with a ready-made fresh cream
raspberry Pavlova.

Then I went to the booze shop and went a bit crazy. I got
some raspberry-flavoured vodka to go with the Pavlova, and
two bottles of expensive wine that I thought even Taylor
wouldn't be able to turn his snooty nose up at.

Oh, yes, and I kept my promise to Sirg and bought him
a luscious fresh mango.

I took it all back to the house and felt a lot brighter for

the trip out. It lasted a good ten minutes, this feeling of brightness, until the house telephone rang and I took a call from my mother.

She'd rung briefly on Sunday, to let me know that she'd arrived safely back, and she'd sounded fine at the time. Upbeat and determined.

Now, though, she sounded more sort of—well…frenzied.

'I just thought you should know what's happening,' she said, in a strange sing-songy voice that made me wonder if she'd been smoking something illegal.

'What do you mean?' I asked her cautiously.

'Between me and your father, of course.'

'What's happening between you and my father?'

'He's having an affair with someone he works with,' she said in a scarily matter-of-fact sort of way, 'and I'm off to Goa.'

I could only take in one shock statement at a time, so I opted for what seemed the *most* shocking statement.

'*Goa?*' I said. 'As in that place where hippies hang out in India?'

'Precisely!' she sang back to me. 'And I am just so excited. Melanie's coming with me. You know Melanie, don't you?'

'I think so,' I said in a daze. 'The woman who shampoos pets for a living.'

'She does more than shampoo them,' my mother giggled, and I knew I was right about the illegal substance. 'She trims them as well. It's a very skilled job, if you must know.'

'I believe you,' I said, 'but what's this about her going with you to India?'

'Isn't it fab?' she said, slipping easily into Sixties-speak. 'We were just chatting away the other day when I bumped into her—you know, about unfaithful husbands and what bastards they are, that sort of thing. And because she's in the same boat, more or less, we said, Fuck them! Let's raid the joint bank accounts and do something we've always wanted to do. And it turned out she's always wanted to go to India as well.'

I was feeling a bit dizzy by now.

'But what's this about Dad?' I said, changing tack. 'What do you mean, he's having an *affair?* And, if it's true, why aren't you screaming and yelling at him?'

Obviously this wasn't a big surprise. The possibility that he was up to something had already been discussed at length, and the fact that he'd not been in touch with me directly proved that he had a guilty conscience. But I was still pretty stunned to have it confirmed.

'I've done all that,' my mother said casually. 'And don't be sorry for me, Tao. I couldn't stand that. Besides, it's given me the kick up my very large bottom that I've needed for years. I've always made excuses before about going to India. Like who'd look after your dad? Who'd cook and clean for him? But he can go take a hike now as far as I am concerned.'

'You mean that the marriage is over?' I was on the point of blubbing now, so I took a deep breath and fanned my face with my free hand.

'Who knows?' she replied, and I could sense her shrug. 'What matters now is that I do what *I* want to do, and we'll just have to see what happens then. And do you know, Tao? I think I have Chris to thank for this—for making me feel positive instead of collapsing into a heap.'

So did that mean I had Chris to blame for the break-up of my parents' marriage?

It might sound unreasonable, but that was definitely the first thought that came into my head.

'So when are you planning to leave?' I said in a daze.

'As soon as possible. I've already left the house,' she said carelessly. 'Melanie has thrown her husband out, so I'll be staying with her till we get all the vaccinations sorted out. And don't even think about trying to persuade your father to come after me, Tao. I wouldn't go back to him if he begged me.'

'But…'

'But *nothing,*' she said firmly, not at all dizzy and frenzied now. 'I've been faithful to the man for thirty years, and I just can't forgive him for this.'

I was about to say 'but' again, but I thought better of it. I decided to leave it till later, when she'd had time to think about what she might be throwing away. I was sure she'd come round eventually.

'Okay,' I said. 'Then you'd better give me your number at Melanie's, so I can ring you there in future.'

She sounded pleased, and when she gave me the number I wished her well. I think that I managed not to sound too emotional.

Of course then, when I'd put the phone down, the first thing I thought of was to ring my dad. I thought about it for a good half-hour, then I decided against it. He would be at work anyway, at the moment, and it seemed to me that it should be him who did the phoning. He was the one responsible for making me the victim a broken home, so he was the one who could do the grovelling. And for the first time ever, probably, I actually felt on my mother's side.

Of course I was looking forward to seeing Sophie all the more now, so it was a lot more than a mild disappointment I felt when she phoned at five minutes to six, when I'd showered and changed into my best jeans and favourite pink sweater, and just started my prep work for the meal, and told me she wouldn't be able to make it.

Oh, she was very apologetic, of course, especially when I told her about my parents, but the upshot was that it couldn't be helped. She'd been asked to stay on to deal with some important work—too important for even me, who'd worked in a bank, to understand—and she wasn't expecting to finish till very late.

'We could do something at the weekend,' she suggested, but I wasn't in the mood for being fobbed off with far-off promises.

'Depends if I'm free,' I said churlishly.

'Suit yourself,' she sighed, and she sounded so tired that I felt a bit guilty.

'I'm sorry,' I said. 'I just needed to talk, and, yes, I'd love to do something at the weekend. Maybe we could do something rash—go to a club and get pissed as farts.'

'Not sure I could manage that,' she said wearily. 'I was thinking more of meeting up for a coffee.'

I realised then that she was more than just tired, that she sounded unhappy. Which reminded me of the possible cause.

'Have you seen anything of Jerome?' I asked, by way of sounding her out.

'No,' Sophie said, 'but it's funny that you should ask just now, because I spoke to someone from his department earlier.'

I felt a sense of foreboding at this, and wished now that I hadn't mentioned his name.

'And...?' I said cautiously.

'And he seems to have disappeared. He hasn't shown up for work all week, and although people have called his flat he hasn't answered.'

'Oh, God! You don't suppose he's been murdered, do you? By his Japanese fence?'

'Don't you think that's a bit melodramatic?'

Maybe it was just my guilty conscience, but it didn't feel melodramatic at all. I pictured Jerome opening his briefcase in front of his contact, and producing Bath Oliver biscuits… What if they hadn't seen the funny side? What if they'd thought they were being made a fool of? And what if the punishment for making a fool of a Japanese fence was…? I shuddered at the thought, but I didn't tell Sophie what I was thinking. 'I suppose so,' I said simply, instead.

'Anyway, one of his colleagues is going round to his place tonight, to see if he's there.' She didn't sound as if she cared very much either way, which I took as a good sign as far as she was concerned. She might be down, but it looked as if Jerome wasn't the resaon.

'Will you let me know the outcome?' I asked. Despite my fears for his possible fate, and my part in it, a little bit of me was hoping that maybe something not *too* horrible *had* happened to him. That would at least keep him away from London till I'd moved on.

When I'd put the phone down I looked despondently at the two salmon steaks which were currently marinating in a little olive oil and lemon juice, and I wished there was someone else I could call.

I'd put the raspberry-flavoured vodka into the freezer earlier, and I took it out now, with a tray of ice cubes. Then I went to the fridge and took out one of the glasses I'd put in to chill, added several ice cubes, and poured in some of the pinky thickened spirit. I swallowed the contents, minus the ice, in one.

It took a moment to hit me, then *Pow!* First the cold in my throat, then the fire in my belly and, within a few seconds, a nice wuzzy feeling in my head. And suddenly life didn't feel so bad after all.

So I had another. Only this time I didn't knock it straight back. I took it instead into Sirg's room, and told him he was the most beautiful bird in the whole world.

I told him all sorts of things, including how much I loved him, and in return he rubbed his head against the side of my face, and performed a couple of snatches of the theme tune from his favourite radio show.

He worked his way down my arm and tipped his beak over the edge of my glass, for a sniff. At which point he pulled it back sharply and screeched at me, as if in disapproval. But I just lifted my arm, taking him along for the ride, and took a quick sip from the glass. The ice was beginning to melt now, but I got some of the flavour of the raspberries, which made me think about the Pavlova, and how the vodka had sharpened my appetite.

So I kissed Sirg on his head and put him back in the cage, with a promise to return with some mango shortly. Then, just as I was in the hallway, heading towards the kitchen, the front doorbell *bing-bonged* behind me.

Not so fearful as I would have been without the vodka, I nipped to door and peered through the spyhole, and felt one of my eyebrows rise with interest.

'I've just had a call from your mother,' Chris said, when I opened the door, and I felt a cringe coming on.

'You'd better come in,' I told him.

He followed me through to the kitchen, where I put my drink down on the table.

'You expecting someone?' he wanted to know, when he looked at the prep work for the meal I'd planned.

'*Was,*' I said with a slight shrug, 'but they cancelled.' Then it occurred to me that I should offer him a drink.

'I've got some wine in the fridge, if you'd like some.'

'I think I'd prefer what you're drinking,' he said with a smile. 'I could do with something strong.'

I glanced at him as I went to the freezer. 'Did my mother do that to you?' I asked him wryly.

'No,' he said, 'that was the work I've been doing, but I'm glad to say that I finished today. About an hour ago, as a matter of fact.'

I got the vodka and out and used the chilled glass that I'd prepared for Sophie.

'Is this the book I've heard about?' I said as I poured.

'Oh, yes,' he said after a moment. 'I understand that we've been talking to the same person lately. Someone other than your mother, that is.'

I passed the glass to him and he sniffed the contents appreciatively before swallowing the contents in the same manner as I'd knocked back my first.

'Good stuff!' he gasped, as if he'd been kicked in the backside.

It seemed to me that he wasn't going to say any more about Mary, so I decided to get the call from my mother over and done with.

'She told you about her plans, I suppose?'

'Yeah. And she wanted to know about places to stay, that sort of thing.'

'And you were able to advise her, of course.' There was a bit of an edge in my voice, a small residue of the blame I'd laid at his door for putting such daft ideas into my mother's head in the first place.

'I did my best,' he said nonchalantly. 'But the reason I'm here is to reassure you. She thought you'd be worried about her, so I said I'd try and put your mind at rest.'

I pulled out a chair and sat down. 'I suppose I had hoped

that she'd go off the idea,' I said with a sigh. 'She's always been a talker, but not much of doer.'

Chris sat down opposite me. 'Well, that's obviously changed,' he said. 'She seems a very determined woman now.'

I nodded and looked over at him. 'I don't suppose she can come to much harm, can she?'

'I wouldn't have thought so, and it's not as if she'll be on her own.'

'Mmm,' I said gloomily. 'But I don't see what help someone who shampoos pets for a living would be in a crisis.'

He laughed then. 'You sound like you are the parent here.'

'That's what I feel like. What I've always felt like where she is concerned.'

I reached over and picked up my glass again, and saw that the ice had melted completely now. Then I looked at the bottle I'd left on the table and asked if he'd like another.

He said that he would, and I told him to help himself. When he had, he lifted his glass to prepare for a toast.

'Here's to your mother,' he said, 'and to finding herself in Goa.'

I smiled and raised my own glass, half-heartedly, but I knocked back the contents with gusto. The effect was immediate again, and the next thing I knew I was asking him if he was busy that evening. When he said no, I suggested he stayed and helped me out with the food I'd prepared.

We had a surprisingly good couple of hours together—but that could have been down to the wine, I later supposed. We did drink rather a lot of it and, on top of a couple of vodkas, I think it is safe to say that we got fairly drunk.

And we did it in front of Sirg, I'm ashamed to say. It was Chris's idea to eat in his room, to keep him company, and the eating was done with most of the drinking, which caused the bird to 'tut–tut' a lot, when he wasn't devouring his mango.

But he definitely enjoyed our company, even if we did keep him from his perch for a good hour longer than usual. It was Chris who eventually noticed the time and said he should go, so that Sirg could get his feathered old head down.

I really wanted to ask him to stay a bit longer, because—well…*probably* because I didn't want to be left on my own again in the house, to worry about Jerome. But, despite my lowered inhibitions, I couldn't quite bring myself to say it.

As I went with him to the front door, a little unsteady on my feet, I realised that we hadn't talked about Mary. About lots of other things, certainly, but not about her—and not about the wealthy blonde with the ridiculous high heels, either. While even with so much booze in me I couldn't bring up that particular subject, I was sufficiently loose to finally mention the TV offer. He had, after all, referred to it himself already, and although the reference had been pretty oblique we'd got on so well that it occurred to me now that I might be in with a chance of some work after all.

'So should I ask for your autograph now?' I said, only I think it came out as a slur.

He looked at me for a moment without responding, and I realised I'd been a bit cryptic for someone as inebriated as we were.

'The offer to do a series of TV shows on gardening?' I spelled out slowly.

'Oh, that,' he said with a frown, and then he shook his head. 'I turned her down.'

And when I stood there, with an unattractively slackened jaw, he said, 'I may live to regret it, but I don't think so. I'm not too keen on the limelight. I'm not even happy about the publicity stuff that might be involved when the book is published.'

And then he left me, with a wide, slightly drunken smile, and even in my befuddled state it struck me that there was another potential work opportunity definitely gone down the tubes.

19

At least we seemed to have broken some of the ice between us—which was something, I supposed, as I lay in bed unable to sleep. I did manage to drop off for a while, but I kept waking up, thinking that I could hear noises in the house but too afraid to investigate.

I got out of bed when the sun came up and I was quite relieved to discover that the house hadn't been ransacked during the night. That the sounds had probably just been floorboards settling or the invention of my lurid imagination. Everything was completely as it should have been, and, taking some comfort from this, I went into the kitchen and loaded the dishwashing machine with the previous night's dishes.

Then I made some tea and took it back to my bedroom. I felt pretty grim, but maybe not as bad as I deserved to feel, and because I thought some fresh air might improve matters more, I rashly decided to go for a jog. Unfortunately

I didn't have much in the way of cool jogging gear, which I imagined was an obligatory requirement in this neck of the woods. But I did have some trainers and a T-shirt, and, teamed with some ancient black leggings that I mostly used for sleeping in these days, I thought I would probably get away with it. There wouldn't be many people around at ten past five in the morning, I figured, and if I ran fast enough they probably wouldn't see the hole in my leggings.

I locked up carefully and, having remembered my bum bag, put the keys in it after setting the security alarm. Thankfully I didn't come across any twenty-four-hour bagel shops on my half-hearted jog around the smart streets of Hampstead, because I would have been tempted, but I met rather more people than I expected to. Fellow joggers, mostly, only a bit more practised than I was, clearly. I wasn't really sure where I was going, but when I saw a couple of runners heading purposefully in the same direction, I tagged quite a long way behind them and eventually found myself huffing and puffing on a wide open green space that I guessed must be the famous Heath. It was rather more misty here than on the streets, and I might have been spooked if there hadn't been so many Lycra-clad bottoms passing me. And most of them did pass me. In fact the only person I managed to overtake on the path was an octogenarian (or at least he looked over eighty) dressed in voluminous khaki shorts.

I decided not to go too far because, a) I was slightly nervous about not being able to find my way home, and b) I was fading fast. Weeks without exercise and a night of overindulgence had taken its toll, and there was a nasty burning sensation in my chest.

I could see a group of trees ahead, so I made the decision

to turn back when I got there. Only I didn't get there, because I saw something that brought me up short in my tracks. The shape of a man, right by the trees, who, from the distance between us, looked exactly like Jerome Audesley. I didn't stick around to confirm my fears, but turned and hot-footed it in the opposite direction.

By the time I reached the street again, the one that would lead me safely home, I'd convinced myself that I'd been hallucinating due to oxygen starvation to the brain brought on by unaccustomed physical exertion. It had been misty, after all, and I had been quite some distance from a shape that just happened to look like someone I had been fretting about. And the clincher, the thing that persuaded me once and for all that I had just been imagining things, was the place where I'd thought I'd seen him. On Hampstead Heath.

'What the hell would he have been doing there at six in the morning?' I asked myself out loud, and when no plausible answer came to me I put the matter out of my mind.

I kept my head down for the rest of the day, and, apart from Sirg, didn't see another living soul.

I did speak to my mother, at Melanie's house, and she sang the praises of Chris again.

'I wish you could find yourself a man like him,' she said dreamily, and for some reason I felt vaguely miffed. I think it was because she'd obviously dismissed him as a serious possibility. As if the idea of him finding me attractive and interesting had not seriously crossed her mind, and the best I could manage as far as she was concerned was a pale imitation of someone *like* him.

'And what about Dad?' I said, changing the subject abruptly. 'Have you been in touch with him since you left?'

'No. I went round while he was out and got some of my things, but we haven't spoken.' She didn't sound remotely troubled by this, but I was.

'Does he even know where you are?'

'Of course he knows where I am. He's rung here often enough. I'm just not taking his calls.'

'So he wants to talk,' I said hopefully.

'Of course he does. But it isn't about what *he* wants any more. He forfeited the right to reasonable behaviour on my part when he took up with that floosie of his.'

'When you say "floosie", do you mean that she's young?' I found it creepy to imagine my dad with someone the same age as me.

She didn't respond immediately, and I had to press her.

'She's older than I am, if you must know,' she finally admitted. 'And *fatter*. And I don't know why, Tao, but somehow that's a lot more galling than if she had just been a slip of a bottled blonde.'

I could see what she meant. That was the sort of image I'd had in mind, the typical fantasy of a middle-aged man, and to hear it was someone other than that seemed a lot more shocking somehow. And worrying.

'Do you want him back?' I found myself asking in a very serious voice. I know she'd said she couldn't forgive him, but that wasn't quite the same thing.

'To be perfectly honest, I'm really not sure what I want,' she said, and all the bluff and bravado was absent now. 'Apart from going to India. And I am very sure about that. The rest can wait till I get back.' Then she laughed. '*If* I come back, that is.'

I didn't take much notice of that, because I couldn't conceive of her living in India for the rest of her days. With her fair skin, I wouldn't be at all surprised if she was back within the week.

Then she told me that she and Melanie had booked their tickets for just over two weeks hence. And that sort of jolted me, and put paid once and for all to my doubts about her determination.

Five minutes after I ended that call my mobile started ringing, and Sirg, who had mastered the new sound of it brilliantly, repeated it, so it was as if two phones were going mad. Which, with my lingering hangover and my mother's latest bombshell, was almost too much to cope with.

'Shut the fuck up!' I yelled at Sirg as I darted to the phone, and regretted it instantly. Because he immediately stopped making the ringing tone and repeated what I'd said instead. And I just knew, by the relish in his voice, which sounded so like mine when he said it, that he would be adding this new expletive to his repertoire. And that Mrs Audesley would know exactly who he had learnt it from.

It was Sophie on the phone, and she sounded very excited. I could tell by the breathy way that she said hi, and how she ploughed right in without the usual pleasantries.

'I've just heard,' she said.

'Heard what?'

'About Jerome.'

'Oh, yes?' I said, and stopped breathing momentarily.

'Yes. You know I said that someone was going round to his place? Well, they did, and he's done a bunk! All his personal stuff's gone from the flat, but that isn't even the half of it.'

'So what's the rest of it?' I asked her ominously. Nothing she'd said so far could affect me directly, but what with my possible sighting of Jerome that morning a deep sense of unease returned to me.

'He told everyone that the flat was his, but it was actually rented. And because he hadn't paid the rent for ages…he was *evicted*. And it turns out that he didn't even own the furniture.'

'Yeah. Okay,' I said, 'but that doesn't explain why he hasn't turned up at work.' It might explain why he was roaming the Heath at six in the morning, though, I thought worriedly, but I didn't say anything about that yet.

'Ah, well, there hangs yet another tale,' Sophie said. 'He was on the point of getting the sack, apparently, which he knew about…'

She paused for a moment, as if waiting for some reaction from me, but I was numb.

'But don't you see?' she said. 'That's probably why he stole the miniatures. He owes money to everyone, and with no job now…'

'He'll be a desperate man. Is that what you're trying to tell me?'

And then I told her about my possible sighting of him on Hampstead Heath, and it didn't seem remotely unlikely any longer. In fact I was never more certain of anything.

'But what the hell would he have been doing?' Sophie sounded completely baffled. 'Surely he wouldn't have been sleeping rough?'

'I don't know,' I said, and I felt eerily calm now. 'But if he is then the fact that he's doing it so close to this house has to mean something.'

'Shouldn't you call the police, then?'

'And tell them what, exactly? That I'm worried that someone might be planning to break into the house? That he's already done it once, but that I got the stuff back with the help of a probable known criminal by entering a flat without permission? And what do you think they'll make of the Bath Oliver prank? Do you think *they'll* find that amusing?'

'Okay,' Sophie said soberly. 'I get your point. But you can't just sit around worrying that he'll appear any moment. You should at least ring Mrs Audesley and tell her what's happening. It's up to her to make a decision about what to do then.'

'I can't do that,' I sighed. 'It'll only upset her, and what can she do from Portugal? And even if she sets off straight away, he could have done his worst by the time she gets back.' I sighed heavily. 'I don't suppose you'd like to come over tonight and keep me company?'

'I'm sorry, Tao, but I can't. I'm expected at Jemima's pre-engagement party, which she's having this evening at the flat.'

'Jemima is getting engaged!' I said, my worries pushed into the background by this extraordinary news. 'But I didn't even know she had a boyfriend.'

'It's an ex who's made a reappearance. He turned up at the flat at the weekend, out of the blue, and next thing we know they're madly in love and planning to marry. He's perfect, apparently. Same sort of background, knows all the same people that Jemima does... Fiona is heartbroken, of course, because not only will she be losing her crony but it means that she's alone on the shelf now.'

I was flabbergasted. 'So does that mean she'll be leaving the flat?'

'Yes, and soon. Edward—that's the soon-to-be fiancé—has a fancy apartment in some nice part of town and she's moving in with him next week.'

Despite everything, I could see a window of possible opportunity opening up for me. 'Does that mean her room will be available?'

'Yes, and I'm ahead of you. I've already spoken to Fiona and it's okay with her if you move in when Mrs Audesley comes back. Jemima's paid her share of the rent up till the end of the month, but if you do want the room you'll have to take over after that, even if you won't be using the flat for a while.'

Which was perfectly fine by me.

'And you're invited to the party, if you think you can make it,' Sophie said.

'I don't see how I can,' I answered gloomily.

'Why don't you ask Chris if he can take over for you tonight? It would make more sense if he's in the house anyway. If Jerome does decide to pay a visit.'

It was a very tempting suggestion. I realised then I hadn't kept Sophie up to date on the Chris front, but I decided I could do that later. If I could only persuade him to take over tonight. 'I'll try,' I said, and with that she told me that she'd have to go.

'Fingers crossed for tonight,' she said. 'But you'd better warn Chris about Jerome if he does agree.'

I went straight down to Chris's flat before I had a chance to think about things and find a good reason not to. I hadn't seen him all day, but since nothing untoward had taken place the night before I wasn't too concerned about seeing him now. In fact, since we'd got on so well, I'd started to hope that I might even have gone up a notch or two in his estimation.

So I was somewhat puzzled when he opened his door and frowned at me. Heavily, as if I was the very last person he wanted to see at that moment.

I managed to keep my smile going, however. I needed a fairly big favour from him so it wouldn't have done to respond in kind. But first I thought it was only fair that I did as Sophie suggested and warned him about Jerome. If he was going to take over from me, he should be aware of the facts. And even if he insisted on telling Mrs Audesley, as I thought he probably would, well, at least I had somewhere to go now if she decided to cut short her stay with her son.

'Can we have a quick chat?' I asked, meaning could I come in for a while. Because it seemed a lot to say on his doorstep.

Although it didn't seem possible, the frown actually deepened, and he glanced quickly behind him. I looked in the same direction and saw the middle-aged blonde sitting with her back to us on one of his red sofas.

'I've got someone here,' he said.

'I can see that,' I told him coolly, 'but I promise not to keep you long.'

He sighed and stepped outside the door, closing it to behind him.

I opened my mouth to start telling him about Jerome, and then I thought, Bugger it! If I told him that, chances were he'd turn me down flat and insist I stay put at my post until Mrs Audesley got back to the house.

And I wanted so badly to get out of the house, even if it was only for a couple of hours.

'I need to go somewhere this evening,' I said, with slight emphasis on the magic *need* word. 'And I wondered if you could look after Sirg for me?'

'How long will you be away?' he asked, impatiently.

'Between, say…eight and eleven o'clock,' I said, thinking that would be as long as I could take of Jemima's smugness and Fiona's misery.

He sighed, and for a horrible moment I thought he was going to say no. Then he glanced at his wristwatch, looked a bit thoughtful, and finally nodded his head.

'Okay,' he said. 'That should be fine. But I might be a little bit later than eight.'

'Thank you,' I managed to say, but I didn't feel very grateful. I was pretty pissed off, as a matter of fact. I had thought he was over whatever problems he'd had with me, but it was as if last night had never happened now. And there was something else.

Something I hadn't been able to admit before.

It seemed that I was as jealous as hell of the wealthy, middle-aged blonde.

I took a taxi to the Shoreditch flat and, partly for Chris's benefit, I was dressed up to the nines. I'd put on the dress I'd bought for the disastrous date with Taylor, and made a big effort with my hair and make-up. The effort turned out to be a waste of time as far as Chris was concerned, though, because he hardly even glanced my way when he turned up at ten past eight. He seemed deeply preoccupied and, partly as a result of this major slight, I made up my mind to have a bloody good time. Despite the fact that I was extremely tired, and still not fully recovered from my hangover, I'd picked up a bottle of champagne to take along for Jemima, plus two bottles of cut-price German wine as a general contribution to the party.

I was a little surprised by Edward, who actually seemed like a pretty nice bloke. A bit plum-in-his-mouth for my personal tastes, but nice-looking and really quite funny in a slightly effeminate way.

Fiona didn't even attempt to put on an act of being pleased

for her friend. In fact she spent the whole of the ten minutes I spoke to her slagging her off.

'And of course Edward is as gay as a goose, you know,' she
eventually said.

I couldn't believe what I was hearing. 'That's a terrible
thing to say,' I said.

'It's true,' she insisted. 'Jemima is just his *beard,* a cover for
his family and work colleagues. But he'll be shagging anything in trousers on the side, of course.'

It was at this point that I excused myself and moved on
elsewhere...

There were only about a dozen of us there that night. The
real engagement party would take place in Jemima's family
home eventually, and the current gathering—apart from
myself—was made up of her closest friends.

I hinted at my surprise at being invited when I got Jemima
alone for a couple of minutes and wished her good luck.

'This probably wouldn't have happened if it hadn't have
been for you,' she told me gushingly.

'How do you make that out?' I wanted to know.

'Well, if we hadn't taken you to Hampstead I'd never have
encountered that vicious parrot, and I'd never have needed
to buy some first aid equipment...which means I wouldn't
have bumped into Sara Byfleet in Boots.'

I must have looked bewildered, because she laughed and
shook her head.

'Of course! You don't know Sara, do you? She's an old
mutual friend of mine and Ed's and—well, to cut a long story
short, she called him, you know, and said we'd met, and next
thing I knew he turned up here! And we just sort of picked
up where we left off years ago.'

She looked at me as if I was some kind of magician, and

I couldn't help wondering if she'd be so fast to *blame* me if there turned out to be any truth in Fiona's spiteful claims about Edward.

It was Fiona who, clearly unable to bear this happy bon-homie at such close quarters, suggested that we all moved on to a club at around nine o'clock. It wasn't a particularly sensible idea, bearing in mind that most people had to work the next day, but everyone was having such a good time that there wasn't a dissenter amongst us. And although I knew that I would have to leave early, I was as up for the outing as everyone else.

We travelled in three mini-cabs to an undistinguished club near Fiona's place of work, where she knew the staff and would have no trouble getting us in. We were no sooner inside and ordering our drinks at the bar when Sophie nudged me.

'Don't look now,' she hissed, 'but that Wiseman wanker is at the end of the bar with some woman.'

On hearing those first three famous words I, like most people, would normally do the opposite of what I was told and look round immediately. But on this particular occasion I froze. Because I knew exactly who the 'some woman' was. We'd exchanged wary glances on the way in, as she was leaving the ladies' toilets.

'It's Amber,' I hissed back at Sophie. 'The one I told you about who works at the agency.' It had to be her with Tay-lor. It would have been just too much of a coincidence if they'd been here independently. And I'd seen the way she'd looked at him when he was talking to Jerry, and re-membered the way she'd tried putting me off him. The clues had certainly been there that she fancied him rotten herself.

'Ah,' said Sophie, 'well, she certainly looks like the cat who got the cream. And she's looking directly at you at this moment.'

'And Taylor?' I asked Sophie anxiously. 'Has *he* seen me?'

'He doesn't seem to have noticed you yet,' she said quietly now, even though there was a lot of distance between us and the end of the bar, and the music was so loud I could hardly hear her.

'Then I'm leaving before he does,' I said, and Sophie didn't try to stop me.

I wasn't in the mood for any embarrassing encounters, and, while it was tempting to take Amber aside and tell her she'd been right about him all along, I soon got over it. I knew exactly how that would have been construed, and it seemed to me that she deserved him anyway. So I made my apologies to Jemima and Ed, and got the hell out of the place.

I was back at the house before ten o'clock.

Chris was obviously surprised to see me so soon, but he still seemed fairly distracted. I'd been thinking about him on the way back, and I'd half planned to bring up the blonde in conversation, to see his reaction. But he didn't seem in the mood to talk. He didn't even seem remotely curious to know where I'd been. So I thought, Sod you, then, and allowed him to leave without even a thank you very much.

I didn't bother to make any tea, and as soon as I'd locked the door behind Chris I went up to my room. I was in bed ten minutes later, and because the previous night's lack of sleep had finally caught up with me I was out for the count not long after that. And I might well have slept soundly till morning if I hadn't been for Sir Galahad.

To begin with I thought I was dreaming. It didn't seem

possible that I could hear him shrieking from such a distance, but when I'd assured myself that I was indeed awake I knew it was happening for real.

I'd never heard him at night before, and I just knew that something was wrong. I was rigid with fear as I tried to make out any additional sounds in the house—something that might have caused the bird to behave this way, like a crazy, screeching banshee...

I don't know how long I sat there like that, bolt upright in my bed, without moving a muscle. Maybe only a minute or two, but it felt like a great deal longer. And then, just when I'd begun to believe that he'd had a nightmare and was looking for someone to comfort him, just when I'd decided to get out of bed and do just that, I heard a creak on the stairs.

At which point I panicked wildly and slipped onto the floor at the far side of my bed. Between it and the window, away from the door.

I hadn't closed the curtains before I got into bed, and the moon, though hardly more than a crescent that night, was shining brightly into the room, so that I felt as if I was under a spotlight. As a result it occurred to me that if anyone came into the room, even if they didn't see me straight away, they would guess I was there due to the unmade bed. So I took a deep breath and quickly reached up to pull the duvet over the bed in order to give the impression that it hadn't been slept in.

By now I was convinced there was burglar in the house, of the mad-axeman variety, and, horribly conscious that I was completely alone, I'm ashamed to admit that I was actually quaking with fear. So much so that when I reached up again, to grab my phone off the bedside table, I could hardly get my trembling hands around it.

Then, when I finally managed it, I realised that I didn't have Chris's number handy. He was the obvious person to call, being so close at hand. But he might as well have been in Outer Mongolia for all the use he was to me without his telephone number.

So I called up my memory facility, tapped Sophie's number in, and just prayed that she hadn't switched her mobile off for the night.

She answered the call on the third ring, thank God, and when I convinced her this wasn't a wind-up, that I couldn't possibly be more scared than I was at that very moment, she disconnected immediately. Without even telling me what she planned to do.

I didn't have a chance to worry about that, though, because just at that moment I heard the bedroom door click open and felt a presence in the room. And I nearly peed myself with fear.

My senses were unnaturally sharp at that moment, and I could hear whoever it was in the room moving about on the carpet. At which point I felt underneath the bed, wondering if there was room for me there. But it was a divan, and the base went all the way down to the floor.

And then, although my eyes were tightly closed, I just knew that someone was standing very close to me.

'I suppose this is what they call the Ostrich Syndrome,' a well-spoken male said snidely, and I opened my eyes and saw Jerome.

'If you can't see me, then I can't see you… Is that how it's supposed to work?' he added sarcastically.

I was oddly relieved to find it was only him. By now I'd conjured up the most hideous image of some kind of monster who was about to throttle me at the very least. But I did feel a bit of a fool, crouched next to the bed with him sneering at me in the moonlight.

'Or are you just looking for something down there?' he said, when I failed to respond. 'A contact lens, maybe?'

'I might be,' I answered stupidly, as I struggled to my feet. I was suddenly conscious that I was scantily clad in only an oversized T-shirt, so I covered my modesty by slipping quickly back under the duvet.

He sat down on the end of the bed and looked at me steadily.

'You've caused me a lot of trouble,' he said, and I stopped feeling quite so relieved.

'Thanks to you, I am now homeless and jobless. Not to mention a laughing-stock in international art circles.'

'*Dodgy* international art circles,' I found myself saying. 'And I don't think you can blame me for being homeless. It's not my fault that you didn't pay your bills, and as for your job—well, that had nothing to do with me at all.'

'Ah, so you know all about it,' he said, and I wished that I'd just kept my big mouth shut. 'No doubt you and your friends have had a good laugh at my expense,' he added dangerously. As if that was my fault as well.

It didn't seem sensible to antagonise him any more, so I decided to try a different tack. 'I think people have just been worried about you,' I said.

He laughed sardonically at this, and then shook his head. 'It isn't people's concern I want. That certainly won't put my life back on track.'

'But this will, I suppose?' I couldn't help myself. I couldn't bear to hear him feeling so damn sorry for himself. Not someone who'd had it so easy, who'd had it all laid on a plate since the day he was born. 'You think breaking into an old lady's home and stealing her things will sort everything out? I take it that's the reason you're here?'

'That, and to have a word in your shell-like,' he said, clearly unmoved.

'And how the hell did you get in anyway?' I wanted to know. I knew that I'd set the alarm, and even though I'd clearly slept through the warning bleep when it must have been triggered, it didn't explain how he'd managed to disable it.

'My aunt has never been very imaginative. I didn't have any trouble guessing the security code of the alarm system. If it hadn't been for the fact that I'd left a window open in that parrot's room you'd never have heard a thing.'

'African Grey,' I corrected him automatically, while I thought about this. He must have left Sirg's window off the latch while I was showing Sophie around the house. So that he could come back later for the Reynolds, no doubt. And although I'd made sure that most of the other windows were locked, I'd completely overlooked that one. Damn it. Then I thought of something else.

I realised that Sir Galahad *had* seen Jerome that day, after all. So did that mean he'd been trying to warn Mrs Audesley when he mentioned her great-nephew's name on the phone?

Or did the fact that I was even considering it as a possibility just mean I was losing the plot? Which reminded me that I hadn't heard him screeching for a while.

'You haven't hurt Sir Galahad, have you?' I said in alarm.

'What do you take me for?' Jerome said in disgust. 'He might have given me away tonight, but I happen to like the bloody animal.'

Relieved again, I suddenly realised how ridiculous this

was. Me here in the bed, him at the end of it. Just what did he hope to achieve?

'You do realise that I'll tell Mrs Audesley that you were here? I didn't the first time, and that was a big mistake. But I won't make it again. If you take anything at all from the house, she's going to know about it.'

'But she won't do anything about it,' he said with a lazy shrug. 'I'm family, and it would just be too much of a scandal for her to cope with if the police were to become involved.'

I shook my head and sighed. 'Don't you have any scruples?' I asked in despair.

'Scruples won't pay the rent, unfortunately, but the Reynolds and those miniatures certainly will.'

I thought about this for a moment, and then let out another sigh, softer this time. There didn't seem any point in pursuing the matter. I could talk till I was blue in the face and he still wouldn't change his mind. The trouble was that he actually seemed to think that it was his due, that he was entitled to take whatever he wanted from his great-aunt. And I certainly didn't feel capable of stopping him on my own.

'If you need money,' I said to him now, 'why don't you go to your parents?'

'That's none of your damn business,' he responded angrily. 'And if I'd wanted advice from someone employed to look after a parrot,' he added nastily, 'I'd have asked for it.'

'*African Grey,*' another voice corrected him before I could, and I turned round sharply towards the door of my room and saw a life-size shadow standing there.

'What the—?' began Jerome, and then things happened so quickly I only had time to register that there wasn't just one extra person in the room, but two. A lot of grunting was involved in the subsequent tussle that took place, as well as swearing. There was even the sound of the odd thrown punch, hard against flesh, and then, quite suddenly, nothing but heavy breathing.

It was then that I finally reached for my bedside light.

And there at the foot of my bed, crouched over an exhausted, prostrate Jerome, was Chris Harris. And behind him, looking like a grizzly bear who had just landed a prize salmon from the rapid torrents of some dangerous river, was Peter Parker. Minus his wig. Either it had been knocked off in the tussle, or he'd taken it off to protect it.

'What the hell are you doing here?' I said, as I pulled up the duvet again when I realised that my twisting to get at the light had left me uncovered.

'I was just passing outside the flat when Sophie got your call, and she piled me into the posh bird's car and told me to get over here fast.'

'Fast! You must have broken some kind of record...'

He looked pleased with himself and I turned my attention to Chris.

'And you?' I said. 'How did you get in on the act?'

'He knocked me up when he got here,' he explained, 'as per your friend's instructions.'

And then I looked at Jerome, who seemed pretty pathetic now, after all his big talk.

'He is okay, I suppose?'

'He's fine. But we're going to have to decide what to do with him now.'

'Let him go,' I said immediately. It went against the grain, but I knew he'd been right about Mrs A. The last thing she'd want was a scandal, and if he was arrested it would be hard to avoid one.

'What? So he can come back later and try again?'

This was Peter speaking now, and he sounded pretty indignant for someone who sailed close to the wind as far as the laws of the land were concerned.

Jerome lifted his head towards me now, and when I saw the self-satisfied smile on his face I was tempted to change my mind.

'He wouldn't dare come back again,' Chris said. 'Not if I move into the house as well and change the security code, of course.'

I looked at him briefly and felt a flutter at the thought of him being in the house with me. But then I heard Peter speak again.

'And I'll keep an eye on the place as well, if you like. Call over now and then, just in case the bastard gets any more clever ideas.'

'That's very good of you,' I said, and I felt oddly pleased with life. I was enjoying these men being protective towards me. And then Chris went and spoilt everything.

'That's not a bad idea,' he said to Peter. 'The last thing I want is Adrienne being upset when she gets back. In fact I'd be willing to pay for your time.'

'Nice one,' said Peter. And with that he moved around Chris and hauled Jerome onto his feet in one easy move.

'Time to put the rubbish out, I think,' he said, and shoved and pushed Mrs Audesley's nephew until he was gone from the room. I listened as the shoving continued on down the stairs and out through the front door, and then I let out a long sigh of relief.

'Are you okay?' Chris wanted to know, but I didn't get the chance to reply because then my mobile phone went off and I dived for it on the floor, where I'd left it.

It was Sophie, and she sounded alarmed.

'It's over,' I said. 'Thanks to you.' I told her exactly what had happened, and I thanked her from the bottom of my still thumping heart.

By the time I ended the call I was alone in the room, but I could hear muffled voices downstairs so I got out of bed and slipped on my none-too-glamorous dressing gown.

I found both Peter and Chris in Sirg's room, and to my great surprise Peter seemed to be getting along just fine with the bird. He wasn't exactly being all sweetness and light, but he wasn't being vicious either. In fact, at that very moment he was on top of his cage, advising them both to 'Shut the fuck up,' in a perfect imitation of my Manchester accent.

'He's a genius,' Peter sighed in admiration. To which Sirg took a deep bow, then looked up and squawked when he saw me.

'Well done, old feller,' I said, when he flew onto my shoulder and I ruffled the feathers at his throat.

'He seems to know that he's done good,' Chris said. 'He's been showing off something rotten.'

I looked at him and realised that I hadn't thanked him, or Peter, for coming to my rescue. Which I made up for now, and then asked them if they wanted a cup of tea.

But while Peter accepted eagerly Chris said that he'd better get back to the flat. That he had to get up early in the morning. Though he did say he'd look in some time to make sure that all was well.

I put Sirg back in his cage and walked with Chris to the door.

'Were you serious about moving into the house?' I asked him casually, and he looked surprised.

'I did say that, didn't I?' He shrugged. 'I'm not sure it will be necessary now. I think the thought of bumping into Peter will keep that oaf away from now on.'

'If you're worried about entertaining your…' I was about to say girlfriend, but it seemed odd to describe a middle-aged woman like that '…your *friends,*' I continued, turning it into a plural so that it didn't seem too overly pointed, 'you can always do that in the flat, if you're worried about us getting in each other's way.'

'Does that mean you'd like me to move in?' he said, with a sort of frown and a sort of smile.

'Maybe just for a few days. I was pretty shaken up tonight.' Which was perfectly true, as it happened.

'Okay,' he said. 'But if it's all right with you I'll bring my stuff up tomorrow. It's a bit late for moving home at this time of night.'

When I'd closed the front door I felt a bit restless and disappointed, which I put down to anti-climax. When something shocking happens, like a man appearing in your bedroom just after midnight, it helps to talk about it afterwards, and I'd have liked to talk about it to Chris. I knew I had Peter, but, as familiar as I was with him now, he still kind of gave me the creeps.

I called him into the kitchen and asked him to keep his eye on the kettle while I settled Sirg down for the night. When I'd done that, I found, somewhat to my surprise, that the tea was made and a plate of gingernut biscuits had been set out on the table. Peter was also wearing his wig again, which I found a bit disconcerting.

I asked him if he'd had any more trouble with the Social, and he told me he hadn't, that it was all cool again now, and then he changed the subject abruptly to Sophie. He spent the next ten minutes questioning me about her, and I got the impression that he was looking for some encouragement. But I couldn't do that to Sophie.

'Do you think it would help if I sent her some flowers?' Peter asked me shyly, and I really felt sorry for him. I didn't want to hurt his feelings by saying she wouldn't look at him twice. What I really needed was a foolproof way of letting him down very lightly, and through a fog of desperation came inspiration...

'I don't know if it's my place to tell you this,' I began cautiously 'but the fact is that Sophie is, erm, well...gay.'

He stared at me in disbelief for a full ten seconds, and then his face crumpled in dismay. For a moment—until his expression turned into a leer. 'You and her...do you...?'

'That's none of your business,' I told him tartly. It had occurred to me that it might be a mistake to deny being gay myself. For all I knew he might think of switching his affections to me in his disappointment, so I was happy to leave some doubt in his mind.

'What about the other one?' he asked me then.

'Which other one?'

'The one who's staying on at the flat when her friend leaves to live with her boyfriend.'

'Fiona?'

'Yeah. Is she a dyke too?'

'No,' I said, and I felt a bit wicked. I'd obviously been right about his fickle affections, and it was clear he was thinking of moving them on to Fiona now. Since I didn't have the same sense of loyalty to her I decided that she could look after herself.

He left five minutes later, with a definite spring in his step, and although I felt a tad guilty I only had to think about the way that Fiona had rubbished her friend to make me feel better.

And when I went back to bed I slept like log until my alarm went off at seven-thirty.

21

First thing the next morning, before I sorted Sir Galahad out, I did what I should have done the night before and checked that all was well in the dining room. I was relieved to find that the miniatures and the Reynolds portrait were still in position, and I wondered what Jerome was up to now. My hope was that he had moved on, and that if he had been sleeping rough locally he would have found some sucker to put him up by now. I didn't believe that he'd be down for long. People like him tended to come up smelling of roses, but just so long as he left me well alone in the future I didn't much care any more.

The phone rang when I was making my first cup of tea.

I was surprised to hear Amber's voice on the phone, until it occurred to me that she'd probably just called to gloat.

But it seemed I was wrong.

'Jerry asked me to ring and say that we have a job for you,' she said—thankfully before I could tell her what to do with herself. 'It's for an ad agency. Some new campaign they're working on.'

She sounded efficient, and without ulterior motive, and I decided that she must have got the problems she'd had with me out of her system now. Now that she'd landed Taylor herself. She gave me an address in Romford, Essex, and when I made plain my dismay at the distance I would have to travel the old Amber reared her ugly head.

'Do you want the job or don't you?' she snapped, and I sighed and said that I did.

I asked for a contact telephone number but she said that she didn't have one.

'Just be there at three-thirty,' she said, 'and do try not to be late.'

I was worried when I put the phone down. Chris had said he was going out early, and for all I knew he might not be back for the rest of the day. In which case I would have to cancel the appointment and, because I didn't have a number, I would have to do it through Amber. That wasn't something I looked forward to.

I went down to Chris's flat and slipped a note through his letterbox. I said what was happening, but that if I didn't hear from him by twelve o'clock midday I would go ahead and cancel.

Then, as I was walking up the steps away from his flat, I looked up and saw Mary Deacon.

It was a morning of the unexpected.

'What are you doing here?' I asked, and realised it probably sounded rude.

'I've come to see Chris,' she said, when I drew level with her. 'To try and persuade him to do a pilot at least.'

'Well, he's not in, I'm afraid.'

I looked at her closely and could see no signs of distress. She was obviously well over Taylor, and I couldn't help admiring her recovery facilities. I wondered if she knew about Amber yet, and if she'd even give a damn if she did.

'Bugger,' she said, and then she looked at me speculatively. 'Do you think you could change his mind?'

I laughed at this. 'I doubt that I have any influence on Chris whatsoever, and he sounded pretty adamant to me when I brought up the subject. He said that he wasn't one for the limelight.'

'Which is another reason I want him so badly,' Mary said. 'It would make such a nice change to have a reluctant celeb. Fame might not go to his head so quickly.'

I imagined she was talking about Taylor now, to whose head fame had gone *very* quickly. But I still wasn't hopeful about persuading Chris, even though the incentive for me might be a really good job.

'I'll give it a go, if you like.' I shrugged.

'Good girl,' she said. 'And make it quick, if you can, otherwise I'm going to have to look elsewhere.'

And, like a hotshot TV producer in a hurry, she turned on her high heels and departed.

I spoke to my mother later that morning, and she didn't mention my father once. When I did, she sounded annoyed and said something that knocked me for six.

'He's moved the elderly frump into the family home,' she said. 'But if you think I'm upset about it then you are mistaken. I've had it with him completely now, and I can't bloody wait to leave the country.'

Then she said that she was ever so sorry but that she'd have to go. Melanie and she were off on a shopping ex-

pedition for the trip. She sounded so pleased about it that
I felt a little forlorn, like a child whose parents had better things going on in their lives than their only daughter. Stella only cared about India, and my dad seemed to
have forgotten I even existed.

At two minutes past twelve, just as I was about to call
Amber and tell her to cancel the appointment for me, the
doorbell rang.

It was Chris, just back, with my message still in his hand.

'Not too late, I hope?' he said.

'The nick of time,' I replied with a smile, more glad than
I could ever have imagined to see his sunny smile.

When I asked him about getting to Romford for half past
three, he suggested I took his van again, and even helped me
plan out a route. We decided I should probably allow an hour
and a half, what with the traffic and everything, and when
he came back up to the house at two o'clock I was glad to
see that he'd brought some overnight things with him.

'That TV producer woman came round to see you,' I said,
just as I was about to leave. 'She said that she'd like you to
consider doing a single pilot show,' I added nonchalantly. 'Just
to see how things go.'

'Some people have a hard time taking no for an answer,'
he said with a frown.

'Does that mean your friend hasn't managed to persuade
you?' I said.

He looked at me vaguely. 'Which friend?'

I'd said it now, so I had to go on. 'The one whose idea it
was in the first place. She was at the flat when I called round
yesterday.'

'Oh, Helen?'

So that was her name.

'No,' he said. 'She was hell-bent on trying to change my mind, but she didn't succeed and Ms Deacon won't either. It's just not for me, I'm afraid.'

I was quite pleased that his girlfriend didn't have quite as much influence as I'd imagined, and kind of impressed that he was sticking to his guns. I'd liked to have stuck around and discussed the matter, but I had to leave or there was serious danger of being late for my appointment.

'I'll cook tonight, if you like,' he called out when I reached the gate. 'You don't have any major dislikes, I hope?'

'Nothing apart from champagne,' I said back, with my tongue in my cheek, and then I was off once more, in the van that smelt strongly of compost.

I got back to the house just before seven, after a torturous journey in rush hour traffic. And what got me most was the fact that it was too late to call Amber and tell the bitch exactly what I thought of her.

But since I had to tell someone, and Chris happened to be handy, it was he who had to listen to the whole sorry tale of how I'd fallen for her nasty, mean-minded hoax.

'You mean she made the whole thing up?' he said across the kitchen table, when I'd been ranting at him for a good five minutes. 'But why the hell would she do something like that?'

'To make me look a fool, of course.' He'd poured some red wine for me, but I'd been too busy raving to touch it yet. 'And she certainly succeeded. I mean, how stupid must I be not to have checked that the company she sent me to even existed?'

'Why would you check, though?' Chris said reasonably. 'If someone called me and gave me an address I wouldn't doubt it either.'

Which made me feel marginally better.

'But why did she want to make you look a fool?' he asked me then, and I forgot to put my guard up before responding.

'Because of Taylor bloody Wiseman, I imagine.' I said. 'She fancied him, and when she thought I'd got in before she did she wasn't best pleased with me.'

There was a short pregnant silence, then, 'And did you *get in* before she did?'

I found myself cringing. I hadn't meant to blurt it all out like that—not after the warning he'd given me about the man. 'Not exactly,' I said sheepishly. 'I went out for a celebratory meal with him, that's all. And then I found out about Mary Deacon and that was that.'

Chris looked a bit sceptical at this reply, and I knew for certain that he knew the full story and all its gory details. I let out a long heavy sigh and felt spectacularly sorry for myself.

'I don't give a damn about him, though.' Which was perfectly true. 'What matters to me is getting some work, and I'm not going to get any through that agency now.'

'There are other agencies,' Chris said, 'and you could always work for me in the meantime.'

He'd said it so casually that I thought I must be hearing things.

'I need someone to take pictures for the book I've just finished,' he went on, though, 'and although the publishing house have suggested a couple of photographers, I don't see why you couldn't do it.'

It wasn't the most graciously put offer I'd ever had, but it was certainly one of the best. I knocked back a slug of wine, screwed up my face at its vinegary taste, and then looked at him closely.

'Are you serious?' I said. 'Mary said something about me working with you if you agreed to do the TV thing, but—'

'Then that's another good reason for turning her down,' he interrupted. 'I don't want people controlling me. I like to make my own decisions. And, yes, of course I mean it—so long as you don't get any fancy artistic ideas. I want to keep it as simple as possible.'

I thought about this for a moment, then, 'I can do simple,' I said.

And he finally smiled. And I smiled as well. Then we had a great dinner of ready-made chicken and mushroom pie and chips, washed down by cheap wine, and I felt happier than I had in ages.

We ended up playing *Monopoly,* which I found in a drawer in the living room. I had the dog for my marker and he had the racing car, and he bought Mayfair and Park Lane and lots of hotels and I ended stony broke. But then Sirg came to my aid by stealing the hotels and Chris's car, so we called it a draw. Which seemed only fair.

I slept well that night, secure in the comforting knowledge that Chris was just along the hall in the bedroom right next to mine.

22

'So you don't think he's so bad after all now,' Sophie said.

We were having coffee in a nearby branch of Starbucks. It was Saturday morning, so she wasn't working, and for the past half an hour she'd listened to me banging on about my parents. I got the impression she was glad when I changed the subject to Chris.

She had a knowing twinkle in her eye when she spoke, and I felt strangely like a kid caught with my hand in the biscuit barrel.

'I'm not saying that I fancy him or anything,' I protested as I scooped chocolate powder off my second frothy cappuccino. 'I don't get the same sort of tingle I got around Taylor. I've just changed my opinion about him, that's all.'

'What, now that he's offered you a job?'

'It's not just that,' I said, but when I looked at her she was smiling.

'He's really, well…nice. And I feel sort of comfortable when he's around. That's all.'

'And you don't mind in the least he's involved with a woman who's possibly old enough to be his mother?'

'Why should I?' I said with a weak shrug. 'He's entitled to see who he likes.'

'For some reason,' Sophie said as she stirred her black coffee, 'that doesn't ring entirely true. Have you spoken to him about…what did you say her name was?'

'Helen. And, no, I haven't, and, yes, you're probably right,' I finally confessed. 'For some unfathomable reason I do feel a bit jealous of her.'

There, it was out, and I felt a bit better for it. It had been coming on for a while now, this feeling I had for Chris. It wasn't at all lustful, like the feeling I'd had for Taylor, and I didn't really know what to make of it. I tried to explain this to Sophie, and to my surprise she nodded sagely.

'I think those lustful thoughts you're talking about can be quite misleading. They can make you go after all the wrong people, and I know what I'm talking about.'

'Yes, maybe,' I said. 'But they are important, surely? And I don't feel them at all for Chris. All I know for certain is that I'm jealous.'

'So what are you going to do about it?' Sophie wanted to know.

'What *can* I do?' I said miserably. 'Challenge the woman to a duel? Sharpened fingernails at dawn…' I shook my head and spooned off more froth. 'I'll just have to content myself with being friends with him now.'

'You don't even know for sure that they're an actual item,' Sophie said, ignoring my self-pity.

I was sure enough though. And look what happened last time I ignored the evidence...

'You said you had something to tell me,' I said, changing the subject. She'd said so when she rang to arrange to meet me, but I'd forgotten about it till now.

'Two things,' she said with a nod of her head. She was looking especially good today, in a tight-fitting top and with her hair casually ruffled up, and I'd noticed the glances that she was getting. 'The first is about Fiona,' she said with a smile, and leaned closer to me over the table. 'You're never going to believe this, but Peter Parker came round last night and asked her to the Karaoke night at the Peeler.'

I put my hand to my face to cover my open-mouthed shock. I hadn't expected him to go ahead with it. Not really. Not when he'd thought about it. Not once he'd realised he was hardly her type. And then I had a very worrying thought.

'Oh, God,' I said. 'I hope she didn't insult him too much and he's given you notice.'

'On the contrary,' Sophie said with a wide grin. 'She's only agreed to go with him.'

I shook my head in amazement. 'Don't tell me she actually fancies him?'

'Of course she doesn't, but she thinks it might be a laugh to hang out with "common people", as she so quaintly puts it. At least that's what she says. But I think it's more about trying to prove something to Jemima. You know—that she can have a fun and interesting time without her.'

'Well, let's just hope it doesn't backfire,' I said, feeling guilty for my part in it all.

'She'll be fine,' Sophie said, with more confidence than I felt. 'I think that Peter's a decent bloke at heart. What surprises me most is why he asked her.'

And so I told her about our conversation, and how he now thought we were both gay.

'It might not even be such a bad idea,' she said at last, when she'd stopped laughing. 'I mean, I haven't exactly got a great track record with men.'

'Who has?' I said, and we both let out a long troubled sigh.

'Talking of sexual preference,' I said after a moment, 'do you think there's anything in Fiona's snide little comments about Edward?'

'I wouldn't be surprised, if I'm honest. But I'm not sure that Jemima gives a damn. So long as she gets the nice flat in town and weekends in the country, I think that will do her nicely.'

'How sad,' I said, and we sighed again.

'What was the other thing you wanted to tell me?' I said, when we'd been silent for a while.

'I've been offered a job in New York, and I'm seriously thinking of taking it.'

'New York!' I was completely dumbfounded. Two minutes ago I'd been looking forward to moving in with her at the Shoreditch flat, and now this... 'You're kidding, right?'

She looked completely serious when she shook her head. 'Things haven't exactly worked out well for me here in London, and I think a new start is probably just what I need.'

I wanted to argue with her, but all the reasons that came into my mind were purely selfish. 'When do they want you to go?'

'Soon. Next month, if I can sort everything out by then.'

'It sounds exciting,' I managed—only I don't think I sounded all that convincing.

'I know. And it's a great career move and everything else, but...'

'But what?' I snatched hopefully.

'But nothing. And that's what I find a bit sad. Apart from you, and a couple of friends at work, and maybe Felix's Place, I'm not going to miss anything here. And I can go home to Manchester from New York almost as quickly as it takes on the train from London.'

It was a bit of an exaggeration, but I knew what she meant.

'It sounds pretty much like your mind is already made up.'

'I think it is,' she said as she looked at me over the table. 'But it will mean replacing me in the flat, of course.'

'Well, the upside is that you won't have to pretend to be a lesbian for Peter's sake,' I said with an attempt at a smile, 'plus I get a choice of two rooms now.'

We left the coffee house soon after that, and on the spur of the moment Sophie decided to go up to Manchester as soon as she could get on a train, in order to break the news to her parents in person.

Convinced that things couldn't possibly get any worse, I trudged miserably back to the house, to find Chris in a flap about Sir Galahad.

'Look at his chest,' he said, when I found them together in Sirg's room.

I did, and I was stunned. The day before he'd looked perfectly normal, but now there was a bald patch there the size of a fifty pence piece.

'My God!' I said. 'What's happened?'

'Anxiety,' Chris pronounced gloomily. 'I think the break-in upset him rather more than it seemed to at the time. That's what they do when they're stressed. I'm afraid that we're going to have to tell Adrienne.'

'About Jerome?'

'I think she'll guess that something pretty major has happened. But, either way, she needs to know what condition the old feller is in.'

'Can't we just call the vet?' I said, feeling a lousy failure.

'I've already done that, but she'll never forgive us if we don't let her know.'

As we were talking, Sir Galahad was looking down at us from the top of the cage, as if he understood every word we said.

'What do you think, Sirg?' I asked him then, and by way of an answer he started plucking again, and spitting the feathers all over us, as if he was showering us in his own novel version of confetti.

'Go ahead, then,' I said with a sigh. 'Only try not to worry her too much. I'm sure he'll be fine,' I added, though I didn't feel remotely sure at all.

He made the call in the other room, while I tried offering comfort to Sirg, assuring him that everything was going to be all right. And then, because it was almost one o'clock, I put the radio on, and he stopped plucking his feathers and listened attentively.

I joined Chris just as he was finishing the call.

'She's going to book a flight straight away,' he said.

'Did she sound okay?' I asked anxiously.

'Considering. In fact, in some strange way I suspect she was pleased. I think she thinks it means that he's missing her, and I get the impression she's not having such a great time anyway. She's very a independent woman, and I don't think she likes fitting into other people's routines—not even her son's.'

I was slightly relieved to hear this. 'Did you mention Jerome?' I asked him then.

'No. I think it's probably best if we leave that until she gets back.'

Being an 'emotional problem', as the vet referred to the feather plucking, there wasn't very much he could do. He gave us some conditioning drops to add to Sir Galahad's water, charged an enormous fee for his trouble, and left within five minutes.

And then Chris had to go out for a while, and I was left to brood on my own. About Sirg, and Mrs A coming back. About Sophie leaving, and my parents splitting up. About Chris and Helen…

Until the doorbell rang again and I opened the door to a young woman with a very small nose and strange pale grey eyes.

'Alina!' she reminded me brightly, and I shook my head and said I was sorry.

'I was miles away,' I said, as I let her in. 'But then I thought you were as well—in Scotland, wasn't it?'

'Yes, but that was two weeks ago now. I told your friend to say I'd be back this weekend.'

'She did,' I said as she followed me to the kitchen. 'I just didn't realise that it *was* two weeks.' I put the kettle on automatically. 'How did it go?' I asked her then.

'It was wonderful,' she said with a gush of feeling. 'I had the best time of my life, and the really brilliant thing is that I've been asked to stay on. They want to develop my character.'

'That is brilliant,' I told her cheerfully, though I had to force it. Nice as she was, I wasn't really in the mood to share joyful news with someone I hardly knew.

'I was hoping to see Chris,' she said then, and I remembered that they were acquainted.

'He's gone out for the afternoon,' I told her. 'Some job or other that couldn't wait.'

'I heard that he's been offered a TV show,' she said, sitting down at the table.

'Yes,' I answered vaguely as I waved a teabag at her, to which she nodded. And then something struck me. 'How did you know?'

'My mother told me. She also told me that the crazy man has turned it down.'

'But how did your mother know about it?' I pressed her as I added the teabags to a couple of mugs.

'She's the one who set it all up.'

Now she really had my attention. 'Is your mother's name Helen, by any chance?'

Alina nodded. 'I met him first, and then Chris designed a new garden for her and they became really good friends.' She laughed indulgently then. 'I think she quite fancied him herself, but I told her to behave. She's already made a fool of herself with one younger man recently, and fancying your daughter's boyfriend is pretty naff.'

I stopped what I was doing now and looked at her. At her wood-creature face. And it all suddenly began to make more sense. '*You're* Chris's girlfriend?'

She let out a noisy sigh. 'It's a bit complicated,' she said uncomfortably. 'And that's why I came round to see him.'

I made the tea quickly, put it down on the table, and realised as I looked at Alina that I'd already transferred my jealous feelings over to her. But then, like the masochist I can be at times, I needed to know more details. 'Do you want to talk about it?' I offered.

She put her small hand around the mug, and sighed again. 'We started seeing each other a couple of months ago and, well, maybe I went a bit over the top and scared him a bit.'

'What makes you think that?' I asked, perhaps a little too eagerly.

'Because he said no when I suggested moving in with him. And don't get me wrong, he was nice about it, but it didn't stop me from being upset.'

'I can imagine,' I said truthfully. 'So, erm, what happened then?'

She looked slightly embarrassed now and made a face. 'I think I made an idiot of myself. I certainly made the most terrible fuss, but then the next day I heard about the acting job. I came round to tell him the night before I left but he wasn't in.' She shrugged. 'Or maybe he just didn't answer the door because he knew it was me.'

I remembered what Chris had said about that particular evening. That he'd been busy working and was *not at home* to callers. 'And have you spoken to him since then?' I asked.

'No. I was so mad with him I didn't ring. He knew where I was, though, because my mum came round to see him a couple of times while I was away. She finds him a very good listener and she's had her own problems recently.'

I didn't admit that I knew all about her mother's problems. Besides, I was much more interested in Alina's problems with Chris. 'But you're not mad with him any longer?' I said.

'Not now,' she said, and her face broke into a beautiful smile. 'I just want to get everything sorted out with him.' She glanced at her watch. 'You know, clear up any misunder-standings.'

Despite feeling hopeful for a while, I'd sort of known all along, I supposed. She meant that she wanted to patch things up, and I had a good idea that she wouldn't find that too difficult. He'd been so grumpy a couple of weeks ago, especially just after she left for Scotland. At the time I'd thought it was all about me, that he just didn't like me, but now I could see how self-centred I'd been. It hadn't been about *me* at all. In all probability he'd been so distracted by their falling out that he'd hardly noticed my existence.

It also explained why he'd been on such good form for the past few days. Because he'd known from her mother that Alina was coming back.

She sipped at her tea to test its temperature, and when she found that it wasn't too hot she knocked the contents back in one, in a very unwood-creature fashion.

'Thanks for the tea,' she said, 'but I'd better go. I've got an idea where he might be, and if I leave now I should catch him there.'

'Well, good luck,' I said, through near gritted teeth as I showed her to the door.

'Cheers,' she replied, with that almost blindingly radiant smile, and then, as I was watching her graceful departure down the steps, she stopped and looked back. 'We should try and get together again before I head back to Scotland. I'd really like to hear how you're getting along.'

'Phone me,' I said. And, much as I wanted to, I found it very hard to hate her.

23

Mrs Audesley arrived home in a taxi at two-fifteen the following day, and I had never seen a reunion quite like the one I witnessed between her and Sir Galahad. She didn't even bother speaking to me as she rushed on through to Sirg's room, and although I followed her in I quickly departed again, because it felt as if I were intruding on something very intimate.

I must admit I was happy for her, despite my worries about facing the music when the reunion was over. Along with everything else, I'd been dreading a lacklustre welcome from the bird. He'd been in my care for two weeks now, and never shown any obvious signs of missing his 'mummy', as Mrs A called herself when they exchanged tender words. But now he was behaving as if he'd been pining every minute of every hour of their separation. And, while I felt privileged that he loved me a bit, I was glad that he still loved her more.

I moved on to the kitchen to make a cafetière of Mrs Audesley's favourite coffee blend, which I hoped would soften her up a little when we hit her with the news about Jerome. When I say *we,* I meant Chris and me, because he'd promised to be there to back me up. Which was why I picked up the kitchen phone then, and called his flat.

I hadn't seen him since he left the house the day before. He'd arrived back after I went to bed and left again before I got up. I'd heard him tap lightly on my door around midnight, when he came in, but since I didn't want to see him all happy and cheerful, now that things were back on with Alina, I pretended that I was fast asleep. I got up when I heard him leave, and found a note on the kitchen table telling me he would be spending the day drawing up garden plans for a new client. He'd added a PS, saying he'd like to start work on the photographs for the book next week if that was okay with me.

Business as usual, in other words, but I'd been wondering since if I could bear to work with him now. I knew it was crazy to even consider missing out on such a great opportunity, but I honestly didn't know if I could cope with listening to him talking to me about Alina. It had been bad enough when I'd thought he was seeing her mother, but this seemed much, much worse.

Which was completely mad, because I didn't even fancy him in the usual sense. And it was all very well Sophie saying that lust could be misleading, but it seemed pretty important to me. I was confused, well and truly, and it didn't help when he turned up a few minutes after I'd called him, all happy and smiley.

We didn't say very much as we waited from Mrs A to join us in the kitchen, except to agree that he would do most of the talking. Which suited me fine.

He took quite a while to tell her the whole story, and I mean the *whole* story—including the snatch of the miniatures, their recovery, and Jerome's most recent attempt to make good his previous failure. And she sat throughout sipping her coffee, not interrupting once.

I was sitting opposite her, and I noticed a slight tug at the corner of her lips on occasions, as if she was about to smile, but I thought that I must have been imagining it. That maybe it was more of a sneer, in actual fact. Until Chris's tale came to an end, and her face broke into a wide grin.

Then she started guffawing, and I glanced at Chris worriedly, thinking for a moment that this was some kind of hysterical response, that really she was having a breakdown.

But he seemed completely unperturbed.

'So you see, Adrienne, you couldn't really have left your house in better hands,' he said, and as he said it he reached for one of my hands, which had been resting limply on my lap.

He brought it up on to the table and held it in his, and I was aware of a tingly feeling that ran up my arm and ended up deep in my body. It was like a mild electric shock, and when I glanced at him I was embarrassed to see that his eyes had narrowed in what looked like a knowing smile. As if he knew exactly the effect he was having on me.

'I couldn't agree more,' Mrs A said, smiling warmly at me now. 'But then Sir Galahad has always been a good judge of character.'

'So you're not mad with me?' I said in amazement.

'On the contrary, I think you've done an excellent job. And changing the miniatures for Bath Oliver biscuits was an absolute masterstroke.'

She started laughing again, and I shook my head in bewilderment.

'But I thought you were going to tell me what an idiot I'd been. And what about Sir Galahad?' I said then. 'He wouldn't be in the state he is if I'd looked after him properly.'

'You seem determined to punish yourself,' Mrs Audesley replied, 'but I'm afraid I shall have to disappoint you. He's perfectly fine, and now that I'm back he'll desist with that silly nonsense of his.'

She sounded so confident that I let out a sigh of relief. 'But what about having to cut short your holiday?' I said, still not entirely convinced I was really forgiven.

Mrs A and Chris exchanged a glance, and then she looked at me more seriously now.

'To be perfectly frank, my dear Tao, I'm delighted to have cut short my holiday. My son has been trying to persuade me to move out to Portugal permanently, and I was beginning to cave in under so much pressure. Now that I'm back, though, I feel quite my old self and have no intentions of accepting his very kindly meant offer. And now,' she said, standing up stiffly, 'I feel rather tired after my journey, so I think I shall take a short nap.'

I wanted to ask if I should pack my bags and leave straight away, but then I noticed that Chris was still holding my hand and I got the tingle again.

When she left the kitchen, I forced myself to look at him. 'You can let go now,' I said, in a jolly voice that sounded false even to me. 'It could be misinterpreted.'

'Who by?'

'Alina, of course.'

'Why should she mind?' he said with a frown, and I of course felt like a fool. It had obviously just been a friendly, supportive gesture on his part, and here I was trying to make something of it.

I tugged my hand away from his and got up from the table.

'Do you think I should leave while Mrs A's taking her nap?' I said, anxious to change the subject.

'Why would you want to do that?' he said.

'Because I'm not needed now that she's back.'

'Well, I'm sure she'd be horrified if you left without saying something first,' he said, and he sounded annoyed with me.

'I don't want to be rude,' I protested. 'I just feel in the way, and a bit awkward about being here when she wakes up.'

'Well, it's up to you, I suppose,' he said with a shrug. 'But do you have anywhere to go?'

'I'll go back to the flat in Shoreditch.'

He got from the table as well now, still a bit moody with me, I thought, as he headed for the back door.

'You'd better lock up after I leave,' he said coolly. 'I wouldn't want Adrienne asleep in the house with the door unlocked.'

I turned away and listened for the sound of the door closing behind him, but it was his voice that I heard instead.

'How are you going to get over to Shoreditch?'

I shrugged as I turned back to him. 'By taxi, I suppose.'

'If you'll give me half an hour, I could take you over there myself, if you'd like.'

I hesitated, not sure if this was such a good idea. But then again it was a very kind offer and it might only seem churlish to refuse...

'Thanks,' I said. 'I'd appreciate that.'

I spent the next half-hour packing my things, stripping my bed of its sheets for the washing machine, writing an explanatory note to Mrs A, and saying goodbye to Sirg.

And that was the really hard bit, because he seemed to know what was going on and became all clingy and sad.

'Shut the fuck up,' he said softly into my ear, as if to re-mind me of the good times. As if he was trying to tell me how much he was going to miss me.

'Shut the fuck up yourself,' I whispered back, and then I put him back on his cage and left him without looking back.

I was on the doorstep with my things when Chris came out of his flat with the keys to his van. Neither of us spoke a single word until we pulled up outside what was to be my home for the foreseeable future. It was late Sunday afternoon now, and the street was covered in debris from the market. It all seemed so shabby after beautiful Hampstead.

And then, just as he was opening the door to get out, Chris finally spoke.

'What did you mean about Alina?' he said, with a frown.

I didn't really want to go into this, but I couldn't just ig-nore the question.

'I meant that now that the two of you have patched up your quarrel.'

He didn't answer for a moment, he just looked sort of puz-zled. And then the frown lifted suddenly. 'You think that we're back together? Is that it?'

'Of course. I saw her yesterday and—'

'Well, you couldn't have got it more wrong!' he inter-rupted. 'She came over to tell me personally that she's met someone else. I already knew anyway, from her mother, but I think she just wanted to clear the air.'

I felt my spirits lift a little, but I was still confused. 'You don't seem very sorry,' I said, 'but you did when she went away. I assumed that was why you were so offhand with me.'

He laughed. 'I was *offhand* with you because I thought you were a stuck-up little madam,' he said. 'Looking down your nose at me because I had dirt on my jeans.'

'But it wasn't like that,' I began to protest, and then I realised it had been almost exactly like that—though there were extenuating circumstances. 'I thought you were a weirdo,' I said. 'I wasn't used to people being friendly in London.'

He laughed again, and I noticed how nice his eyes were. I remembered that tingle I'd got in my arm, and I got it again now just looking at him.

'And you're not troubled about Alina?' I said.

'Far from it. There was never anything much between us as far as I was concerned. And I'm sorry if that sounds arrogant, but—'

'She told me she'd suggested moving in with you,' I butted in.

'That's when I knew it had to come to an end. And the great thing is that she sees how right I was now.'

I wasn't sure what to say. I couldn't believe how much I'd got wrong about him. Practically everything, in fact.

'Is there anything else we need to clear up?' he wanted to know.

'I can't think of anything,' I said.

He looked at me quizzically for a moment.

'What?' I said uncomfortably.

'I was just wondering what you'd do if I kissed you.'

Although I could feel my cheeks burn, I was definitely feeling bolder now. 'Well there's only one way to find out,' I said.

I'm not sure how long it lasted. It was one of those time-standing-still moments. But I do know that I thought of Taylor briefly while it was going on. But only by way of comparison. Only to note that compared to Chris he had been a mere amateur in the kissing department. And as for the knock-on effect on my body, well, that was in a different league altogether.

24

One Month Later

It was a cold mid-November night, but it was baking hot inside Felix's Place, where we were gathered for Sophie's surprise farewell party. It was Jemima and Edward's job to get her there, under the pretext of a quiet something to eat in her favourite café before she left.

Luckily the windows were drenched in the usual condensation, so she wouldn't be able to see us inside as she passed by to the door. To make absolutely sure that she couldn't, Felix had switched off the harsh overhead strip lighting and put candles on the counter and tables. It looked quite swishy by candlelight, a bit French bistro in style, but strictly no French food was to be on the menu.

There were a lot of her friends from work, plus Chris and me, and Fiona and Peter, but they weren't actually together. It turned out that he'd dumped her on the first night because—as he told me quietly later—her stupid posh accent and her constant giggling had done his head in. I don't think she realised that she had been dumped, because I'm pretty certain she never thought for a moment that it was an actual date he'd taken her on. In fact I think she'd have been horrified if she had known.

Peter's mother was there as well, although I don't think anyone had invited her. As soon as I saw her she told me again what a wonderful man that Taylor was. She was deeply upset to hear that his current series was to be his last on this side of the Atlantic and that he'd headed home to the States to do some TV work there.

I'd heard this from Mary, who'd found another young gardener now, a female one, and was in the process of filming a series with her.

I had no idea what had become of Amber, and I couldn't care less. I'd signed on with a different agency now, and the work was coming in steadily. All sorts of work, but strangely nothing whatever to do with food. And what with that, and the job that I'd done for Chris, I was hopeful that I would eventually be able to make my way as a fully-fledged professional *general* photographer.

Stella was doing her long overdue thing in India now, and if her postcards were anything to go by then, she was having a whale of a time. As for my dad—well, I don't think she'll be going back to him. I haven't met his new woman as yet. I'm putting that off as long as possible, because it feels sort of disloyal to Stella, and besides, I'm still pretty mad with him. He finally got round to calling me. He told me he still loved Stella but the truth was he was happier with someone who was a bit more down to earth and ordinary. And I couldn't really blame him for that. Not when I thought about it. Not when I knew Stella was happier too.

Everything was fine with Adrienne, as I called her these days, although she wasn't too pleased at first with some of the additions to Sir Galahad's repertoire... As far as I know she hasn't been bothered by Jerome lately. She did track him down, I understand, and told him that if he ever tried to pull another stunt she wouldn't hesitate to contact the police in future. She also sent him a pretty large cheque, according to Chris, which he used to take himself off to South Africa. Why there, I don't know, but I'm glad it's a very long way away, and just as long as he leaves his great-aunt alone I couldn't give a fig what happens to him.

Rightly or wrongly, I blame him for Sophie leaving, and I'll never forgive him for that.

And then, just as I was thinking about her, the door of the café opened and we all went quiet.

'Surprise!' thirty or so voices bellowed as she walked in, just behind Edward, and we all laughed when her mouth gaped in shock.

Then Felix put on some Eighties music—which was as grim as it had been when most of us were growing up with it—and champagne corks popped and the party began in earnest.

Though I stuck to wine, I got as drunk as Sophie did, despite all the delicious stomach-lining pies that Felix and Angie had prepared, and by the end of the evening I was crying with her.

'I'm going to really miss you,' I blubbed all over her as we sat at our favourite table next to the window.

'Me too,' she blubbed back. 'But at least you've got a decent bloke now, so I don't feel too bad leaving you.'

'And I'll come over and see you soon,' I promised passionately.

'You'd better,' she said.

'And watch out for Taylor Wiseman,' I warned her. 'Now that he's back in New York.'

'It's a big city,' she said, and that for some reason made us blub again.

Eventually, someone who wasn't as drunk as we were reminded Sophie that she had to leave first thing in the morning, so she hugged everyone, promised to keep in touch with them all, and after hugging me longest and hardest—which earned us a leering wink from Peter—she finally left with Fiona.

When everyone else left, I stayed on with Chris for a while to help Felix and Angie clear up for the morning.

And later, because Chris was staying over with me, we walked back to the flat together. At least he walked, while I wobbled drunkenly on my high heels.

'How's Sirg?' I slurred, because I hadn't seen him for ages and I was feeling fondly for my old friend in my heightened emotional state.

'He's great,' Chris said, and squeezed my hand. 'The feathers have just about grown back on his chest now.' And then he stopped suddenly and turned to face me.

'You could see him more often if you moved in with me,' he said.

I chortled at this. 'You're only saying that because I'm drunk and you think I'll forget by tomorrow.'

'Then I'll ask you again when you're sober.'

'What about Fiona?' I said with a frown, the idea that he might be serious registering now. 'I can't leave her on her own.'

'I've already spoken to her,' Chris announced. 'She's got several possible replacements lined up for you and Sophie already.'

'You've got it all worked out between you, then,' I said, beginning to sober up rapidly. 'But what if it doesn't work out?' I was thinking of Mal and our little Manchester starter home.

At which point Chris kissed me, and suddenly I didn't give a damn about the far distant future. All that mattered right now was that my toes were curling and jolts of something very high voltage were going off all over my body. And, don't get me wrong, I think Shoreditch is great, but the thought of switching it for Hampstead helped to clinch the matter nicely for me.

'When shall I move my stuff in?' I said, when he let me go.

'How does tomorrow sound?'

I thought about this for a moment, and decided it sounded pretty good.

On sale in April from Red Dress Ink

The Matzo Ball Heiress

by Laurie Gwen Shapiro

Q. How does Heather Greenblotz, the thirty-one-year-old millionaire heiress to the world's leading matzo company, celebrate Passover?

A. Alone. In her Manhattan apartment. With an extremely unkosher ham and cheese on whole wheat.

But this year is going to be different. The Food Network has asked to film the famous Greenblotz Matzo family's seder, and the publicity op is too good to, ahem, pass over. But the Greenblotz's aren't your average family, and an unexpected walk-on from Heather's bisexual father, his lover and her estranged mother proves just that. This is sure to be a family affair you will never forget.

RED DRESS INK

™

Visit us at www.reddressink.com

RDI04041TR

On sale in April from Red Dress Ink

My Fake Wedding

by Mina Ford

Katie's given up on love…
so she'll make the perfect bride.

When Katie's gay best friend suggests that she
marry his Aussie lover so that he can stay in the
country, she agrees. After all, things are looking
a little bleak for her on the love front. But just
as she starts trying on white dresses, romance
comes from the unlikeliest source. Will Katie
let the man she loves ruin her wedding day?

Visit us at www.reddressink.com

RDI04042TR

Also on sale in April

Inappropriate Men

by Stacey Ballis

Newly separated from her husband, Sidney Stein
dives into the dating pool. And after more than
a dozen dates, a disastrous transitional guy
and reconnecting with a high school crush,
she can't help but wonder if it might not just
be easier to let herself drown.

Experience the love, joy and heartbreak
of Sidney Stein in Stacey Ballis's debut
novel. Neither pat nor predictable,
Inappropriate Men is laugh-out-loud funny
without compromising intelligence.

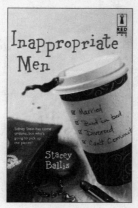

**RED
DRESS
INK**
™

Visit us at www.reddressink.com   RDI04043TR

Also available from Kelly Harte

Guilty Feet

Life is so much easier when you
are in someone else's shoes!

Evaluating her current situation, Jo decides she
is not so happy. Her solution? Be someone else
for a while—just until she figures things out.
So thanks to the wonders of technology and
the anonymity of e-mail, she does just that:
reinvents herself and strikes up a virtual
friendship with Dan, her ex. And if that isn't
confusing enough, Jo also has to deal with a
scheming neighbor, a disapproving mother and
a gorgeous Italian waiter. Without a doubt this
novel will keep you on your toes!

RED
DRESS
INK
TM

Visit us at www.reddressink.com

Are you getting it at least twice a month?

Here's how: Try RED DRESS INK books on for size & receive two FREE gifts!

Here's what you'll get:

Engaging Men *by Lynda Curnyn*

Angie DiFranco is on the age-old quest to get her man to pop the question. But she's about to discover the truth behind the old adage: be careful what you wish for....

Cosmopolitan Virtual Makeover CD

Yours free! With a retail value of $29.99, this interactive CD lets you explore a whole new you, using a variety of hairstyles and makeup to create new looks.

YES! Send my FREE book and FREE Makeover CD.

There's no risk and no purchase required—ever!

Please send me my FREE book and gift and bill me just 99¢ for shipping and handling. I may keep the books and CD and return the shipping statement marked "cancel." If I do not cancel, about a month later I will receive 2 additional books at the low price of just $11.00 each in the U.S. or $13.56 each in Canada, a savings of over 15% off the cover price (plus 50¢ shipping and handling per book*). I understand that accepting the free book and CD places me under no obligation ever to buy any books. I can always return a shipment and cancel at any time. Even if I never buy another book from Red Dress Ink, the free book and CD are mine to keep forever.

160 HDN DU9D   360 HDN DU9E

Name (PLEASE PRINT)

Address   Apt. #

City   State/Prov.   Zip/Postal Code

In the U.S. mail to:
3010 Walden Ave., P.O. Box 1867, Buffalo, NY 14240-1867
In Canada mail to:
P.O. Box 609, Fort Erie, ON L2A 5X3

RED DRESS INK

Order online at www.TryRDI.com/free

RDI03-TR